THE AGENCY

THE AGENCY

Ally O'Brien

ST. MARTIN'S PRESS ❧ NEW YORK

This is a work of fiction. All of the characters, organizations, and events portrayed in this novel are either products of the author's imagination or are used fictitiously.

www.stmartins.com

Design by Christopher M. Zucker

Library of Congress Cataloging-in-Publication Data

O'Brien, Ally.
    The agency / Ally O'Brien.—1st ed.
        p. cm.
    ISBN-13: 978-0-312-37944-5
    ISBN-10: 0-312-37944-7
    1. Artists' representatives—Fiction. 2. International business enterprises—Fiction. 3. Businesswomen—Fiction. 4. Literary agents—Fiction. I. Title.
    PR6115.B735A37 2009
    823'.92—dc22
                                2008035451

First Edition: February 2009

10 9 8 7 6 5 4 3 2 1

I

1

MY LIFE.

Eight thirty-seven in the morning, en route from Putney Heath to Piccadilly, first crisis of the day. People push the crisis button in my business like a lab rat pushes a lever to get pellets of food, but this is a big one. Lowell Bardwright was just found hanged by his Hermès tie, his fingers clenched in a death grip around his dick.

Lowell is my boss. Well, not anymore.

"Was it erotic asphyxia?" I asked my assistant.

"Erotic what?"

"Was this some kind of sex game?"

"Oh, I don't know," Emma replied. "I assumed it was suicide."

Not bloody likely.

"No, I'm sure it was an accident," I said.

When you are the managing partner of a successful entertainment agency, you don't kill yourself. Lowell made millions of pounds on the ability of people like me to attract scribblers, footballers, Soho chefs, and other celebs who can be hocked to the

public on grocery store book stands or on the eight million chan-
nels of satellite TV. He had a flat by the Thames and a weekend
home outside Cambridge. God was going to have to come down to
wrestle Lowell personally into the afterlife.

"Was he alone?" I asked.

"I guess he was."

"Don't be so sure. If I know Lowell, he found himself a Julia
Roberts look-alike who freaked when he stopped breathing."

"What's erotic asphyxia?" Emma asked with an unhealthy curiosity.

Emma is twenty-five, and what she lacks in her face she makes
up for in the size of her breasts and the tightness of her drainpipe
jeans. I remember what it was like at that age, when your sex drive
revs like a Ferrari. Hell, I'm still like that, although I've down-
shifted a little in my midthirties. Emma is into girls, however, and
I play for the traditional team.

"Some people say that the sensation of orgasm is heightened by
lack of oxygen," I told her. "So they try cutting off their air as they
get close to coming. Unfortunately, a lot of them wind up like
Lowell, so don't try this at home, Emmy. I know you."

"Hmm," she said.

You want to watch every head snap around on the 14 bus? Say
the word "orgasm" on the phone.

"What does this mean for the agency?" Emma asked.

Good question. Every entertainment agency boasts of having
the most influence and the best connections, and they're all quick
as hyenas to pounce on any sign of weakness in a competitor.
Right now, the phone lines of London are buzzing. Did you hear
about Lowell? My God, what a shock. Of course, without him,
they don't have anyone who can reach the senior producers at the
Beeb. Oh, it's true, and he was their top man for Fleet Street, too.
This may be the time to think about switching your representation, my dear.

Meanwhile, inside the Bardwright Agency, where I work, they're
busy soft-selling Lowell's importance. He was beloved, darling,
but he was a figurehead. Hadn't closed a big deal in years. Never

missed an industry party. A "mentor" to every twenty-four-year-old girl in the agency, that scoundrel, ha-ha. No, we'll miss him, but don't worry, nothing will really change without him around.

But that's not exactly true.

There will be one big change, and it affects me more than anyone.

"Cosima will be in charge now," I told Emma.

"Oh, Lord."

In my head, I heard a blast of organ music. You know, like in silent films, when the mustachioed villain in a black cape abducts the blond virgin. Not that you'll find many virgins in this business.

"I hope the police checked for coral Dior lipstick around Lowell's mushroom," I said. "Cosima has been looking to send Lowell to an early grave for years. Maybe she was there to help him along."

"You are so bad."

I did feel a little bad, only because I wasn't crying over Lowell's death. I'd worked down the hall from him for ten years, after he'd hired me out of the book biz. Me, I thought the agents made the money, which was what I needed back then. No one told me that the partners who own the agency make the money, and the rest of us divide up the crumbs that fall from their smacking lips onto the floor. Lowell and I had had our run-ins over the years, but he was a decent guy. Big, loud, with tobacco breath and roving hands. Fifty-five years old, a lifer in the biz, who remembered a time when bookstores sold more than the fucking *Da Vinci Code* and films didn't rise or fall on the box office receipts from the opening weekend. He never pushed me to drop clients who had potential, even if their sales were underperforming. He indulged my fading ideals that it really meant something to find the next Ian McEwan or Salman Rushdie. On the other hand, I saw the numbers on the royalty statements from my clients, and then the numbers on my agency paycheck, and never the twain did meet.

However, Cosima Tate makes Lowell look like Sir Gawain gallantly taking on the Green Knight. I admit I have my own reasons for loathing Cosima, but I'm not alone in feeling that way at the agency. She is our wicked witch—the kind of witch who would have bitch-slapped Dorothy and served up Toto sausages to the flying monkeys.

"What does this mean for us?" Emma asked, which was the obvious question. I like that Emma says "us" when she talks about herself and me. She is as loyal an assistant as you can find. Organizing my life is not my skill set, and without Emma I would probably starve because I would never know when, where, or with whom I was having a single meal.

"We'll be fine—don't worry."

"Yes, but Cosima *hates* you," Emma whispered.

True enough, but I am bulletproof.

"We have Dorothy, darling, remember?"

"Oh, well, that's true."

Dorothy Starkwell, an American eccentric who lives in the Tribeca area of Manhattan, writes tomes about talking pandas that have become the biggest thing in children's fiction since Pooh set foot in the Hundred Acre Wood. She is my client. She is my gravy train. As long as I write eight-figure deals for her—and the latest deal is in the offing—no one will touch me.

And at that moment, I had my big idea.

If I knew the pain that idea would cause me in the next few days, I wonder whether I would have handled things differently. Perhaps I should have been more paranoid and realized that people really *were* after me. Or I should have known how resourceful and vengeful Cosima could be. However, when you are thirty-six, you never think about being forced to start your life over; and the truth is, it is every bit as hard as anyone will tell you. Still, sometimes you have to wipe the slate clean and find out if you are truly the person you always imagined yourself to be.

"Do I still have lunch with Guy on Friday?" I asked Emma.

"Yes."

Guy Droste-Chambers is Dorothy's editor, the man who makes the deals. He is a sleazy bastard, but Dorothy is infatuated with his wordsmithing. Or perhaps he reminds her of her panda hero,

Butterball, with his porky belly and soup dripping down his chin. Regardless, Dorothy will not hear of switching editors or publishers, despite my advice that she could do better elsewhere.

"Take the lunch out of my calendar, will you?" I said.

"You mean cancel it?"

"God, no, keep the appointment but delete it from the agency calendar right away, okay? Don't mention this to anyone. Just remember to remind me about lunch on Friday."

"Okay."

Emma knew better than to ask me why. The truth is, I wasn't entirely sure myself. All I knew was that I didn't want Cosima to find out that Guy and I were close to inking a new contract for Dorothy that would gross around ten million pounds in advance money. In agency terms, that's one and a half million to us. Not that I would see any of that myself.

Which brings me back to that big idea of mine.

I'm thinking of going out on my own. Launching my own agency.

2

THE BARDWRIGHT AGENCY—named for Lowell's father, the éminence grise of the publishing industry, who started the agency in 1960—is located on the south edge of Soho. We can lunch in Chinatown and walk to the premieres in Leicester Square. Forty of us are crammed onto a single floor with glass closets for agents like me, a rabbit warren of desks for assistants like Emma, and corner palaces for Cosima and Lowell. I can see Lord Nelson in Trafalgar Square from my office window, if I lean out far enough. Never lean out a window when you work at an agency, however, unless you are certain no one is behind you.

All hell was breaking loose when I arrived that morning. Everyone was jabbering into their phones and clacking away on their keyboards. I had fifty-one new messages on my BlackBerry. Lowell would have loved it.

If there is one thing the entertainment world runs on, other than money, it's gossip. Lowell's death was the kind of wonderfully risqué event that will keep us all buzzing for days. Truth doesn't really matter. I have no idea whether Lowell was found wearing high heels and women's lingerie, but I'm sure that someone like me will make a joke about it, and a joke will become a juicy rumor, and a rumor will become fact. By Saturday, someone will parrot it back to me as gospel.

I hurried down the hall to my office as quickly as I could, spinning the wheel on my BlackBerry and getting a crick in my neck as I browsed my dozens of messages. I was busy—but much more important, I wanted to *look* busy to avoid getting roped into bull sessions about Lowell and Cosima. I was too full of my big idea and how to make it work without screwing up my life.

"Morning, darling," I called to Emma as I ducked into my office. She waved back at me and held up three fingers, meaning she was on three calls at once.

I draped my leather jacket on the back of my door and closed it. I took my phone off the hook. I hit a button on the stereo and started a disc by Eminem. (God help me, but I think he is a genius.) I sat behind my desk, grabbed a manuscript from the stack of seventy unread scripts on my floor, and leaned back in my chair and pretended to read.

Nice try.

Marty Goodacre drummed on my window with his fingernails and then let himself inside. "Are you busy, Tess?"

"Would it matter if I was?" I asked.

Marty laughed nervously. "I assume you've heard."

"Lowell. Dead. Dick in hand."

"That's rather crass."

"That's me," I said.

Marty was the agency's business manager and handled the messy matters like salaries, contracts, and accounts. Cosima brought him with her from her old agency. He was thirty-two, had limp brown hair that lay in a greasy pile on his head and a long, narrow face on which he boasted a scruffy goatee. He wore a Marks & Spencer navy suit that hung baggily on his tall frame, and his Argyle tie was loosened so far that the knot fell below the second button on his baby blue shirt. He punctuated his remarks with a tittering laugh, which I imagine he developed while spending half his life on all fours, having Cosima spank his bum.

"I know this is a difficult time, but Cosima wants me to assure everyone that life will go on," Marty said. Titter, titter.

"Be brave, Marty," I said.

"We'll all miss Lowell very much, of course, but I'm sure you know that he would want us to soldier on. Every change is an opportunity. Cosima specifically wanted to be sure you know how much she values you in this agency."

"So much that she couldn't tell me herself," I said.

"Oh, you can imagine it's a busy morning—with banks and solicitors and reporters and editors and everyone else wondering what's going to happen next. It's important that Cosima demonstrate that someone is in charge. The agency isn't going to drift."

"No drift. Got it. Is that all, Marty?"

"Well, Cosima wanted me to check on one other thing."

Dorothy Starkwell.

"Dorothy Starkwell," Marty said. "Cosima thinks it would be a great morale boost—what with everyone being down over this tragedy with Lowell—if we could announce Dorothy's new deal soon. Cosima feels this would send everyone a signal that we're still on top and we plan to stay there."

"Tell me, Marty, when you're wanking off, do you tell your dick that Cosima thinks it would be a good idea if you spurted some jism now?"

Okay, no, I didn't say that.

I said, "No news to report yet, Marty. Sorry."

"Cosima was hoping that you and Guy Droste-Chambers were close to nailing down a deal," Marty told me. Titter, titter frown.

"We haven't even started. Guy's been busy. I've been busy. Dorothy's been doing veggies-not-meat, free-the-bunnies kinds of stuff, so she asked me not to hurry. As soon as we sign a contract, she starts feeling guilty if she's not writing, and she promised all of May to the animal rights crowd."

"Oh," Marty said. "Well, yes, we do whatever Dorothy wants. I know that Cosima would love a timeline, though, for when you hope to wrap up the deal."

"You mean start the deal? Soon."

"Soon as in this week?"

"Soon as in soon, Marty."

"Cosima thought she saw a note in your calendar about lunch with Guy on Friday."

God, that woman doesn't miss a thing.

"It was tentative. Guy had to cancel. But I'll keep you posted."

"Oh, yes, please do that. Cosima calls this her number one priority." Titter. Coffee-stained smile.

Marty snaked his way out of my office, and Emma Strand passed him on the way in. He contorted his body like a Cirque du Soleil acrobat in order to make accidental contact with Emma's tits. She closed the door and stuck out her tongue.

"Any news?" Emma asked.

"Just what I expected. They're salivating over Dorothy's deal."

"I take it you don't want them to know about it."

"You take it right."

Emma smiled. She was smart, God bless her.

"You look tired, darling," I said. "Partying last night?"

"Martinis at the bar in the Soho Hotel until two," Emma said. "Sienna was there. The popzees had it staked out."

"Sienna is one of your faves, isn't she?"

Emma panted. "Are you kidding? Did you see *Factory Girl*? I don't care what anyone says, I think they were really doing it."

"The girl is gorgeous, I'll give you that."

"What I wouldn't give for a girlfriend that classy," she breathed.

Emma sat down in my guest chair and crossed her legs, which shunted her candy red skirt somewhere near her upper thighs. She shoved a pencil in her mouth and began flipping through the pages of her diary. Emma still wrote things down, which was another thing I liked about her. She had electric, stick-your-finger-in-a-socket red hair and a scrubbed Irish face that was a mess of freckles. Her teeth were lily-white but were crammed in her mouth like rush hour commuters on a Central Line train. She had a sweet, perky smile, though, and, Lord, what a body. Insanely tall. Pencil thin. Breasts like overblown birthday balloons. She claims they're real, but I'm suspicious.

I hired Emma away from another agency two years ago, where she was a celebrity publicist. If you are twenty-two and a publicist, your job is to sleep with stars. Every now and then, you might leak a photo op to a friendly popzee or call a knuckle dragger at the *Sun* about some fake bit of gossip, but mostly you ride back to the hotel and give blow jobs in the limo. Emma, being gay, didn't really fit the job requirements, except for an occasional threesome. Anyway, she was incredibly organized and loyal, so for me, she fit the bill perfectly.

"Hey, good news," she told me.

"What?"

"We got a Czech deal for *Singularity*."

"How much?" I asked. The ex-commie countries are about as lucrative as finding a penny on the street.

"A thousand euros."

Right. Minus commission and taxes, that will leave the author, Oliver Howard, with about two weeks' rent in another six months or so when the deal gets signed and the publisher coughs up the money. Unless your name is Nora Roberts or Dan Brown, writing isn't likely to buy you a yacht to race around the Isle of Wight.

"Did you tell him that we got turned down in France, Germany, and Holland?" Emma asked me.

"I don't tell writers when publishers say no," I told her. "They can't handle it. Better to wait until someone says yes."

"So do you want me to e-mail Oliver with the Czech details?"

"No. See if he can do dinner on Friday night. Pick someplace nice. I'll pay. Oliver could use something other than a bacon sandwich for once."

"That's nice."

"Speaking of Oliver, what's the word from Tom Cruise?"

Emma's red lips curled into a snarl. "Felicia called."

Felicia Castro is Tom Cruise's agent and business manager. Unless you know Katie, there's really no other way to get to the Man with a proposition for a movie idea. However, I pissed off Felicia about two years ago because I passed over one of her clients who was desperate to option a number one bestseller, in favor of a series buy with HBO at twice the price. Not a tough choice. But Felicia screamed at me that we had a handshake deal, which wasn't true, and she swore I would never sell so much as a Weetabix commercial to any of her clients from that day forward. And she's been as good as her word.

The trouble is that Oliver Howard's first book, *Singularity*, was absolutely written for Tom Cruise. Anyone who reads it can see Cruise in the lead role. If I do nothing else in this life, I want to see Tom Cruise take that book and make a movie out of it. It's not like the guy needs to buff up his box office bona fides, but this would be his *Shawshank Redemption*, the one everyone remembers in a hundred years.

Another confession: *Singularity* was a huge bomb. I sold the UK rights, and we couldn't move ten fucking copies off the shelves. Oliver didn't earn out even a quarter of his measly advance. I know it happens that way, and that's why, as agents, we try not to fall in love with the works we sell. But I thought *Singularity* was absolutely mind-blowing amazing, and I still think Oliver ought to be the hottest literary author since Thomas Pynchon.

So far, though, I am a cheering section of one.

"What did Felicia say?" I asked.

"Mostly, she called you a cunt," Emma said.

"Well, fuck her," I said. I knew what Felicia wanted. If I lay down naked in front of her desk, let her paint the words "I am a lying bitch" on my chest, and then paraded that way through Leicester Square, maybe she would take my proposal to Cruise. But I wasn't about to do that.

I just didn't know how else to get *Singularity* in Tom's hands.

"What else?" I asked.

"Sally Harlingford wants to know if you can do tea on Monday at Fortnum's."

"She read my mind," I said.

Sally runs her own agency, and she's been a friend and colleague for years. I wanted to pick her brain about my big idea. She knows what it's like to go it alone. By the way, tea at Fortnum's is our own little code for pinot noir at the Groucho. On our bad days, we like to head out for an early drinkie.

Emma leaned forward with a knowing smile. "Also, Darcy sent me an e-mail."

"Ah."

I felt a lovely little spurt of arousal between my legs.

"He wonders if you can meet him late on Friday night."

"Tell him yes, I can."

"I thought you'd say that," Emma replied, giggling. She loved being the secret go-between for my affair. I never communicated with Darcy directly, and his name, of course, isn't Darcy. But Emma and I are both suckers for *Pride and Prejudice*, even if Emma's dream Darcy would look more like Sienna Miller.

"Eleven o'clock at the apartment in Mayfair?" I said.

"I'll tell him."

"Order in some champagne, will you?"

"Of course."

My week was looking up.

3

I PACKED A SMALL BAG in my apartment on Friday morning. Nothing much. I was planning on being naked most of the night. Toothbrush, toothpaste, makeup, L'Occitane shampoo, pair of black lace knickers, fresh blouse, and a packet of ribbed Trojans. What every girl needs for a tryst. The zipped pouch fit comfortably inside my purse.

After my shower, I chose the tightest pair of jeans I could wear without risking circulatory failure and the amputation of my lower body. Honestly, I don't know how Emma gets her jeans on or off. I picked out a push-up bra for the girls, not only because of Darcy but because I was having lunch with Guy Droste-Chambers, and the negotiations always go better with him when my tits are front and center. I hooked on a slim gold chain. Diamond studs. I wore an untucked strawberry silk shirt and left the top couple of buttons open. I squeezed my feet into killer black heels. Pointed toes. Mirror shine. Three-inch spikes. I swayed a little from the lack of oxygen up there. The shoes brought me in at five foot ten.

My hair is short, bottle blond, with a few strands of color. Blue. Red. I'm going for that delicate balance of young, hip, tarty, and aggressive. I worked in a pomade with my fingers and spent fifteen minutes messing and remessing until I was satisfied that I was irresistibly sexy. Guy will think this entire look is for him, which it isn't, but I'm okay with that.

Am I beautiful? Well, I have to work at it, and that means working a lot harder at thirty-six than I ever did when I was twenty-six. Even so, I get there when I need to. Wherever I go today, men will stare, but that's no challenge. Men will stare at anything with breasts. The real test is whether women will take a second glance and pinch their mouths unhappily. I still get those jealous looks, but I know my days are numbered.

Beauty is an attitude. It's about confidence. It's the message you send to the world. Someone once told me that nice people aren't beautiful—and that's harsh, but it's probably true. You have to have a bit of edge to be beautiful, like you know you've got something other people want, and they can't have it. Beauty is about ego.

Sexy is something different. I think women who love sex have a chemical makeup that men can whiff like pheromones in the air. I had a boyfriend who claimed he could look at any woman and decide in five seconds whether or not she enjoyed giving oral sex. (Honey, we *all* like to get it, don't we?) He kept a scorecard on his computer. This is what you get when you date an industrial engineer. Unfortunately, I discovered that the entries in his BJ ledger didn't stop after he met me, so it was time to move on.

I spent the morning working from home, answering e-mails, calling clients, reading crappy manuscripts, and sweet-talking editors and reporters. Everyone wanted to talk about Lowell. They all wanted dirt. I dropped a couple of hints about his being dressed in a white corset and garters when he went to the big sex shop in the sky. I couldn't resist.

Someone named Nicholas Hadley left me a voice mail message. He didn't say who he was or what he wanted, so he was way down on my callback list. Probably a writer trying to pitch a book. I'm at the point where I don't tell anyone what I do for a living, because everyone has either written a book, thinks they could write a book, or knows someone who has written a book. I figured Hadley was one of the three.

I also talked to my solicitor and my banker and asked for their confidential assessments of whether I could launch my own agency and what I would need to make it work. They talked about cash flow, client agreements, contracts, currency exchange rates, financial accounting, and administrative support. In other words, I would need to hire people to do the things I didn't know how to do and didn't want to do so that I could do what I do best: make deals.

However, they were very encouraging. If you have Dorothy Starkwell, they both told me, you can do it. That's what it takes to get started, really—a big client and a big deal.

So I was ready for Guy.

Around one o'clock, I took a cab to his office. No need to inhale bus fumes or risk humidity, dust, sweat, body oils, and Tube grease before my big meeting. I sat in the cab as the city went by and let my mind wander. I had all the sales figures and prior contracts in my briefcase, but I had been over them so many times that I couldn't bear to look at them again. I could recite hardcover, trade paperback, mass market paperback, and open market sales country by country from memory. Guy knows where we have to be. He got lucky on the last deal. Dorothy has written six panda books, so this deal will be for seven, eight, and nine. She didn't hit the big time until an indie studio made a computer-animated version of *The Bamboo Garden* and hawked it at Sundance. That was shortly after her fourth book was in the stores. The movie was a respectable success, and all of a sudden, parents started snapping up Dorothy's books. It made the twenty-five-thousand-pounds-per-book advance for four, five, and six look pretty paltry when the royalties began closing in on seven figures for every title in her backlist.

This time, Guy was going to have to break open the piggy bank. He knew it. I knew it.

Dorothy has done well, but this is only the beginning. Books are a small piece of the pie. The real money is in film, television,

Broadway, product licensing, merchandising tie-ins, that kind of thing. Hardly anybody reads anymore. Sad but true. My plan later this year is to start hammering my buddies in TV land and get those damn pandas their own weekly series. Maybe a children's magazine, too. From there you can see them on cereal boxes, jammies, stuffed animals, fridge magnets, lunch boxes—you name it.

If I sound like a tough negotiator, I am. I don't make any apologies for it. Even the editors who are my personal friends know that I will reach into their mouths and pull out the last gold filling on behalf of my clients. After ten years, I have a reputation. A lot of women don't like dealing with me because I'm a pushy bitch. Men are turned on and a little scared. That's okay. I use it to make my clients a lot of money.

People ask where I get it, and I tell them my father. My mum and dad divorced when I was only five, and my mum followed her horny desires to Italy, where she has lived the bohemian life with a chorus line of buff waiters and long-haired street painters ever since. If I inherited anything from my mum, it's an unfortunate tendency to listen to my clitoris even when it is giving me lousy advice. More about that later. Anyway, Dad is and has always been a political editor for the *Times*, married to his job, hard as nails, scary as hell, an old boy from the old school.

I had thought seriously about following in his footsteps. I worked at the paper for three years after college as a political reporter. I learned the ins and outs of Parliament. I interviewed Colin Powell when he was in London. I did a six-month stint in New York at the UN. I had an affair with a married Cabinet minister. It was that last one that got my arse kicked out of journalism, and it was my dad, true to form, who gave me the heave-ho. I didn't blame him for it, and I didn't miss the job. I had been in the media long enough to know it was populated mostly by chain-smoking cynics who despise the people they cover. I was in the wrong biz.

From journalism I did the shuffle into publishing, not as an editor (God help me) but as a marketer negotiating mass media placements. English translation: I was the one who got Carmela to announce on HBO that she was reading our latest gardening book, which propelled it onto the bestseller list for nine weeks. Never underestimate the power of *The Sopranos*.

It was during that period that I first met Dorothy Starkwell. She was a fifty-year-old housewife living in upstate New York in a town called Ithaca, which to this day I still call Icarus. Dorothy worked at the local library, picketed hamburger restaurants on behalf of the animal rights loonies known as PETA, and wrote stories about pandas in her spare time. When I met her, she had published the first of her stories in the United States. This was *The Bamboo Garden*, which would later become a movie. She was in Frankfurt trying to schedule appointments with overseas publishers during the book fair, but she was a babe in the woods with a sixty-four-year-old literary agent from Buffalo who appeared just as naive about the sales game as Dorothy. We met for vegetarian Indian food at a restaurant across the street from the Messe, and I wound up giving them both some informal advice on book marketing. Little did I know how that night would change my life.

I enjoyed the work, but I wasn't cut out to be in publishing. I avoided jumping into bed with my boss (not for want of trying on his part), but I lasted only two years. Despite my working sixty-hour weeks, my salary barely paid the monthly rent on a flat in Rayners Lane. My peers who had been in their jobs five, ten, fifteen, and even twenty years weren't doing much better. Publishing is not exactly about upward mobility.

That was when I first met with Lowell Bardwright about the possibility of joining his agency. He offered me a 30 percent raise over my current salary, and a month later, I was at my new desk in Soho. Six months after that, Dorothy Starkwell's agent in Buffalo died of a heart attack, and Dorothy called me.

Ten years later, here I am.

Don't get me wrong, I have made progress. I made it from Rayners Lane to a two-bedroom flat south of the Thames that is three times as expensive. When I go to Frankfurt now, I stay at the Hessischer Hof. There are at least a few items in my closet that come from Sloane Street. So, yes, I do just fine.

But there comes a time when you wonder if you will always be working for someone else, and whether you will be content to live out your life earning a paycheck instead of profiting from the fruits and risks of your own labor. There comes a time when you have to prove yourself to yourself.

For me, as I got out of the cab and stared up at the Regent's Park Nash house where Guy Droste-Chambers and his publishing house were located, that time was now.

I was totally unprepared.

4

GUY WELCOMED MY BREASTS WARMLY. He hugged them like long-lost friends and stared at them with the protectiveness of a mother lion, as if to make sure they didn't decide to get up on their own and leave the two of us alone together in his office. He waved them into a chair and asked if they would like anything to drink. On their behalf, I ordered Perrier.

"Filippa, darling, it is so good to see you again," he gushed.

No, he didn't get my name wrong. I'm Tess Drake, but Filippa is the nickname Guy has used for me since I did the movie deal for *The Bamboo Garden*. The rich Russian developer who wants to pave over the panda habitat with the help of corrupt Chinese officials (you try pitching this stuff with a straight face) was originally called Liudmila in the book. However, we ran into an unusual snag when negotiating the film rights, because Liudmila turned out to be the name of the executive producer's grandmother. So he insisted that we change the villain's name before signing off on the deal. Like most stubborn artists, Dorothy was adamantly against doing so, until I proposed the name Filippa, which for some reason resonated with her as an even greater paragon of wickedness. Thanks to me, Liudmila became Filippa in the movie, and we were forced to change the name in the books, too, so moviegoers wouldn't become confused.

Guy thought the whole affair was incredibly amusing.

"I have reservations at Locatelli," I told him.

Guy loved Italian. I could practically see saliva gather at the corner of his mouth, so I was stunned when he said, "That's sweet of you, Filippa, but I've ordered lunch in for us right here."

Immediately, my guard was up. One of the few perks of life as an editor is the opportunity to eat out almost every day at trendy restaurants, sucking up beef, shellfish, and expensive wine, with literary agents picking up the tab. Guy had leveraged the generosity of agencies like Bardwright into eighteen stone bulging out of his five-foot-five frame.

I raised an eyebrow.

"New house rules." He sighed. "Ever since the damn Americans took over, they're obsessed with conflicts of interest. We can't accept any gifts, meals, liquor, what have you. It's insanity. Like a few bob for a nice meal would sway me one way or another. It would be one thing if they adjusted our salaries to compensate for the change, when they know perfectly well that all of us count on the occasional free lunch or cocktail hour to make ends meet."

Occasional?

"But, no," he continued, "we still make the same pittance of a wage while our authors buy penthouse flats and agents like you scum off fifteen or twenty percent of the cream while leaving the real work to us."

"It's nice to see you, too, Guy."

He rubbed his balding pate like he was hoping for a genie to pop out. "Oh, I know what I sound like—you're catching me on a bad day. You can't imagine how it feels to see this river of money streaming along, and you have to stand on the shore and wave as everyone else paddles by."

"If it's any consolation, I do know how you feel," I told him.

I was willing to bet that Guy made a lot more money than I, given his senior editorial role and his unique relationship with Dorothy, who was one of their biggest bestsellers. However, Guy was approaching fifty, and he had his eye on a retirement property in Grasmere. Fifteen years ago, a house in the Lake District might have been within reach for someone in Guy's position, but the inflated property market had driven prices so high that you had to work in the financial sector in the City to afford the nicer areas.

"Yes, sorry, of course you do," Guy told me. "You know how unfair it is. We have to look out for each other, because we both get screwed by our employers."

He picked up his phone and told his secretary that I was here. Fifteen minutes later, she delivered cello-wrapped tuna sandwiches and bottles of Perrier in a takeaway bag from Pret. I had to push aside stacks of books to find someplace on the desk to balance my sandwich. Most editors' offices look as if a flu-ridden library had sneezed books over every available surface.

We had the obligatory conversation about Lowell.

"Terrible thing about your boss," Guy said.

"Terrible," I said.

"Imagine copping it while you're wanking off. Pretty humiliating. Like having a heart attack while you're on the loo."

"Dead is dead," I said.

"Still, he lived the high life, didn't he, the rich bastard." Guy wiped a stray bit of tuna from the side of his mouth.

"Someone told me they found him in a white corset and heels," I said.

Guy's mouth fell open. "Seriously?"

"Well, it's just a rumor."

"That is bloody brilliant! Oh, that is a treat! You just made my day, Filippa, you really did."

I smiled. "You didn't hear it from me. Don't tell anyone."

"No, no, of course not. My lips are sealed."

The entire building would know by five o'clock.

Guy leaned forward. I could smell his fishy breath across the desk. "So do you think it's true, that thing about constricting the

airflow when you come? What did the papers call it? Erotic asphyxia?"

"I have no idea."

Guy grinned at me. "Ever tried it?"

"I get my orgasms the traditional way, thank you. Two Nubian
masseurs, a bowl of salad cream, and a Rampant Rabbit."

Guy roared. "My God, you are wicked! You are wicked!"

I smiled, but inwardly I was concerned, because Guy was stall-
ing and appeared overconfident. Usually, he was a nervous, down-
to-business type. Get the details out of the way. Wring his hands
about sales. Leave the flirting for the last few minutes.

Guy knew how much I was asking for the new contract, and he
had already told me he was prepared to make it happen. This should
be a no-brainer. The last thing that Guy wanted was to lose Dorothy, although he knew that my threats to take her elsewhere were
mostly empty. Dorothy thought that she and Guy shared a mystical
literary relationship reminiscent of Eliot and Pound's. Sort of like
"The Waste Land" with pandas. Guy also fancied himself an animal rights activist like Dorothy, although it was obvious to anyone
who met Guy that he was a ravenous carnivore who would eat
grilled polar bear cub if it was served with enough brown sauce.

On the other hand, I wasn't in a hurry anymore to do a deal. I
didn't want anything in writing for a few more days.

"We already agreed that ten million is the right target," I told
him. "Three-book deal, like we discussed. We can haggle out the
royalty terms next week."

Guy leaned back in his chair. The frame squeaked ominously.
He folded his hands over the dome of his belly.

"Oh, yes, no problem, no problem."

He smiled at me. It was a nasty smile. I didn't like it. What was
going on?

"Marty Goodacre called me today," Guy said.

Shit.

"Oh?" I said.

"He told me Cosima was wondering where we were on Dorothy's deal. He sounded pretty anxious to get a contract signed."

"Yes, you know Cosima."

"He also said you told him that our lunch today had been canceled and that we hadn't started talking about the terms of a new deal yet."

"Did he?"

"Yes, he did."

"What did you tell him?" I asked, holding my breath.

"Nothing," Guy said. "Marty left me a voice mail. I thought I would wait to call him back until you and I had talked."

I tried not to sigh with relief, but I must have sounded like a popped balloon.

"However, you'll be happy to know that I'm ready to print out a contract right now," Guy said. He dug into his drawer and pulled out a stapled sheaf of papers. "In fact, I have a model draft already typed up. It's got Dorothy's name as the Proprietor in care of the Bardwright Agency. That's what you want, isn't it? Would you like to take it with you to review?"

I hesitated. The bastard knew exactly what was going on.

"There's no rush," I said.

"I thought you might say that."

"Just between us, I'm contemplating a change in my status."

Guy fanned himself with the contract. "You mean you're thinking about spreading your wings and flying from the Bardwright Agency, now that Cosima is in charge?"

"I haven't made any decisions yet."

"But in the meantime, you'd like to keep your options open. As well as Dorothy's contract."

"As a matter of fact, that's right." My face was burning red. I hated that he was playing me.

"So you'd like me to tell Marty that we haven't started negotiations yet—is that what you're saying?"

I took a deep breath. The girls swelled. Guy liked that. "Yes, that's what I'm saying."

"Ah."

Guy got up from his chair. He came around the front of his desk and sat next to the tiny open space where I had my sandwich. He glanced at the office door to make sure it was closed and then stared down at the half-moons of both breasts that were on display.

"And what's in it for me?" he asked.

I folded my arms, blocking the view. "What do you want?"

"Well, for one thing, I haven't had a decent meal since the Americans put this fucking conflict policy in place. They have eyes all over London. I can't go anywhere without bumping into someone from one of the other divisions. You know how it is, don't you, Filippa?"

"That must be difficult."

"Yes, it is, it is. So I was thinking it might be nice for you and me to have dinner somewhere outside the city. We could celebrate your new venture properly."

"What did you have in mind?"

"I don't know. Brighton maybe? I love the sea, don't you? We could even make a weekend out of it."

Bastard, bastard, bastard.

"Get real. That's not going to happen, Guy."

"No? You think about it, Filippa. Think hard. I really believe this is the time to go out on your own. You'll be a huge success. You're smart, you're sexy, and you know how the game is played. I'd hate to see you miss such a great opportunity."

I stood up. I was furious, but I couldn't simply take off my shoe and drive the heel into his groin, which was what I wanted to do. Guy knew damn well that he held all the cards this time. If he told Marty that we had already talked about numbers, then I would watch my biggest client and my biggest deal slip through my fingers. So much for the seed money to go out on my own. I kicked myself for not realizing how vulnerable I was and for not thinking about all this weeks ago, before Lowell's death, before Guy and I started negotiating. I was too complacent.

"Here's something else for you to think about," Guy said, as I gathered up my things and felt like a fool.

"What?" I snapped.

"You'll make, what, fifteen percent of the gross on this deal? That's a nice piece of pudding to start a business on."

"So?"

"So I imagine you could carve off five percent and not even miss it."

"Are you saying you want a kickback to hold the deal? Fuck you, Guy."

Guy put a plump hand on my shoulder. I felt him rubbing my skin. "Don't decide right away, Filippa. Take the weekend. I won't call Marty back until Monday. But I know Cosima would love to grab one and a half million pounds in new commission money for the agency. On the other hand, I'll bet even a million pounds would let you get a nice start on your own business. Wouldn't it?"

I didn't say a word. There was nothing to say.

5

"WELL, WHAT DID YOU EXPECT, Tessie?" Oliver Howard asked me, as he downed his second shot of Lagavulin and reclaimed his cigarette from the marble ashtray. "Everyone fucks everyone else in this business."

"You don't have to tell me," I said. I was halfway through a bottle of Narbey Pouilly-Fumé and was a little buzzed. I checked my watch. I still had three hours to go before I needed to be in Mayfair, stripped and ready for Darcy.

"Dangle a wad of money in front of anyone, and he'll sell his mum for it," he said.

"Except you," I said.

"Except me," he acknowledged. "But I've never had a penny to my name, so my poverty actually feeds my ego." He inhaled smoke and let loose a phlegm-filled, tooth-rattling cough, which you'd expect from a seventy-year-old woman with spots on her lungs, not a twenty-nine-year-old writer. Oliver smoked the dark European cigarettes that form choking clouds outside

Parisian cafés, but that was the least of his vices. I was worried about him.

"How are you, darling?" I asked.

He shrugged. "I'm all right."

"No, seriously."

"I'm not dead yet."

That was something of a miracle. Oliver was tall and skeletal. He wore a black turtleneck that didn't hide his protruding bones. He had black hair buzzed down to a #1, which basically means your skull has five o'clock shadow. His face was sallow; his sunken eyes looked haunted and sleep deprived, and his skin hung like a wrinkled shirt on a coat hanger. It was the kind of beaten-down face you'd expect to find on a chronic drug user, and you'd be right. Seeing him smoking and downing scotch was better than seeing him with his pupils so wide you could stare into his brain.

But what a brain. *Singularity* blew me away. It was a fantasy novel, which is normally not my genre. I'm not much for sword fights between mole-faced dwarfs and three-eyed unicorns. However, Oliver's world is nothing like the dungeons and dragons of Tolkien or Paolini. Instead, his book was about a kind of post-apocalyptic Eden with burned-out cities and odd cross-species sexuality; and out of this he managed a retelling of *Paradise Lost* with a high-energy hero-devil searching for his soul. Sound crazy? Well, you weren't the only one to think so. No one in the industry knew what to do with *Singularity*. I am still trying to rescue it. What I need is Tom Cruise as the devil.

"If you needed something, you'd call me, right?" I asked Oliver.

His lips cracked into something like a smile. "Sure, Tessie."

I wasn't convinced. On some level, Oliver reveled in his self-destruction. He liked playing the tortured writer, and I wasn't sure what he would do if I could make him into the success he deserved to be, with fat royalty checks twice a year. However, I knew Oliver's story, and it wasn't pretty. When Oliver was fourteen, his father killed his mother with a kitchen knife and then booked his own journey to the afterlife with a supersized injection of heroin. Oliver found the bodies after school. He wound up in a foster home but ran off and spent five years in the blackest streets of Manchester, selling himself, breaking into shops, drowning himself in cocaine. By all rights, he should already be dead or brain damaged, but he was one of the rare kids who wound up saved by his stint in jail. There, he was forced to wean himself off drugs for a few years, and during that time, he wrote stories that attracted the attention of a fantasy mag editor on Charing Cross Road, who recommended him to me.

I've known Oliver for four years now. It took that long to launch *Singularity*. Publishing is a slow game. Meanwhile, Oliver has relapsed a couple times and wound up in rehab. In between, he writes for weekly magazines to stave off complete poverty and starvation. He is a few chapters into his second book, *Duopoly*, which is every bit as astounding as the first, but he's writing it on spec. I'm still fighting with his publisher over a new deal.

I don't always understand Oliver and his demons. Even so, I like him. He is my favorite client. He's the reason I got into this business: to find authors who really have something to say and give them an audience. There are days when I think that Oliver is my ultimate test, and that if I can't succeed with him, then I should give up this business once and for all.

Right now, that doesn't sound so bad.

"Guy Droste-Chambers," Oliver mused. "I don't even know him, and I know exactly what he's like. I guarantee you he has a nine-hundred-page novel in a desk drawer somewhere that he wrote when he was thirty-five, about a posh Victorian gentleman who discovers what great sex is like with a char girl and gets her pregnant."

I laughed. "Guy actually did shop around a romance novel a few years ago. It was pure drivel."

"Drivel usually sells," Oliver said.

"Well, not in this case."

"It's the curse of the editor. Most of them can see what's wrong on a page, but give them a blank piece of paper, and they don't know where to begin."

That's true.

"Yes, Guy has always nurtured the fantasy of being an author himself," I said. "It killed him when he couldn't even publish a bit of genre fluff. I think on some level he hates Dorothy and those pandas."

"Don't you?" Oliver asked, smiling.

"Oh, Dorothy is a bit of odd, but she's all right. Look, you never know where lightning is going to strike. I learned that long ago. Quality has nothing to do with success or failure. *Singularity* should have been at the top of the bestseller list—you know that."

"Perhaps I should sign up to be James Patterson's next co-author," he said.

I gagged.

"Anyway, what are you going to do?" he asked me. "Are you going to whisk off to Brighton with Guy for a weekend of corpulent passion?"

"Of course not."

"Or slip him some of your commission money under the table?"

"Oh, please. You know I would never do that. It's wrong."

"It's a little late to be fretting over your ethics, Tessie."

"What do you mean?"

Oliver shrugged. "Well, you've already crossed to the dark side, haven't you? You're trying to hide Dorothy's deal so you can steal it away from the evil witch Cosima."

I was defensive. "Dorothy is my client. I've put in all the work on her deals and not seen a penny from the millions in royalties the agency has made on her. I'll be damned if Cosima takes it all away from me again."

Oliver waved his empty whiskey glass at the waitress and ignored my frown. He lit up again. We were seated at an outside patio table in a French restaurant near Westminster. The MPs all went here. Half a dozen backbenchers waved to me, because they knew my father. Everyone here lived under the cone of silence. You made sure you didn't listen to the conversations around you, and whenever someone from the *Sun* called for a reservation, the tables were always full.

Oliver's cigarette made me want to smoke again. I quit years

ago, but you never really quit, do you? You're just one fag away
from inviting Satan inside your house again. With the stress I felt
now, I had a good job not ripping the cigarette out of Oliver's hand
and taking a long drag.

"I'm not saying I blame you," he said. "Cosima is the scariest
bitch I've ever met. She oozes all that treacle at you while she's
sharpening the scissors to cut off your balls. I'm sure her first order of business will be to ask why you haven't dropped a loser client like me who's wasting your time and not paying the bills."

I didn't say anything. Oliver was dead right.

"So believe me, Tessie," he continued, "I'll be the first to cheer
when you tell Cosima to shove the Bardwright Agency up her arse
and go out on your own. More power to you. But you know—and
I know—there's only one right thing to do in this situation."

"And that is?" I asked.

"Close the deal with Guy, and then walk away."

I stared at him. "Walk away?"

"Leave it with Bardwright. Forget about it."

I put down my glass of wine. I thought for a moment I might
have stepped over into Oliver's *Singularity* universe. When I
looked around, however, I was still in London, and there were no
mutant reptiles lurking in doorways, sporting forked tongues and
Scarlett Johansson's breasts.

"That's the scotch talking, Oliver," I said. "I am not walking away
from one and a half million pounds. Are you totally bonkers?"

"It's not yours."

"The hell it's not. My client, my deal, my negotiations."

"Except you have an employment contract with the agency that
says otherwise. Right?"

"Fuck the contract."

Oliver shook his head. "I know you, Tessie. You are better than
them. You won't sell your soul. Even for a million pounds. You
don't have it in you."

"I'm not sure you know me at all. Don't you understand? That
deal gives me the cash I need to launch the agency. Without that,
what the hell do I have?"

Oliver shrugged. "True enough. I know that you're not going to pay your bills with the commissions you get on my lavish royalties."

"I'm sorry. You know what I mean."

"I do, but think about it, Tessie. What's the worst that can happen?"

"I think you just described it."

"Okay, so you give up more cash than I'm ever likely to see in my lifetime. That's a huge hit. I'm not denying it. But look at the big picture. You still have Dorothy. You've got the TV and movie rights to sell. Cosima may have three books, but you'll have everything else that goes along with those fucking pandas. That's enough to get a line of credit from a bank if you need it, right? What's more, you'll have played it the way you always play it. With integrity, class, and an arse as hard as titanium."

I laughed. "You smoothie."

"Besides, it's a moot point if Guy spills the beans, isn't it?"

"Yes."

"So there you go."

"I understand what you're saying, Oliver," I told him. "I really do. I just don't have the moral fiber to ignore a seven-figure payout that is rightfully mine."

"Just tell me you haven't changed your mind about shagging Monsieur Droste-Chambers."

"No. I think Guy is bluffing. When it comes right down to it, I think he'd rather deal with me than Cosima. He'll keep his mouth shut."

"Just remember what I said. You may think it's the end of the world if you lose this deal, but it's not. Believe me, I've been close enough to the end of the world to see it from where I was, and it has nothing to do with million-pound deals. The only thing that matters is whether you are true to yourself."

Damn him. I work so hard to keep a suit of armor around me, and Oliver has this annoying habit of knowing how to prick me so I bleed. I swirled the wine in my glass and didn't say anything. I felt guilty, because he was doing his best to help me, and all I could

seem to do for him was pony up a deal worth eight hundred stink-
ing euros from the Czech Republic.

He read my mind. "I suppose you haven't heard anything about
Duopoly in the UK? Or did they say no and you're sparing my
feelings?"

"There's no word yet, but I'm not giving up," I assured him. "If
your current publisher won't bite, then we'll shop it elsewhere.
Don't worry. We'll do a deal. Keep writing."

I tried to sound optimistic. He could see through me.

"I'm not concerned," he said. "Now that we have the Czechs on
board for *Singularity*, the Poles can't be far behind, right? Soon I'll
be up to my balls in kolaches and pierogi. In fact, maybe I should
skip writing in English altogether and switch to something in Cy-
rillic. I like languages that have lots of accent marks. We're missing something in English without them."

That was the cynical Oliver. "It's going to happen, darling," I
said. "Trust me."

I hoped I wouldn't have to eat my words.

"What about Tom Cruise?" he asked. "Any chance of him signing onto a movie deal? If it would help, I'll become a Scientolo-
gist."

"I've been in touch with Felicia Castro. She's the way in to Tom."

"And?"

"We're still talking."

Oliver blew a cloud of smoke at me. "Don't treat me like a child,
Tessie."

"All right, Felicia called me a cunt and said I had a better chance
of bearing Tom's love child than getting the book in his hands."

"In other words, I'm fucked."

"No, I'll find a way around her."

Oliver nodded. If he doubted me, he was kind enough not to
show it. I knew that I was his only hope. No other agent would
touch him, not with the dismal track record of *Singularity*.

The waitress brought the check, which I paid. Oliver had ordered a steak and chips and hoovered up the whole thing. I wondered how often he had a decent meal.

"Here," I said, sliding a small envelope across the table.

"What the hell is this?"

"Call it an advance on my commission." I had put one hundred pounds inside the envelope.

Oliver pushed it away. "Forget it."

"Oh, don't be so fucking noble, darling."

He shook his head. "You're sweet, Tessie. Really, you are. But, like I told you, once you compromise your principles, you lose yourself. I can't do that."

"This is not a compromise. This is a loan."

"It's welfare."

"Oh, fine, you stubborn arse." I took the envelope back.

We both stood up. As I leaned forward, Oliver had a good look at the girls spilling forward in my blouse. Oliver looked at them with detached interest. He was gay.

"Are those for Darcy?" he asked me without a smile.

I nodded.

"You still haven't told me who he is," he said.

I haven't told anyone except Emma.

"Believe me, Oliver, you don't want to know."

I took a cab from Westminster to Piccadilly and had the driver let me out in front of the Athenaeum. I tried to put all thoughts of Guy, Dorothy, and Cosima out of my head, so that I could focus on the night ahead. Darcy and I don't see each other often. One night of horny passion every few weeks was the most I could hope for. Even so, I was falling for him. As if my life wasn't complicated enough.

My father keeps an apartment in Mayfair that he uses during the week. He's usually there only to sleep and eat breakfast; otherwise, he is at the newspaper's offices every other minute of his life. On the weekends, he takes the train west to his farm in Somerset, and I have a standing invitation to use the flat for whatever rendezvous I may need to satisfy my desires. My father knows me and knows I'm my mother's daughter. That is where Darcy and I have been meeting for the past year.

All I wanted tonight was to freshen my makeup, dab on Jo Malone, open a bottle of Laurent-Perrier Rosé Brut, and allow myself to be ravished. Unfortunately, nothing is as easy as it seems.

As I walked from Piccadilly up Down Street toward the inner circle of Mayfair, I passed a small Italian bistro on my left. Candlelight. Trendy pizzas. Very romantic. I glanced idly through the window and couldn't help but notice Guy Droste-Chambers sitting alone at a table on the far wall. Guy is difficult to miss. He was staring into a bell-shaped glass of red wine.

I felt a twinge of regret for this lonely, middle-aged man, despite the games he had tried to play with me. Then I saw a woman emerge from the ladies' toilet and join him at the table. That was when I realized there was already another glass of red wine at the place setting opposite Guy. He wasn't alone.

I saw who it was.

My heart left my chest and went running for the Tube. My breath was stolen away. The woman with Guy was the last person on earth I wanted to see with him.

No, not even Cosima.

Her name was Saleema Azah. She was a literary agent in New York. Once upon a time, going all the way back to college, she was my best friend. Now she was a self-declared enemy. We had done battle over clients for the last five years. She was my alter ego. My evil twin.

I moved on quickly along the sidewalk before they noticed me outside, but my mind was spinning.

For all I know, it was an innocent dinner, and it had nothing to do with me. Saleema had clients in the UK. No doubt Guy was the editor for some of her authors. But you know what they say about being paranoid: That doesn't mean they're not after you.

I suddenly heard Oliver's voice in my head.

What's the worst that can happen?

6

MY NEMESIS.

I first met Saleema in New York when I was doing a term abroad at NYU, studying English and film. I had a hankering for saag paneer on a Tuesday night and found a restaurant called Bengal Star in the East Village. Saleema was there, too, and I recognized her from a class we were both taking on the films of Scorsese. We sat together, shared nan and pilau rice, and struck up a friendship. My favorite was *Taxi Driver*. Hers was *Goodfellas*.

Saleema is DDG—drop dead gorgeous. She has jet-black hair, wavy and full, that hangs halfway down her body. A tiny frame, never more than a hundred pounds. Thick eyebrows and huge brown eyes. A skin tone like cappuccino. After twenty years, she still seems ageless.

Back then, she wanted to be an actress, and I was majoring in wine and marijuana. We both took the long way around to our careers. She made it into a couple of indie films, largely based on her willingness to flash her nipples and supple arse for the camera, while I played around with journalism and publishing. Her acting career peaked with a role as a murderous computer programmer in an episode of *Law & Order*. It's still not easy to make it as a minority woman in acting, and she decided to quit rather than eke out a modest living playing bit parts. Saleema was already in New York, and she had an English degree and a PalmPilot full of contacts in the movie and TV biz. With that background, and looks to die for, she had the makings of a great agent.

I made my way down the same path by coincidence, and so we found ourselves a few years after we first met in similar jobs on opposite sides of the Atlantic. Still friends. I made trips to New York a couple of times a year, and Saleema made an annual spring pilgrimage to the London Book Fair. We always got together for dinner. I stayed at her place. She stayed at mine. We were both good at our jobs, and we both had a solid roster of clients. She's been with the Robinson Foote Agency for nine years, and she complains about it as much as I complain about Bardwright. In a different universe, we might have opened our own transatlantic agency in the wake of Lowell's death, because we were as close as two attractive women can be.

Which is to say, we were always one little mistake away from watching our friendship dissolve into a bitter feud.

As it turned out, the mistake was mine. I admit it. I fucked up. I did a terrible thing.

You'll recall that I inherited my mother's tendency of paying way too much attention to a certain part of my body. Look it up in the dictionary, and you'll see it described as being "homologous" to the penis. I love that word, "homologous." I've never seen it anywhere else. When I think homologous, I think clitoris. It wants what it wants, when it wants it.

About five years ago, I visited Saleema's office, which is on the sixth floor of the Flatiron Building, that wonderful triangular landmark in Manhattan. I was in the city doing the rounds of publishers, and from there, I had a West Coast swing planned to LA. Saleema was in the midst of a crisis, because *People* magazine had just released a scathing review of a memoir by one of her clients that had her at full boil. Me, I'm just glad that *People* still finds room for book reviews at all, in between their shirtless photos of Matthew McConaughey. Anyway, our dinner plans were shot to hell. Saleema said she could make it up to me, however, and she introduced me to another agent in her office, a blond god from Florida, former basketball player for something called the Gators, eyes so blue they were like a swimming pool in which you wanted to strip off your clothes and skinny-dip.

Homologous, definitely homologous.

Saleema called him a friend. That was all. A friend. She gave me no hint of any relationship whatsoever between them. His name was Evan.

Evan asked where I wanted to have dinner, and I think I surprised him when I said the Carnegie Deli. When I get horny, I get hungry. That night, I wanted a hot corned beef sandwich six inches tall and a slice of cheesecake so thick you could rub it all over your body and still have some left for the next day. We ate like animals. We laughed. We talked about British politics. We went to a club. We danced. Okay, look, we all know where this is going. Evan proved to be as long as he was tall, and I spent most of the night under him, on top of him, and holding on to the porcelain edge of the bathroom sink. OMG.

The next day, I couldn't wait to tell Saleema. She couldn't wait to tell me something, either. Fortunately, I let her go first.

She and Evan were engaged. Surprise!

And what did I think of him, anyway?

Some surprises leave you almost speechless.

Well, I said, with my stretched-out insides still aching gloriously, I think he's just as DDG as you, and I'm sure the two of you will be very happy. Congratulations. Smile. Look to God and whisper, "Oh, shit." You certainly do *not* tell your best friend that her fiancé failed to mention your engagement and spent the night rocking your world in more positions than you had previously tried in your life.

Evan, Saleema, and I had lunch at Pastis that day, and I shot him daggers across the table whenever Saleema wasn't looking. He was enjoying my discomfort, and I think he knew that I was still turned on by him, regardless of the fact that he was now forbidden fruit. I left town wanting to tell Saleema that her fiancé was a cheating bastard, but it was hard to make that message stick when the bastard was cheating with me.

Now for my big mistake. That was still to come.

Two months later, Evan called me in London. He was in the city and wanted to see me. Saleema wasn't with him. I should have slammed down the phone, but I finally had a chance to slap his face and use every word in my dictionary of expletives. I could make him grovel. I could savage him. I could get my sweet revenge.

So I met him at a pub in Bloomsbury.

Okay, look, we all know where this is going. Again.

I screamed at him. I slapped his face. Then I spent most of the night on top of him, under him, and braced against the wall of the lift in my apartment building. Thank God the thing is old and slow. The lift, I mean.

Like I said, I don't have the greatest track record of good decisions when it comes to sex.

The next morning, I felt guilty and sick as I let the hot water of the shower pour over my head. I swore to myself I would never see him again. My resolve lasted until he joined me in the shower. But that, I promised myself, was absolutely the last time. I don't claim to understand the power he had over me, but certain men can make you forget everything else in the world. Including your friends.

Not surprisingly, I wasn't the only tunnel into which Evan was driving his stretch limo. Saleema found out about his numerous affairs and broke off the engagement. She cried to me about it on the phone. I felt like shit. I could have confessed then and there that I was one of his conquests, but I knew that would be the end of our relationship, and I didn't think it would make her feel any better to know that her fiancé *and* her best friend had both betrayed her together. You can say I was just trying to cover my arse, and maybe that's true.

I didn't count on Evan being cruel and vicious.

He sent her a break-up box with the things she had left in his apartment, but he included a little bonus. It was a beautifully carved miniature wooden tiger from Calcutta. Saleema had bought it as a present for me on her last trip to India and had given it to me in London. I had kept it in my apartment. I didn't even notice that Evan had nicked it. Needless to say, Saleema got the message loud and clear.

So did I.

I don't blame her for what she said to me. She was right. I deserved it. You can't apologize and make something like that go away. I tried for months to make things right between us, but eventually I realized that for the first time in my life I had made a blood enemy. All the emotions between us had to go somewhere, and Saleema let them flow into hatred. Me, I don't hate her. I feel nothing but regret. But I learned the stakes a year later when one of my best American clients dumped me and signed on with Saleema. My client was a recently divorced woman whose husband had cheated on her. Saleema made sure my client knew exactly what I had done with Evan.

Two other clients followed that year. I really think Saleema would steal all of them if she could. However, it's been a couple of years since anyone else has bolted to Robinson Foote, and I keep hoping that the fire of her vengeance has cooled a bit. Maybe she has other battles to fight. Maybe screwing me until I plead for mercy is lower on her list now.

Maybe her dinner with Guy has nothing to do with me at all.

Maybe.

7

———

I WAS NOT FEELING particularly horny or carefree when I reached my father's apartment in Mayfair. I checked voice mail and had the usual blizzard of messages, but none of them related to Guy or Dorothy. That made me feel a little better. The fact is, if Saleema had visions of using Guy to steal Dorothy away from me, she was going to have to stand in line. Loyalty goes a long way with Dorothy, and she is as committed to her relationship with me as she is to her editorial partnership with Guy. I really think I would have to commit murder before Dorothy looked for another agent; and even if she did, her first stop would undoubtedly be with Cosima and the team at Bardwright, or my friend Sally Harlingford, who have all been very good to her. I just don't see Dorothy agreeing to bolt to a new agent and a new agency at the same time.

Still, if that is Saleema's plan, let her dream.

I was early, so I got the flat ready for Darcy. I put on Nina Simone. I lit fragrant candles. I moved the champagne that Emma had ordered to an ice bucket in the living room. My nerves were still jangled, so I opened the bottle and poured myself a glass. Something about the bubbles soothes me. I undid another button on my shirt. I touched my skin with a damp fingertip.

Okay, I was a little horny. And getting more so as the clock neared eleven. Darcy makes me very homologous. Even so, I was nervous about seeing him tonight. Saleema felt like a ghost, reminding me of past mistakes. You'd think I would have learned my lesson with Evan and become exceptionally cautious about dating men with outside commitments. You'd be wrong.

Darcy is married.

It's a long story.

I can tell you all the reasons why his marriage is hollow and why we are so good together, and you can tell me why none of those things matter. You're probably right, but I don't care. It's not like I can blame this one on fate or say it was an accident. After all, I didn't know Evan was engaged to Saleema when I slept with him. Not the first time, anyway. With Darcy, however, I marched into sin with my eyes wide open. Yes, yes, and my legs, too. That goes without saying. I knew what I was doing, and the little voice inside that said I was a fool was drowned out by the other voice that screamed, "Yes! Harder! Right there! Oh, God!"

I sipped my champagne. I stared out the windows of the flat, which had a view over the nearby roofs toward Green Park. I have this fantasy of being invited to dinner at Buck House someday, and when I meet Liz, after I curtsy, I ask her to do her Helen Mirren impression for me. The fact that I have a fantasy like this tells me that I am not the kind of person who will ever be invited to dinner with the queen.

Actually, I blame Liz for my affair. Eighteen months ago, I was on my usual 14 bus around midday, expecting it to sail past Hyde Park Corner and continue toward Piccadilly Circus, where I have a brisk ten-minute walk to my office near Trafalgar Square. That day, however, HRH was hosting a diplomatic luncheon at the palace, and it was my bad luck to arrive at the Corner just as a line of flag-waving limousines began to parade down Park Lane. Apparently, the risk of assassination of the prime ministers of Abkhazia and Tuvalu is sufficient to shut down London buses. I could have dashed into the Tube easily enough, but as it happens, it was a stunning late fall day, warm and sunny, with color in all the trees, and I was right across the street from Hyde Park. I decided the office could wait. Fifteen minutes later, I was seated on a bench by the Serpentine, licking up a soft-serve ice cream cone with a Cadbury Flake, watching the lovers in their pedal boats, and indulging one of my guilty pleasures, namely the latest jet-setting, bodice-ripping, caviar-eating novel by Jilly Cooper.

And that was where I met Darcy.

I knew who he was, of course, and he knew who I was. We had exchanged pleasantries at parties. A little smiling. A little flirting. Nothing more than that. We had never really talked. I don't know why it was different this time, except that it was one of those rare days when London feels like paradise, and he was walking his little seven-year-old Westie, and I love Westies. I could have spent hours rubbing his tummy.

I mean the dog.

We sat on the bench in Hyde Park and talked. And talked. And talked. I forgot all about the office. His dog nuzzled in the grass. The sun got lower. It got cooler, and he took off his anorak and let me drape it over my shoulders. I felt like I was sixteen. I'm not sure exactly when we both realized that we had crossed the line from strangers into friends, or when we admitted to ourselves that we had already skated past the next line where friends begin to look at each other as lovers. Sometimes an attraction is so obvious that you don't need to talk about it. It's just there.

I really didn't expect anything to happen. This was one chance meeting, a little memory for me to tuck away, a nothing romance with a "what if" or maybe an "if only" question at the end of it. We both knew, without saying, that we would be fools to acknowledge the reality of what was going on between us. After all, you might fall in love with a house, but if it belongs to someone else and has a great big security fence to keep out trespassers, you'd probably think twice about looking for a way to get inside, right? So the easy thing to do was walk away. Smile. Pretend.

Except one of the things we talked about was Chihuly glass. Don't ask me how or why. He told me about the Chihuly ceiling in the lobby at the Bellagio in Las Vegas. I told him about the frieze in the Rainbow Room in Rockefeller Center. We both loved the olive-and-turquoise chandelier at the Victoria and Albert. And it just so happened that a Chihuly exhibit was back at the Tate Modern, and I was planning to take a jaunt across the Millennium Bridge to go there on Friday evening, and would he like to see it with me?

Completely innocent.

Except we both knew it wasn't.

As we stood at the balcony on the second floor of the Tate and stared at this glowing orange sun made up of squiggling snakes of glass, we just naturally held hands. As we paused on the arch of the bridge two hours later, with a mist dampening our hair and the fuzzy lights of the city twisting along the banks of the Thames, we just naturally kissed. It was Friday. My father was in Somerset. The Mayfair flat, sitting empty, just naturally beckoned us, and by morning, we were contemplating the wreckage we were making of our lives and telling ourselves that we had to stop.

That was a year and a half ago. We haven't stopped.

When I heard the drumroll of his fingertips on the door, my heart took off like a racehorse. I scared myself with my emotions, but I was powerless to stop them. The difference between a crush when you are sixteen and a crush when you are thirty-six is merely that you have more gray hairs and fewer inhibitions. As I ran to the door, I may as well have been a teenager fantasizing about Robbie Williams.

"Tess," he murmured to me in that oh-so-English voice. "You are a vision."

Melting. Rubbery knees. Girlish giggle.

I pulled him inside and wasted no time helping him off with his charcoal coat, untying his cravat, and wrapping my arms around his neck and kissing him until we had sprained our tongues. His big hands lifted me effortlessly into the air. I felt weightless, like an astronaut.

"It's lovely to see you, darling," I said when we took a breath.

We both laughed. I poured him champagne. We flopped down on the sofa, and I lost myself in his chest. He smelled like Dunhill Original. His chiseled jaw was barbershop smooth. His teeth were a row of snow-white soldiers.

Darcy is a few years older than I, a youthful forty. He has this swept-back mane of salt-and-pepper hair like one of the Landseer lions. His clothes are Manning & Manning, and they make an expensive hummock of silk and wool on the bedroom floor. He is a towering six foot four with the easy grace of an athlete. In his twenties, he was a tennis player, seeded at Wimbledon, but he suffered a groin injury that short-circuited his career. I assure you that his groin is fully recovered.

When you are a young male sports star, you assume that the river of money will flow forever, and you spend it accordingly. Darcy has a weakness for the finer things in life. It was a rude comeuppance to find himself broke no more than a year after he played his last match. No purses. No promotional appearances. No endorsements for shoes and T-shirts. Just a shriveling bank account. In those circumstances, a man does what he must, and that means marrying up. Find an older woman with a hunger for eye candy and the wallet to pay for it. That's what Darcy did. Fifteen years later, he professes no love for his wife, but she has him neatly sewn into her pocket, like a teacup dog you pull out at parties. For a man of Darcy's size, it gets cramped in there.

"God, it's been forever," I said.

We both kicked off our shoes and propped our stockinged feet on my father's coffee table. The champagne went down smooth and fast.

"Three weeks, and it feels like three months," Darcy said. "I'm sorry, my dear, it took her forever to leave town."

"Where is she tonight?"

"Paris. Eurostar. Back tomorrow."

"So you can stay all night?"

"I can."

"Heaven," I said, nibbling his ear.

"What's new in your world, Tessie? I heard about Lowell, of course."

I understood his curiosity, but I wasn't especially interested in making small talk about work. We had other things to do.

"They found him in a white corset, you know." My voice a seductive whisper. My throat rumbling with laughter.

"Are you serious?"

"No."

"You are so bad."

"That's what Emma tells me."

"Your sense of humor is going to get you into trouble someday."

"Why don't you get me into trouble now?" I said.

"Now?"

"Now."

Some things you do not need to ask a man twice.

His slim, long fingers undid each of the buttons on my shirt and peeled back the strawberry silk. The girls made a dramatic appearance, sky high, bursting in black lace. Emma has nothing to fear from me in the tits department, but mine were at their best tonight.

"Oh, my," he said.

I popped the buttons on the sleeves myself, extracted each arm, and dropped the shirt from my fingers onto the floor behind the sofa.

His face found my cleavage. Kissed my skin. Inhaled my perfume. His hands squeezed my breasts like a greengrocer testing ripe grapefruits. There is nothing like a thin layer of silk buffing and twisting your nipples. They puckered into two rocklike nubs.

"Fast or slow?" he asked.

"Fast now, slow later," I said.

He left my bra on. He stood up from the sofa, all big and strong, and began to undress. He knows I like it when he is naked, and I'm not. Cuff links, then white shirt, then undershirt, then braces, then socks, then pants pooling at his ankles, then low-rise black briefs peeled down and flicked aside. For a breathtaking moment, it was just the two of us in the room. Me and his dick.

"You're looking healthy," I said.

"I took a vitamin V."

God help me, I really need to buy stock in Pfizer. That is a wonderful, wonderful company.

He held up one hand, pointed his index finger down, and made little circles with it. Turn around.

"Ah," I said.

I got the picture.

I faced the other side of the sofa, jacked my arse in the air, and he came up behind me. When he tugged my zipper down, I expected to hear seams popping as my hips reinflated to their natural size. He pried my jeans over my backside, pulling my knickers with them. I've never seen that particular angle on myself, and I really don't want to, but I heard him let out a decidedly pleasurable gasp behind me, and then Darcy, his dick, and the good people of Pfizer all squeezed in together under my bum and almost launched me into orbit with the first thrust.

Oh, shit, I said silently, and then not long after, much louder, I heard myself say for the first time, "*ohhhh.*"

You'd think I would be satisfied with great sex. You'd think that after two hours of tongues, dicks, nipples, and orgasms, I would be sated enough to fall asleep without doing any further damage to my life. Is that so much to ask? One light-speed ride in the living room, one achingly slow ride in bed, long minutes of touching in the dark, everything a girl could want from a passion-filled, commitment-free affair with another woman's husband. You'd think I would wrap my slender arms around his barrel chest, sink my face into his back, and close my eyes and dream my way to morning. You'd think there was not one more thing I needed from such a perfect night, and no way that even a master of romantic mistakes such as myself could screw it up.

But no.

We were spooned together. He was almost asleep. I was almost asleep. Which was when I said it. I don't know where the words came from. Someone else must have taken over my body, like a character from Oliver's book. It couldn't have been me.

"I love you."

Yes, it was me, after all.

Oh, fuck.

8

―――

I'M GOING TO launch my own perfume brand. You know, like all the stars do. Still by Jennifer Lopez. Fantasy by Britney Spears. Lovely by Sarah Jessica Parker.

Mine will be called Stupid by Tess Drake.

When I woke up, Darcy was gone. No note. No message on my voice mail. Just gone. I love you? Now that's what every man married to a rich older woman loves to hear from his mistress. I'm not clingy or possessive, and I'm not prone to emotional overreactions every time I have an orgasm. So I must really love him. Why I felt the need to say so is a mystery. I probably just took a dagger and stabbed this relationship through its heart.

I was so disgusted with my lapse in judgment that I decided to go into the office and spend Saturday morning working on client matters in order to get my mind off Darcy and what he must be thinking about me. I like working in the office on Saturdays. It's dark and quiet. No interruptions. I bring in a triple-shot Italian coffee from Caffè Nero, shut my door, and get more done in a couple of hours than I can get through in an entire day during the week.

You have to understand that the life of an agent is mostly about solving crises and soothing fragile egos. Somewhere in between, we do deals, but closing a deal doesn't take nearly as much time as reassuring a blocked chick-lit writer that she still has God's gift or explaining to a *Telegraph* reporter why my client compared the latest Galaxy award winner to a vile, steaming chamber pot evacuated into a crowded alley. Much of the time, I feel like that boy with his finger in the dike, plugging up holes as fast as I can while my clients burst through somewhere else.

Don't get me wrong. I love my clients. Well, most of them. Many of them. It's just that I am not the world's most patient person, and spending an hour listening to Dorothy fret that the Italian cover of *The Bamboo Garden* makes the pandas look too thin taxes my will to live. However, I do it with a smile. "I understand," I say. "You are totally right," I say. "Let me look into that," I say.

Usually, by the time I am done with one call, three more have gone to voice mail, and my BlackBerry light is flashing with nine more e-mails. That's life during the week. Fortunately, the office phone doesn't ring on Saturday, because there is a general assumption that no one in publishing works on the weekend. That's mostly true. And good luck if you want to reach an editor on Friday afternoon, too.

I sipped my espresso. I went through my voice mails.

Still nothing from Darcy.

Nicholas Hadley, whoever he is, called again and urgently wants me to call him back. I pressed delete.

Dorothy Starkwell called "just to chat, my dear."

When your most lucrative client calls to chat, you call her back immediately, but when I did, I got no answer. Dorothy has neither voice mail nor an answering machine and no e-mail account, so I have to try again and again when I need to reach her, because most of the time, she is either writing on notebook paper in a Tribeca coffeehouse or attending her animal rallies.

Frustrating, but you will never hear me say so.

Oliver Howard's editor left a message, too. He is a complete fucking idiot. "I'm sorry, Tess, but I think we're going to take a pass on *Duopoly*. The sales on *Singularity* just don't warrant us continuing with the series. So we're giving up our option, and you can feel free to shop it elsewhere. Sorry to hear about Lowell, by the way. Cheers."

Idiot, idiot, idiot.

I called him back. He wasn't there, of course.

"Malcolm, it's Tess. When you open your mouth to talk, does everyone around you wonder who farted? Go shag yourself."

No, I was more discreet.

"Malcolm, it's Tess. I hate to see you miss this opportunity. Tom Cruise may be interested in *Singularity* for a film. You know what that would do to the price for *Duopoly*. Last chance, call me."

Okay, well, Tom *might* be interested. If Felicia Castro ever let him read it, he would be interested. Close enough.

I texted Emma what was really on my mind:

TOLD DARCY I LOVE HIM. AM I NUTS?

She replied almost immediately:

NOT NUTS. YOU GO GIRL.

Despite Emma's optimism, I was discouraged, so I called a couple of clients and discreetly floated the idea of starting my own agency, and if I did, would they join me? They said yes, absolutely, you're our girl, follow you to the ends of the earth, that sort of thing. I was pleased, but I'm no fool. Clients hate change. They like everything to stay exactly the way it is. Having your agent go out on her own induces paroxysms of doubt and a lot of thumb sucking. What about my past deals? what about my future deals? what about my international deals? what about my movie rights? who will pay me? what will my editor say? what about my taxes—that sort of thing. I know that, eventually, I will simply have to pull the trigger and hope that many of my clients have the courage to follow me.

I read manuscripts for another hour. Finished my coffee. Checked voice mail on my cell phone. Still nothing from Darcy.

My office phone rang. Rare for a Saturday. I thought it must be him, so I grabbed it up and said "Tess Drake" in as breathy a voice as I could muster.

It wasn't him. It was Guy.

"Oh. Filippa. You're there."

"I'm here." Breathy turned to frosty.

"I thought I'd get your machine."

"Well, you got the real deal, Guy. What do you want?" And what the fuck were you doing with Saleema last night?

"Ah, actually, this is a little awkward."

"Now you know how I felt yesterday."

"Yes, about that." He stopped.

"I'm listening."

"The thing is, I'm calling to apologize," Guy said.

Apologize? Guy?

"Ooookay," I said, drawing out the word so he knew that I was suspicious.

"Truly, I was out of line."

"I know."

"I wonder if we could forget all about that conversation and start over."

"Why the change of heart, Guy?"

I was trying to figure out Guy's ulterior motive and whether it had anything to do with Saleema.

"Isn't it enough that I'm telling you I'm sorry?"

"No."

I heard him sigh theatrically. "Look, I was having a bad day. Money problems. I won't bore you with the details."

"Please don't."

"So that whole commission thing—I hope you'll just forget I said anything of the sort. I wouldn't want rumors like that to get out."

"I forgot it as soon as you said it, Guy, because it was never going to happen."

"Ah. Yes. Well, good. And the other thing, I mean, about you and me. You know, Brighton and so forth. I thought perhaps, well . . . you *are* very attractive, Filippa. I've always thought so."

"End of discussion, Guy."

"Yes, of course. Again, I'm sorry. What I wanted to tell you is that I am happy to put our negotiations about Dorothy's next contract on hold for a while. Until you clear up your own situation. Okay? We'll consider the deal discussion so far to be no more than idle chitchat. The real work will begin when you say so."

That was exactly what I wanted, so I couldn't help wonder: What game was Guy playing?

"I appreciate it, Guy. We'll talk soon."

"Indeed."

He hung up.

Ten years in this business have made me a cynical, suspicious bitch. Whenever someone caves too easily for no apparent reason, I wonder what he's hiding. Try as I might, however, I couldn't see any downside for me in Guy's postponing the wrap-up for Dorothy's next deal. Assuming I went out on my own, and assuming Dorothy was still my client, then Guy was giving me a huge ace to play against Bardwright. Such things don't normally come free, and Guy isn't the kind of man to offer something for nothing.

Hmm.

Maybe Saleema is harboring dreams of stealing Dorothy away, and she's convinced Guy to wait until her schemes bear fruit. After all, if Cosima gets the deal, then we all lose.

I thought about it and then did something I hadn't done in a very long time.

I called Saleema's cell number.

"It's Tess," I said when she answered. "Don't hang up."

Saleema was silent, and then she said, "What do you want, Tess?"

Her voice was butter smooth. She still had an erotic hint of an Indian accent, despite all her years in the States. I could picture her face clearly. A tiny, gorgeous firebrand.

"I thought we could bury the hatchet," I said. "But maybe somewhere other than in my head."

I thought that was funny, but Saleema didn't laugh.

"Who are you sleeping with these days, Tess?"

I was taken aback, and I didn't answer. She said it as if she knew something. But that was impossible. Emma was as loyal as a palace guard, and Darcy and I had plenty of reasons to keep our mouths shut.

"Look, I'll tell you I'm sorry a few more times if it would help," I said.

"It wouldn't."

"Ah." I didn't know what else to say. "So where are you? You sound faraway."

As in, are you in London, you scheming bitch?

"I'm in the toilet in first class on a seven forty-seven."

"You know you could be interfering with the aircraft's communication and navigation systems."

"I'll take my chances."

I was looking for something, anything. The truth is, I really did want to put the past behind us. I missed her. Of course, I knew it was a lost cause. Once you've pricked your skin and become blood enemies, you don't change.

"I really miss you, Saleema. If I could go back and do things differently, you know I would. I wish I could make things right between us."

I heard a long pause, and for a moment, I thought maybe the relationship we had shared in the beginning might peek through. But no. "You made your choice, Tess."

"Will you be in London anytime soon? We could talk."

I heard a smile in her voice as she replied. As if, somehow, she knew that I knew. She had been in London yesterday. With Guy.

"I never know when my plans will take me to London. Sometimes it's on short notice."

"So call me next time."

"I don't think so, Tess. Good-bye."

She hung up on me.

I didn't learn anything from the call, other than what I already knew. Saleema still hated me. Five years hadn't softened her. I didn't know if she and Guy had plans with regard to Dorothy, but as far as I knew, I was still bulletproof. They were handing me Dorothy's deal on a silver tray. Sometimes the bad guys do the good guy a favor, even if they don't want to.

I was so caught up in my thoughts that I didn't even hear my office door open.

When I looked up, my other enemy was there, framed in the doorway, the dark office behind her. Thin. Arrow straight. Hands on her hips.

The wicked witch. The new head of the agency.

Cosima.

9

MY BOSS.

I have worked with Cosima Tate for three years, and I have known her as long as I've been in the industry. Everyone knows her, in the way that you know war, pestilence, and plague exist in this world but you hope they don't come to your neighborhood.

For twenty-five years, Cosima ran her own agency. She was one of the most successful female entrepreneurs in the city, but let's be honest. She was and is a bitch with a capital *C*. Single-minded. Ruthless. She will tell lies, go back on deals, cut you off at the knees, plot behind your back, and do whatever it takes to ensure that she comes out on top. It's all about power, and power comes through money. You might tell me that I could learn something from Cosima, and you're probably right. If business success is your model, she's a paragon. She does nothing that men don't do every day, without an eyebrow being raised. If I am as successful in running my own agency as Cosima was in running hers, I will be a wealthy woman.

At least until Satan comes calling to get his soul back.

The entire agency world was taken by surprise when Cosima agreed to merge her agency with Bardwright three years ago and accept a number two role behind Lowell. Everyone speculated—correctly—that Lowell would become a figurehead leader and the real power would reside with Cosima. The question was, why do it at all? My friend Sally told me at the time that Cosima had big plans, world plans, and she needed a larger platform to mount her assault. Merging her own company with Bardwright created a combined entity that was the second-largest entertainment agency in London. I have no doubt that she intends to be number one very soon. Not just in London but in New York, LA, and elsewhere.

She could let me and Dorothy walk away without blinking. Her plans don't rise or fall on a few children's books about pandas, however popular and lucrative they may be. But it isn't about that. When you are Cosima, you win every battle. You offer no consolation prize to your opponent. You take everything, leave nothing. For her to finally win complete control of Bardwright and then have a story in the *Bookseller* about one of her agents leaving with a multimillion-dollar client? That would be intolerable.

It's also true that, on some level, this is personal. Cosima and I hate each other. Always have. I don't know whether she sees something in me that makes her question some of the choices she made along the way or whether I see in her some twisted monster who symbolizes what I don't want to become. Maybe it's just that I don't toe the line. I challenge everything. I do things my way. Cosima loathes anyone who thinks differently from her, which is why she is always trying to rein me in using Marty Goodacre to do her dirty work. It hasn't worked, and it never will.

Or maybe there's something more to all of this. Maybe she *knows*. I tell myself this can't be true, but there are days when I'm certain she has sniffed out my secret.

You see, there is another reason why I cannot abide Cosima Tate.

I know how she keeps her husband under her thumb and treats him like a kept man. I know her money is like a chain around his neck. I know he yearns to be free, and he cannot be, not the way things are.

Her husband is Jack Tate.

Jack is Darcy.

"That's a beautiful scarf," I told her.

Cosima was wearing a purple-flowered wrap around her chest and shoulders. Purple, the color of royalty. I figured she had purchased it on the Champs-Élysées on her visit to Paris. Her blouse was white silk. Her black pencil skirt hugged her knees. She was not particularly tall, but her stilettos shot her into the stratosphere, and she maintained a posture so rigid I wasn't convinced she could really bend at the waist.

"Thank you, Tess," she said.

She stood in the doorway without coming into my office. Cosima never entered offices. If she wanted you, you came to her. She was sixty years old. Her face had the uncomfortably stretched look of a face-lift. Probably more than one. Her hair was as black as it had been in her twenties, but the dye job looked startling, as if gray would have come to her more naturally. Nonetheless, she was impeccably put together, right down to her elongated fingernails and her French makeup.

"Good trip to Paris?" I asked.

She arched a black eyebrow.

"Marty told me," I explained. "Where is Marty, by the way? Don't tell me you let him off the leash. He'll wander into the park and get lost."

A thin smile. Lips only, no teeth.

"Marty is extremely efficient," Cosima said, "although he does resemble a whiny dachshund at times."

"A yipper dog. Yes, you're right."

"I hope Marty passed along my message to you. You're very important to us, Tess. To me. I have extremely ambitious plans for this agency, now that poor Lowell has passed the torch, and I want you to know that you are a big part of those plans."

"That's kind of you to say."

Flattery wasn't her usual game. In Cosima's mouth, it felt particularly dangerous.

"You remind me a little of myself when I was younger, Tess," she said.

Now I was really scared.

"Oh?"

"Yes, absolutely. Tough. Smart. Willing to take on the world. Those are admirable qualities."

"Thank you."

"Of course, you need a savvy business sense, too. Without that, you can find yourself all alone."

"I do okay alone," I said.

"How old are you, Tess?"

"Thirty-six."

Cosima nodded. "When I was your age, I had been running my own agency for several years. It was tough going in those days. Many times I wished I had never done it."

"You did rather well," I said.

"I did, but, you know, I only went out on my own because I didn't have an agency that saw my potential. There were many days that I wished I had a support network around me. I stared into the abyss more than once, and if a lucky wind hadn't pushed me back, I might have fallen. Success is all about hindsight, Tess. It looks like an easy, straight path when you're on the other side of it, but the road is rather more curvy and treacherous along the way."

"That's good advice, but why are you telling me this?" I asked.

Cosima's shoulders inched upward in a barely perceptible shrug. "I want you to think of me as a mentor, Tess."

Run! Run!

"I appreciate the offer."

"I know you were often frustrated while Lowell was in charge," she continued. "You saw yourself as able to deliver much more, and you were right. I understand how you feel. However, as much as we will miss him, Lowell is gone. The agency is on a new path.

You could wind up as a partner here, which means a much greater share of the agency's income."

"That's very interesting."

"Achieving your potential means making hard decisions, however."

"Such as?"

"Well, we're not artists here. We're not museum directors. Agencies thrive on revenue and profitability. Partners in particular have to understand that."

"Of course," I said.

"However much we may like them, not all our clients deliver the returns we need. In that circumstance, it's really better and kinder if we help them find other representation. We don't simply want clients, we want *profitable* clients."

"Did you have someone in mind?" I asked.

But I knew. She wanted me to dump Oliver.

"The agency has invested hundreds of hours in Oliver Howard," Cosima continued. "Many of those hours are your own precious time, and there's substantially more among our international and film teams. Unfortunately, we haven't seen a suitable return on our investment, and it's unlikely we ever will. I think it's time we cut our losses and move on."

"Oliver is a genius."

"Oscar Wilde was a genius, but he died penniless."

"Maybe he needed a better agent," I said.

Cosima folded her arms. "Touché."

"I won't drop Oliver."

"Well, I applaud your loyalty and faith in him. I think it's misguided, but *you* are the agent, Tess. Ultimately, the decision is yours."

It is?

"I'm pleased to hear that," I said.

"You're not measured by your hours, you're measured by your results. For example, Dorothy Starkwell."

"What about her?"

"Marty tells me that you're holding off on a new deal for her with Guy. Is there a reason?"

"Dorothy wants more time."

"Ah, of course. But I was under the impression that you and Guy had already come to terms on the shape of the deal. If Dorothy wants a more relaxed deadline, that's perfectly fine, but we may as well close the book on your fine efforts and put pen to paper. Marty may have mentioned that this is a priority for me. It would give us such good press, coming so soon after Lowell's unfortunate tragedy."

I smiled.

Cosima smiled.

"There's no deal," I said.

Sorry, Oliver, I can't just walk away from that kind of money.

"No?"

"Guy doesn't want to talk terms until Dorothy is ready," I said.

"Ah."

"I'll talk to Dorothy again tomorrow," I said.

If Cosima's face got any tighter, I thought it would snap like a rubber band.

"Yes, please do. You know how important this is."

"Absolutely."

Cosima turned to leave. Half her body disappeared into the shadows outside my door, as if being gobbled up by the dark side of the moon. She turned back to me and added, "Will you be at Lowell's funeral on Wednesday?"

"Of course."

"Good. We all need to pay our respects. Such a terrible thing."

"Yes."

"I wonder if they will find out what happened."

I looked at her. "What do you mean?"

"Well, you know how people talk. I've heard rumors."

"Rumors?"

"Of murder," Cosima said.

"Murder? That's crazy."

"Yes, I'm sure it will all come to nothing. Lowell was beloved. No one had a reason to kill him."

I thought to myself: no one except you, Cosima.

"Oh, Jack will be at the funeral, too," she added.

"Jack?" I asked, barely able to breathe.

She smiled. "My husband."

"Yes, of course."

"He told me how well you and he got on at the last Christmas party."

"He's a very pleasant man," I said.

"Yes, he is. I thought that the four of us could go to lunch after the funeral. You, me, Jack, and Marty. Toast Lowell, and take a look forward to a new era. What do you say?"

Forget it, I thought.

"I'd love to," I said.

10

I TOOK A BUS back to my apartment around noon.

Still no message from Darcy. Normally, that wouldn't worry me. We make it a point never to call each other directly, because we don't know who might happen to overhear a message or see a number on a call log. That's why we use Emma as our go-between. Even so, I thought that he might make an exception this time, because of what I said to him last night. I was unreasonably nervous, and talking to Cosima only made it worse.

I tried Dorothy again but didn't reach her. I figured out one time that it took me an average of six tries to get a hold of her. If you're thinking of ditching the modern world by turning off your answering machine and throwing away your mobile, just remember those of us out here who may want to reach you. We are likely to be annoyed.

Emma sent me another text:

MET NEW GIRL LAST NIGHT. WOW. IN LOVE. HOT.

I smiled. Emma falls in and out of love every week with a new girl, but who am I to tell her to go slow? I wondered if this one looked like Sienna Miller. Emma's girlfriends have a way of mirroring her latest celeb crush.

I decided to go for a run. The sky was drizzling, but no more than a spitting rain, not enough to keep Londoners indoors. I took the bus up to Battersea Park and did a few laps around the Carriage Drive. I don't run often enough, but I try to get out two or three times a week to clear my head. You would think that, being single, I have plenty of alone time, but that's not really true. I eat most of my meals with editors, clients, reporters, producers, and everyone else who needs to sell or be sold; and my other waking minutes are normally spent on the phone and the BlackBerry. Other than in the shower and on my runs, I feel like I have invited the rest of the world to share my life.

I try not to think about anything when I run. I listen to my breathing. I feel my heart race. I watch the trees, the river, the people, the vendors selling ice cream, and the squirrels chasing each other around the grass. But not today. I had too much on my mind. The drizzle soaked my hair and face, and that mirrored my mood. I felt as if I were running *from* something now, but I didn't know what, and I didn't know how far I had to go. In my business, it pays to be suspicious of other people's motives. If you assume the worst, you're rarely disappointed. Even so, I couldn't escape the feeling that someone was out there, plotting against me. Call it ego, if you like. I mean, I know the world doesn't begin and end with me. I don't believe in conspiracy theories. But I kept looking over my shoulder anyway.

After running for an hour, I collapsed on a bench by the Thames. The white spires of the Albert Bridge were on my left. It's my favorite city bridge, particularly at night. My brow was wet with sweat and rain. I unhooked a water bottle from my waist and squirted a long stream into my mouth. I threw my head back and closed my eyes.

"Excuse me?"

I looked up. A young woman, protected by a giant black umbrella,

stood next to the bench. A plastic London map dangled from between her thumb and index finger. She was in her early twenties,
heavy, mousy brown hair, red glasses.

"I'm so sorry to bother you."

I managed a smile. "That's okay. What do you need?"

"Well, I'm down here from York, and it's my first trip, and I'm
afraid I'm totally lost. I wonder if you could show me on the map
where I am exactly?"

"Sure."

I took the map from her outstretched hand. The plastic was
sticky and greasy, as if she'd been looking at it while eating a bag
of chips and a leaky cup of soda. My hands stuck to the plastic.
I found the panel for Battersea Park and pointed at it. "You're
here," I said. "Right between the Albert Bridge and the Chelsea
Bridge."

"Oh, thanks so much," she told me. She reclaimed her map and
headed east away from me along the riverbank.

I watched her go. When I looked back toward the Albert Bridge,
I jumped. A man had taken a seat next to me on the bench.

"Shit!" I said involuntarily.

He smiled and lit a cigarette. "I'm sorry to startle you, Miss
Drake."

"Who the hell are you?"

"My name is Nicholas Hadley. I've left a couple messages for
you, but you haven't called me back. So I thought I would visit you
in person."

Hadley was a small man in his fifties with thinning hair and a
trimmed gray beard. He wore a chocolate-colored Burberry. Tan
trousers, muddy black dress shoes. He coughed as the smoke hit
his lungs.

"How did you find me?" I asked.

"That's my job," he said.

"Your job?" I felt an itch to run away. "Look, if this is about a
book you're writing—"

"It's not."

"Then what do you want?"

I smelled the smoke as he exhaled. I really wanted to beg a cigarette off him.

"I'm a detective inspector with the Metropolitan Police, Miss
Drake," he said. "I'm looking into Lowell Bardwright's death."

He showed me his identification, and I studied it carefully enough
to see that he wasn't lying.

"What does that have to do with me?" I asked.

"Well, you worked with Mr. Bardwright for ten years, is that
right? I was hoping you could answer a few questions for me."

I hesitated. "Why? I thought his death was an accident."

"That's one possibility."

"What's the other?"

He smiled. "That it wasn't an accident."

I thought about Cosima hearing rumors of murder. "The papers all said Lowell was alone in his apartment. That he accidentally hanged himself as part of a sex game."

"Oh, you know the media, Miss Drake. They don't always get it
right."

"Meaning?"

"Meaning we don't think Mr. Bardwright was alone."

"Oh."

I remembered what I'd said to Emma when I first heard about
Lowell's death: If I know Lowell, he found himself a Julia Roberts
look-alike who freaked when he stopped breathing.

"So again, what does that have to do with me?" I asked him.

"We're talking to everyone at the agency," Hadley said. "It's
routine background."

"Well, what is it you want to know?"

"What kind of person was Mr. Bardwright?" Hadley asked.

"Lowell? He was a player. Knew everybody. Liked to be in the
limelight, attend the parties, see and be seen."

"Did you work with him regularly?"

"Of course."

"In what way?"

I shrugged. "He was the head of the agency. Every deal went
across his desk."

"Was he a person of integrity?"

I thought about it. "Yes, Lowell usually played fair. I could trust him not to go behind my back. That's not always the case in this business."

"Did he have any enemies?"

"When you're the head of an agency, you always have enemies," I told him. "But nothing worth killing someone over."

"No? Doesn't the Bardwright Agency handle a lot of multimillion-dollar deals?"

"Sure."

Hadley nodded. "Then, believe me, he had things worth killing over."

"Are you saying he was murdered?" I asked.

"I'm not saying anything of the kind." Hadley added, "Did his death surprise you?"

"Of course."

"Not that he died, but *how* he died. The sex thing."

"Nothing surprises me anymore," I said.

"Are you familiar with erotic asphyxia?"

"I've heard of it. Beyond that, no. I've never tried it."

"Did Mr. Bardwright like to experiment sexually?"

"I have no idea," I said.

"Did he ever make a pass at you?"

I nodded. "Once or twice, in the early days. He made it clear that if I was interested, he was interested. But I wasn't. He had the good taste to drop it. It was never an issue between us."

"So you never slept with him?"

"No. Is that something you're asking everyone at the agency?"

"Do you think I should?"

"I have no idea. I just wondered why you're asking *me*."

Hadley didn't answer. "Have you ever been in Mr. Bardwright's apartment?"

"What the hell is this about?"

"It's a simple question."

"No, I've never been in Lowell's apartment."

"Never?"

"Never. I've never been in his apartment. I've never slept with him."

Hadley nodded. "I understand you've been telling people that Mr. Bardwright was found dressed in a white corset."

"I have a crass sense of humor," I said. "Is that a crime?"

"Not at all. Except that Mr. Bardwright really *was* wearing a corset, and we deliberately didn't release that information to the press. So I was wondering how you knew about it."

Oh, fuck, fuck, fuck! What are the odds of that? Did God think this was funny?

"It was a joke!" I insisted.

"That's quite a coincidence."

"I'm sorry, but that's all it is. I simply made it up, because I know how the rumor mill works in this industry. It was stupid. I had no idea he was really dressed that way."

"Where were you the night that Mr. Bardwright died?" Hadley asked.

"In my apartment. Sleeping."

"Alone?"

"Yes, of course, alone. Look, I can understand why this corset thing would make you suspicious, but I swear to you, it is just a hideous coincidence."

"You never had any kind of sexual contact with Mr. Bardwright?"

"None."

"You were never in his apartment?"

"I already told you, never."

"Did you have any dispute with him? Problems at the agency?"

"No. I think this conversation is over, Mr. Hadley. I'm not answering any more questions."

I got up from the bench. My legs felt like rubber.

Hadley made no move to stand up. He reached inside his Burberry and slid out a magazine that had been folded in half. It was a month-old, wrinkled copy of the *Bookseller*. He opened it and found a dog-eared page.

"Do you remember this photo?"

I thought about walking away without looking, but I gave in to my curiosity. It was a photo of Lowell and me at a Christmas publishing event. His arm was around my waist. We were both mugging for the camera.

"Yes," I said.

"The two of you look pretty cozy."

"Oh, for heaven's sake, it was a Christmas party. Two hundred people, most of them drunk. There are probably photographs of Lowell with his arm around half the women at the party."

"I'm sure you're right," Hadley said. He added, "Nice dress."

I looked at the photo. I was wearing a navy blue cocktail dress, low cut, just barely above the knee.

"So?" I asked.

"I was wondering if you still have that dress," Hadley said.

"What?"

"You heard me."

I stared at him. "Actually, no."

"Oh? Where is it?"

"The dry cleaner lost it. That was a couple of months ago."

"Ah, I see. Too bad."

He smiled at me again and sat there, tapping the ash off his cigarette onto the wet ground. I turned and jogged away, but I was so shaken I was afraid of falling down. It was obvious what was going on, but I couldn't bring myself to believe it.

They couldn't possibly think I had anything to do with Lowell's death.

Could they?

11

I FINALLY REACHED Dorothy Starkwell from my office on Monday afternoon, which is Monday morning in New York. It was my ninth attempt to call her, which is by no means a new record. I had to dial the calls myself, which is a hardship, because I'm hopeless with international dialing codes. Emma had decided to take the day off, either to get past a hangover or to spend the day in bed with her latest whirly girl.

My end of a conversation with Dorothy usually goes like this: "Dorothy, it's Tess."

At that point, I put down the phone, answer a few e-mails, head out for noodles at Wagamama, take the Tube to Oxford Street, pay my mobile bill in the Orange store, buy a new skirt at Selfridges, walk back, toss some bread cubes to the pigeons in Trafalgar Square, and then saunter into the office, by which time Dorothy is ready to take a breath.

"Dorothy, it's Tess," I said when she answered the phone.

"Oh, Tessie, how lovely to hear from you! I called you three days ago, and I was beginning to wonder if you were ill, because I hadn't received a call back. You are all right, aren't you? You work too hard, Tess. I know it's all day and all night for you agents, but honestly, dear, you're going to have to take some time for yourself. Did I tell you that I'm fostering a kinkajou? Yes! He is adorable! Although I understand you can't give them strawberries, which I find a little odd. Can you imagine any creature being allergic to strawberries? I'd die, I really would. I just got back from breakfast in SoHo, and I had strawberry-stuffed French toast, which was lovely, dear, absolutely lovely, we will have to go there when you're in New York. Are you coming over soon? It's been eons, simply eons. Oh, by the way, I heard from my publisher in Milan, did I tell you, and even though I still think the pandas on the cover look anorexic—and pandas are roly-poly, dear, not anorexic—which reminds me, did you see what that Nicole girl looks like these days? My God, her forearms look like chopsticks, it's so sad. Where was I? Oh Milan, yes, anyway, Maria tells me that the books are selling over there like, well, what sells well in Italy? Pasta, I suppose. See, that's another reason why the pandas shouldn't be so thin. People in Italy love to eat. Although it is true that they themselves are thin as rails, and I don't know how that's possible. Do you think they work out? I mean, if I ate Italian every night, I'd be the size of, well, one of my pandas, don't you think? Can't you just imagine that?"

I heard Dorothy inhale, and I broke out of my coma and jumped in with the most important question.

"What's a kinkajou?" I asked.

Okay, second most important question.

"Well, this fellow looks a little like a monkey, or maybe a ferret, although I'm told he's part of the same family as the red panda, which I thought was very ironic and appropriate for me, don't you think? However, if truth be told, the red panda isn't in the same family with the giant panda at all, and since they don't really look at all like each other, you have to wonder why they wound up with the same name. Both Chinese bamboo eaters, though, so perhaps that's the reason. Strange. That's life in the animal kingdom, I guess. I imagine they think all the names we give them are pretty silly. Someone says 'kinkajou,' and I want to say gesundheit! Do you think they come up with names for us?"

"I heard that lions give names to other animals," I said. "They call them dinner."

Dorothy giggled. She is in her early sixties, no bigger than a kinkajou herself, with a helmet of gray hair. She wears jewelry that is so gaudy and heavy her earlobes droop and her back is permanently slumped. Her body, bathroom, condo, and car smell of Crabtree & Evelyn. When she laughs, she has all the innocence of a ten-year-old girl. "Oh, Tess, what am I going to do with you? You are too funny, dear."

"What do the girls think about the kinkajou?" I asked.

Dorothy has five female white standard poodles that she walks every morning and every afternoon. They're clipped like balls of cotton candy and look like a poofy street gang taking over downtown Manhattan.

"The girls are in Starkwell North, dear, and I keep the kinkajou in Starkwell South. I don't suppose they'd get along."

Dorothy owns the two top floors in a Tribeca loft, which should tell you that her panda books have generated an awful lot of bamboo.

"I guess you can't risk having an apartment full of kinkajoodles," I said.

Dorothy giggled again and snorted. "Kinkajoodles. Oh, that's funny, I love that."

"I suppose you want to hear about lunch with Guy," I told her quickly, before she could recover.

"Oh, yes, that's why I was calling! Now I remember! Dear Guy, I suppose he was as crusty as ever, the pudgy ol' poop. I really do love him, almost as much as I love you, dear. There aren't many people who understand my pandas so well, who really get their personalities. I was so lucky to find him. I know you had lunch on Friday, so just send me the contract, I'm ready to start, I've got some wonderful ideas."

"Yes, about that—" I began, but I wasn't fast enough.

"Speaking of lunch, did I tell you who I was seeing today? No, I don't suppose I did, he just called me over the weekend. His name is David Milton. Have I ever mentioned his father? Tom? Tom was a dear, dear friend back in Ithaca, he worked at the library alongside me for years and years, but he died of a brain aneurysm, terrible thing, it was like losing a brother. I still miss him. I mention Tom in the acknowledgments of *The Bamboo Garden,* do you remember? He was so supportive of my career, so inspirational to me. David is his son. I don't recall meeting him more than once, because he was busy in the city, and Tom would visit him here from time to time, but I suppose I understand now that once you live in the Big Apple, you don't really think about going back to quiet little Ithaca. Did I ever tell you the town slogan in Ithaca? Ithaca is gorges! Really, because they have these wonderful gorges with waterfalls around town, but of course, it's a pun, you know. Gorgeous? Get it? Well, David called me out of the blue and said we should have lunch, so I'm seeing him at Ono in the Gansevoort. They have some amazing vegetable sushi there."

Dorothy is a vegetarian, which is probably no surprise. I have to suppress my carnivorous instincts when I'm around her. I would happily devour roast kinkajou with mushy peas.

"About Guy," I said.

"Yes, dear, tell me everything, I am yours."

I took a breath. I tried not to think about the fact that my whole life depended on what Dorothy would say to me in the next five minutes. I felt like a Mexican cliff diver with a fear of heights. Yes, I have other clients, but if I want to launch my own agency, I need Dorothy with me. It's as simple as that. Her deals are my moneymakers.

"Well, I have a very important question for you, darling," I said.

"Now, Tess, I know what you've said in the past, and, yes, I'm sure I could get more money by going elsewhere, but Guy is the dearest person in the world to me after you, and he's a crazy animal lover like me, and my books would be nowhere at all without his guidance. So don't start in on me again about switching to a different house, because I just won't hear of it. I love Guy, and I have more money already than I know what to do with, so there's just nothing more to be said."

"No, it's not that," I told her, although I do wish she would give up her little crush on Guy and move to a house that does proper marketing. But that ship has sailed. "Some things have been happening here at Bardwright," I added.

I told her about Lowell. She was shocked.

I told her about Cosima. She was appalled.

"So the long and the short of it is that I'm thinking about launching my own entertainment agency next week, which means leaving Bardwright, and I was very much hoping that you would allow me to keep representing you in my new business." I said this all so quickly that I was afraid I had condensed the words into a little *urp* sound that was unintelligible to the human ear.

"Oh, well, Tessie, of course," Dorothy said.

"I know you have a long history with Bardwright, and there are some fine people here, and anyone would be thrilled to have a gem like you as a client. But I truly value our relationship and would love for it to continue when I take the big step."

In fact, I can't afford to take the big step without you, so please say yes, or I will be forced to swoon in front of the next Tube train that presents itself or follow Lowell's example and play an abortive game of erotic asphyxia. I have to say, as death goes, the latter doesn't sound so bad.

"Tessie, dear, get the wax out of your ears. I already agreed."

"You did?"

And then my brain caught up with my ears, and I realized that she had said yes. I think I may have had a little orgasm right then. Just a quick one. Oh my God, I'm free at last!

"Dorothy, I can't tell you how much that means to me," I told her honestly.

"Please, dear, you'd have to murder someone before I went with another agent. You know that. You're everything to me."

I knew what she meant about killing someone, but I didn't tell her that Nicholas Hadley seemed to be under the impression I had done exactly that. Better to leave that discussion for another day.

"We can talk about the details later, but I'll be hiring coagents for the international deals and accountants and bankers and people like that, and so for your purposes, it should be basically seamless. I'll have even more time to focus on bigger and better things for you and your little black and whites."

"Will Sally still do the deals in Europe?" Dorothy asked. "You know I love Sally."

"Yes, I'm sure I'll use Sally for Europe. I'm seeing her for a drink later. The only thing that will change at all in the short run is that I want to slow down the train a little with Guy and get the deal done as soon as the agency is launched. Does that sound okay to you?"

"That sounds lovely," Dorothy told me.

Oh yes, lovely, lovely. I felt like a heroine in a musical. I felt pretty. My hills were alive. I was making the music of the night.

"Was there anything else, dear?" Dorothy asked me. "I know you like to go on a bit, and sometimes I have to cut you off, or neither one of us would get a thing done. I've got to see that boy David Milton for lunch, and I haven't taken the girls for their morning walk, and they get cranky if they don't get to prance through City Hall Park."

Try to imagine five clipped poodles strutting through the canyons of New York ahead of a woman barely taller or larger than a Russian gymnast. Scary thought.

"Thank you, Dorothy, you're the best," I told her.

"Oh, you're very welcome, Tessie dear, don't give it another thought. Go do all of your little agent things, and don't worry about me. Give Sally a hug. I could swear, though, that there was something else I was going to tell you. What, what, what was it, and it was on my tongue just a second ago. Oh, yes, I know, I have greetings from a friend of yours, that's what it is."

"Friend?" I said.

If someone introduces himself to Dorothy as a friend of mine, I have an awful feeling that he's not.

"Yes, I was getting an award at the animal rights dinner last night, don't you remember? Very posh, swanky, in the ballroom at the Pierre. I love that ballroom, do you remember what it's like? Anyway, it was all vegetarian, of course, and I was telling everyone about my kinkajou, and they all wanted to see pictures, not only of Kinky—that's what I call him, isn't it wonderful?—but of the girls, too. Naturally, I was happy to oblige. Oh, and the ceremony was lovely. I cried. They talked about everything I do for animals, and, yes, I know it's a fancy way of saying I write big checks, but they were gracious about it and they even did a little reading from my books."

"Friend?" I repeated.

"Oh, yes, I met this lovely woman, and we spent most of the evening together. She is extremely passionate about animals, too, just a lovely little thing. But I was so surprised that she knows Guy, and she knows you, too! Isn't it a small world?"

"Tiny," I said. "Minuscule."

"Her name was very exotic—now what was it?"

"Saleema?" I said, feeling all my stomach juices slurp through the hole that had just formed, like sand squeezing through an hourglass.

"That's it! Saleema, isn't that pretty? Saleema Azah. She said I should be sure to say hello when we talked. I thought that was very sweet, don't you think?"

"Sweet as sugar, that's Saleema," I said.

If you're diabetic.

12

"MY GOD, I'M EXHAUSTED," I said, collapsing onto the burgundy sofa in the downstairs bar at the Groucho Club. I blew a kiss at the bartender, who knew me and kept me well supplied with white wine and cosmopolitans. Always make friends with your bartender.

"Dorothy?" Sally Harlingford asked me with a knowing smile.

"Dorothy. I feel like I'm a year older every time I talk to her. This time, however, it was worth it."

"So I gather."

I had texted her the good news about Dorothy and my agency. It was a code she would understand: PANDAS R FREE.

I made short work of the first glass of wine and relaxed into the red velvet with a satisfied sigh. It was only four thirty, but I knew my afternoon would be a loss after chatting with Dorothy, so I asked Sally if we could move up our date. Sally never says no to early drinkies. You'd think the bar would be empty at that time of day, but the Groucho is a haunt for the publishing industry, and we do as much work over afternoon drinks as we do at our desks. Probably more.

A few book biz women started the Groucho back in the 1980s in revenge against the old boys' clubs (no girls allowed, only crusty old men like my father) and because publishing still carried a whiff of Fleet Street that made us socially questionable. We both use ink, and we gossip, and we spill secrets to the world at large. Bad form all around. However, for twenty-plus years, the Groucho has been a home we can call our own, where rumors fly in the course of the evening from the bar to the brasserie, based on who is talking to whom. Lowell was a fixture on the club's board for years. I imagine Cosima will inherit his chair.

"So how is the Bard of the Pandas?" Sally asked, carefully crossing her legs and tugging her lavender skirt over her knee.

"Oh, as scattered as ever. She sends her love."

Sally made a kissing noise with her lips. "Back at her."

Sally loves New York and makes any excuse to cross the pond. A few years ago, when we were both at Book Expo America, I arranged for the two of us to have dinner with Dorothy at a restaurant in Little Korea. We all hit it off, and our girls' night out during BEA has become an annual pagan rite.

"You know I want you to handle Europe for me?" I asked Sally, who is something of a language savant and speaks fluent French, German, and Italian. To be honest, I think Sally hates London and would love to live just about anywhere else. Most of the time, she's in Paris, Munich, or Rome, meeting with publishers on translation rights for her clients, which is a wonderful excuse to suck down wine and goose liver terrines. How she stays so damn skinny is a mystery. Anyway, I handle the deals in the United States and Britain and all the film and publicity work, so I need someone who knows the European terrain to sell to the inscrutable publishers on the Continent.

"I'm a little overcommitted, Tessie," Sally replied.

"Dorothy wants you and only you."

"Well then, anything for her."

"Thank you."

"When's the big day?" Sally asked.

"Next Monday, I think. That will give me time to figure out what the hell I'm doing. Besides, I want to wait until after the funeral on Wednesday. It looks bad to bail on Bardwright before Lowell is even in the ground." I saw a tightness in Sally's face, and I knew I had stuck my foot in it. "Damn, that was a stupid thing to say, I'm so sorry."

Sally shrugged, as if it were nothing to her, but it wasn't. Sally is many things to me. A friend. A mentor. A gossip. An inspiration. She is the soul of elegance, a blond beauty from the old school, diplomatic and British, but with all the toughness and independence of a woman who has struggled to survive on her own. If Cosima had her grace, I probably wouldn't be leaving Bardwright. I have known Sally for years, but she is still a bit of an enigma to me. She never really invites you inside her soul, like a Frenchman who still uses *vous* instead of *tu* with a neighbor of thirty years. Me, I spill my heart to bus drivers, but for Sally, some things are meant to be kept under lock and key.

Among her secrets is a big one that I know only because Lowell blabbed it to me, not Sally. Once upon a time, Sally and Lowell were married.

It's hard for me to imagine. Lowell, hard smoking, hard drinking, womanizing, and not above masturbating in a corset with a tie around his neck. Sally, whose lips never left a lipstick ring on a cigarette in her life and who had expressed so little interest in sex during the course of our friendship that I had to wonder if she even knew what an orgasm was. This was the woman who stole Lowell away from his second wife when Sally was twenty-five and Lowell was thirty-five, and who spent six years at his side in the Bardwright Agency. Then Lowell moved on to wife number four, and Sally launched a solo career as a quiet deal maker, which she has done ever since. I know she doesn't make a fortune, and I think Lowell won the battle of the solicitors during their divorce. She lives in a flat no bigger than a closet in Fitzrovia, which may be why Sally has never been wild about London.

Not surprisingly, she's never been wild about Lowell, either. Given their history, he was never shy about using his position to screw her out of deals and clients over the years. However, you may not grieve when your ex-husband dies, but you don't expect your friends to make jokes about it, either. Not Sally, anyway.

I changed the subject. "So do you know Tom Cruise?"

Sally raised an eyebrow into a perfect semicircle. "If I knew Tom Cruise, do you think he'd be married to Katie?"

"Good point."

"What do you want with Cruise?"

I explained again about me, Felicia Castro, and my quest to get Tom Cruise to read *Singularity*. Sally shook her head.

"I know you don't want to hear this, but I think you're fighting a losing battle with Oliver Howard, sweetheart. If you expect Tom Cruise to ride in on a horse and rescue Oliver's career, it's just not going to happen. Better to hand him off to another agent, particularly when you're about to be consumed with all the details of getting your agency off the ground."

"I owe it to Oliver," I told her.

"You owe it to a client to be honest and realistic," Sally replied, which was true. "Feeding false hopes won't help him, and you can't make up for the disasters in his past. His addictions aren't your fault."

"I know."

"What's the word on *Duopoly*?"

"His publisher bailed. I'm going to be getting pitches out around the industry this week."

"Do you think it will fly?"

"No," I admitted.

"Time is money, sweetheart."

"You sound like Cosima," I told her, winking.

"Speaking of Cosima," Sally said.

"What?"

"I wonder if you've considered staying put and giving Cosima a chance," Sally told me with a casual air that belied the bomb she had deposited in my lap.

"Are you kidding?"

"I'm not saying to do it," Sally said. "I only asked if you'd considered it. I did European work for Cosima when she ran her own agency, and once you get past the fact that she's a power-hungry bitch, you realize she's very effective at what she does."

"She hates me. I hate her."

"I know, but that's the business. What else is new? You're trying to screw her, and she's trying to screw you. That doesn't mean you can't make a lot of money right where you are."

"There are other reasons," I said obliquely. Namely Darcy.

"I've worked on my own for years," Sally reminded me. "There are rewards, but there are also a lot of days when I wish I had a team behind me. I've actually thought about going back into the ring."

"You?"

"Sometimes. Doing everything yourself is nice, but it means you have to do everything yourself."

"You've been the one encouraging me to make the big leap. Now you're telling me to skip it and stay where I am?"

"No, I just want you to be happy. This is a cruel business, and more and more, it's being run by a few big players who pull all the strings. It's harder and harder for solo agencies like me to make a go of it. If you want to do it, Tessie, you go for it, but do it with your eyes open. And for the right reasons."

"Point taken, but this isn't a sudden decision," I said.

"I know."

"I've been wanting to run my own shop for a long time."

"And you'll be great at it, but don't think the world will automatically beat a path to your door. It just doesn't work that way. Even for someone with your gifts."

"Are you trying to depress me?"

"God forbid. I just don't want you to find out the hard way that running your own agency isn't everything it's cracked up to be, and then have you blame me when you find out you hate it."

"I won't," I assured her.

"You won't hate it or you won't blame me?"

"Both."

Sally smiled, but the truth is, I *was* feeling depressed. When you make up your mind to do something, you don't want to hear that you might be making a mistake that will screw up your life. Not that I haven't made plenty of those mistakes in the past with my eyes wide-open. The hard part was knowing that Sally was right. I really didn't know what I was getting into, but you don't turn up your nose at opportunity.

"Will you be at Lowell's funeral?" I asked her, not wanting to hear any more about the risks of my life-changing decision.

"Oh, yes, I have to pay my respects to the old bastard." She raised her wineglass toward heaven and took a drink.

I hesitated. "Did the police talk to you? A detective named Nicholas Hadley?"

"The police? No, why?"

"There are rumors about Lowell's death."

"What, the murder talk?" Sally asked, tossing her styled blond hair back. "What a load of tosh. I was married to Lowell, so let's just say I'm familiar with his predilections. The way he died wasn't exactly a surprise to me."

"Hmm," I said.

Sally pursed her lips. "Are you saying the police talked to *you*?"

I nodded.

"What on earth about?" she asked.

"I really don't know, but the questions were strange."

"Strange?"

"Like they thought I might have been involved. Like I might have been in his apartment."

Sally narrowed her eyes at me. "Just so we're clear—you didn't help Lowell into the afterlife, did you? I would have bought champagne."

"Of course not."

"Then don't worry about it. You have plenty of other things to worry about this week."

"That's true."

"I guess I shouldn't tell you the latest rumors," Sally said.

"Rumors about what?"

She shook her head. "It's nothing. You know how rumors get repeated and twisted and wind up as fact in this business."

I do, and I spread my share of them. Except, like Lowell being found in a corset, some rumors turn out to be true.

"What have you heard?" I asked.

As a solo agent with ties to nearly everyone in the business, Sally's usually first in line for the good gossip. She is my unattributed source for entertainment industry dirt.

"You shouldn't give it a thought," Sally said. "Obviously, you just talked to Dorothy, so there's nothing to it."

"What about Dorothy?" I asked. Then I made a guess. "Are people saying she's in play? Because that's just Saleema trying to get under my skin. Dorothy's not going anywhere, least of all to Saleema."

"What's up with Saleema?" Sally asked.

"I saw her having dinner with Guy."

"So what? I see Guy all the time."

"You don't live in New York and have to fly seven hours to meet him," I pointed out.

Sally shrugged. "I wish."

"I found out that Saleema showed up at an animal rights benefit where Dorothy was getting some kind of award. She sees Guy, and then she sees Dorothy? I don't like coincidences."

"Well, Saleema or not, it wasn't that," Sally said.

"Then what?"

"Word on the street is that Dorothy may be having legal problems shortly."

"Legal problems? What kind of legal problems?" I asked.

"Big ones," Sally said. "That's all I know."

13

I HAD NO LUCK reaching Dorothy on Monday night, and I didn't think she wanted me waking her up when I got to the office on Tuesday morning. Sally was probably right. It was probably just a rumor started by Saleema to put pressure on me. If Dorothy really had legal problems, I'd be the first to know.

I was barely behind my desk when Emma parked her mile-long legs in the chair in front of me. Her frizzy red hair was damp, and her makeup looked hastily applied. One of her bare knees twitched nervously like a puppy getting its tummy rubbed. It's not hard to tell when Emma is in love.

"Good day off?" I asked, smiling.

"Oh my God."

"Nice girl?"

"Oh my God."

Ah, to be young again. I don't miss my twenties, except when I remember having a springy body that can drink all night and make love all day. When I do that now, I get bags under my eyes that make me look like one of Dorothy's pandas. Not that this stops me, mind you. That's what makeup is for.

"Okay, details, darling," I said. "Who is she? Where did you meet her?"

Emma squirmed forward in her chair. "Sally told me about this hot new club when she phoned last week," she breathed. "It's in a basement off Drury Lane. Girls only. Very exclusive. Very discreet. A lot of celebs hang there who don't want publicity for their sex lives."

"Since when is Sally your What's On guide for lesbian nightclubs?" I asked. "Do I need to worry about her seeing me naked?"

"No, no, she's got a gay client who mentioned that this club is where she goes for hookups when she's in London. Sally thought of me."

"How'd you get in?"

"Sally talked to her client, who put me on the list."

"So who was at the party?" I asked. "Anyone I'd know?"

"Lots."

"But you're not telling?"

"I had to sign an NDA. Can you believe it? These people are serious about security. That's why the celebs go."

"So who's the girlfriend? Or is that a secret, too?"

"I asked, and she's okay with my telling you. I told her all about you."

"You didn't spill anything you shouldn't, did you?" I asked nervously.

Emma knows everything there is to know about me. Including Darcy. Right now, that makes me feel a little vulnerable.

"No! God, no!"

I breathed a little easier. "So who is she?"

"Her name's Jane Parmenter. She's an actress."

Aren't they all?

"What does she look like?" I asked.

Emma dashed out to her desk and ran back, chest bouncing, with a copy of *Hello!* She flipped the pages urgently and then wrapped the cover back and pointed at a photo taken on a red carpet at a Leicester Square premiere.

"That's Jessica Alba," I said. "You're dating Jessica Alba? Did she turn gay?"

"Not her, behind her, in red."

I squinted at the magazine and saw another young woman, in her early twenties, doing what wannabe actresses do—flashing cleavage for hungry photographers. She had pageboy blond hair, a toothpick physique like a 1960s model, cheekbones cut with a circular saw, and a red designer dress that was long on sequins and short on fabric. I had to admit that she was beautiful, but beauty only buys you a ticket to the cheap seats in the film world.

"She's a stunner," I said with appropriate enthusiasm for Emma's benefit.

"Isn't she?"

"Looks a little like Sienna," I said.

"Yes, I thought so, too!"

Welcome to Emma's crush of the week.

"How did the two of you hook up?" I asked.

The red of Jane Parmenter's dress bloomed in Emma's freckled cheeks. "It's so crazy. I was sitting on the toilet, sending texts. I mean, I wasn't doing anything, but you can't find places to sit down in those clubs. Jane really needed to go, and she just sort of waltzed in and closed the door with us both inside. We talked while she did what she had to do and then we got friendly."

"Apparently."

"It was very sexy."

"Sounds like it."

No, it really didn't, but a male model has never followed me into a toilet stall, so who am I to judge?

"We wound up at my place. She spent the night and most of the day. She's amazing."

"Why not her place?" I asked. "I've seen your place, Emmy—it's not exactly the Ritz."

"Jane still lives with her mum, if you can believe it."

If a man told me that, I'd say he was married, but I wasn't going to throw cold water on a horny assistant.

"Have you ever worked with Godfrey Kahn?" Emma asked me.

"The film director? Sure, I've placed a couple of projects with his company. I've never met him personally. Why?"

"Jane's up for a big part in his latest movie. It's her and two other actresses, but the others are bigger names. Jane's wondering what she can do to get in good with Kahn."

"Take her clothes off," I said.

"Short of that."

"Kahn mostly does teen comedies. They're brainless. Any actress in one of his flicks is going to have to lose her top. Maybe her bottom, too."

"Oh, sure, Jane knows she'll have to do nude, but she doesn't want to sleep with him."

"Then she's already behind the eight ball."

"She thought some publicity would help. Get some more photos in the tabloids. Make sure people know who she is."

"That's a good thought," I said. "The trouble is that the tabloids don't have much room for wannabes, after they've crammed fifty pages with Brangelina, Paris, Britney, Becks, and Posh."

"Well, if you think of anything, can you let me know? I'd love to see Jane get the part. It would be a big break for her. Maybe you could make a couple of calls? You said you knew some people in Kahn's production company."

"I'll do what I can, Emmy," I assured her.

"Really?"

"Really."

Her snaggly smile lit up the room. "That's brilliant! Thank you *so* much!"

I knew that Emma was going to be scattered all day. I'd come out of my office and find her staring into space and chewing on a pencil. It's that way whenever she meets someone new.

Emma lowered her voice. "Have you heard from Darcy?"

I frowned. "No."

"Oh."

"I'm afraid I screwed things up."

"All you did was tell him how you feel."

Exactly. The one thing you never do when you're having an affair is allow yourself to be honest with your partner. The silence from Darcy came through loud and clear: We're through.

"I'm not sure that's what he wanted to hear," I said.

"Maybe he'll send a message through me today," Emma told me.

I shrugged. I wasn't optimistic. Rather than dwell on it, I dug in my purse and pulled out a miniature flash drive, which I handed to Emma. "Oliver Howard's editor said no to *Duopoly*, so we need to make a wider pitch," I said. "I did a letter and put together a list of eight other editors I want to target. Let's get packages out today with copies of *Singularity* and the synopsis and first ten thousand words of the new book. Okay?"

Emma nodded.

"Sally tells me I should pull the plug on Oliver," I said, mostly to myself.

"Except he's brilliant."

"Yeah, so why can't I sell him?"

"That's not your fault."

"I'm his agent, so I don't know who else I can blame," I said.

The fact is, when you're an agent, you have no control over people saying no. You can lobby and cajole and bluff and threaten and beg, but in the end, the editor will decide what he or she likes and that's that. It doesn't matter if you know damn well they're making a pigheaded mistake. I've had crappy material that sells like chocolate biscuits and winds up with a seven-figure film option. I've had really great material that doesn't make it out of the starting gate. Go figure. It's not my call to make, but I still get infuriated when I swing and miss, and I scream at the editors, and I blame myself, and it doesn't change a thing.

Oliver isn't the first client I've failed. He won't be the last. I just feel like he's a symbol of my frustrations. And I worry that, in the real world, my failure will kill him. Literally.

"Get me Felicia Castro on the phone," I told Emma quietly.

"Are you sure?"

"I'm sure. Maybe if I eat a little crow, she'll pass *Singularity* to Cruise." Eat a little crow. Swallow a little pride. I don't do that well, but if you believe in something, you have to screw your ego. It also occurred to me that I have more enemies than friends, and maybe that's not such a good thing.

"Okay," Emma said. She got out of the chair, looking all gangly and tall, with her long legs, a perfect hourglass shape, and those breasts that defy gravity. Damn, I hate being envious of another woman's body, but what can you do? Tempus fuck it.

"Oh, one other thing," I told her.

"What?"

"Dorothy is on board for the new agency. She's with us."

Emma beamed. "Congratulations!"

Yes, I should be feeling good, shouldn't I? With Dorothy in my camp, I'm nearly free. I should be on top of the world right now. So why do I feel like a fly on the window right before the swatter makes me into a little smear of goo?

"Sally says there are some odd rumors out there about Dorothy, but I don't think there's anything to worry about," I said, trying to reassure myself.

"When do you drop the bomb on Cosima?" Emma asked.

"Next Monday."

"I can't wait."

I smiled at her. "It occurs to me that there's something I really need to say to you, Emma. I mean, I've been sort of assuming all along that you would be with me, but I guess I shouldn't assume that. If I were in your shoes, I wouldn't want to give up a job here, where you've got stability and benefits and upward mobility. You know I want to train you as an agent, but there will be lots of grunt work, and I don't know how much I can pay you, and it will probably be a struggle while we get started. Sally says I'm nuts. She thinks small shops face an uphill battle these days. So what I'm saying is that I really want you to join me in the agency, but if you don't think you can do it, I'll understand. Just because I'm willing to throw away everything on a huge gamble doesn't mean I expect you to do the same."

"That's sweet," Emma said. "But I'm with you."

"You don't have to decide right away—" I began.

"I already did, Tess."

I had been waiting to exhale. "That's brilliant, Emma, thank you."

There's something about having someone put her faith in you that makes you want to come through for her. Emma. Oliver. Dorothy. I realized that I had been using the Bardwright Agency as a safety net all these years, so I didn't have to face my fears. After all, it's easy to pretend you are bulletproof when no one is shooting at you. Now I was about to shuck off my security. Put a target on my chest. Strap a parachute to my back and jump and hope the damn thing opens.

What if I wasn't good enough?

What if I lost everything?

For a girl who never spent much time doubting herself, I was scared to death.

14

THE CONVERSATION with Felicia Castro did not begin well.

"My assistant told me the cunt was calling," Felicia said by way of introduction, "but I didn't believe even you would have the fucking gall to call me."

Felicia sounded pleased with herself. The old Tess would have taken the bait, given her a snarky riposte, and slammed down the phone. But this is the new and improved Tess. The patient, charming Tess. The graduate of the school of how to win friends and influence people.

"Felicia, when you talk like that, you get me hot," I replied through gritted teeth. "Really, you do. I'm fanning myself right now. I'm going to swear off men from now on, because there's nothing like a Spanish girl cursing at me to turn me on."

"Fuck off."

"See? If I were wearing panties, I'd be taking them off."

"What do you want, Tess?"

Okay, charm wasn't working. Once upon a time, Felicia and I

had traded dirty jokes and sex stories over drinks every month. No more. Time to try another approach.

"I want to grovel in abject submission, Felicia. I want to take out a full-page ad in *Variety* to say you were right, and I was wrong. I want to give you a tongue bath. Frankly, I want to know what it will take for me to get back on your good side, because I will happily do anything. Nothing is too degrading, and I say that as someone with a generous view of degradation."

Felicia laughed. It wasn't a kind laugh. "I told you that you'd come crawling back to me someday."

"You're right. You're absolutely right. This is me on my knees. I'm really sorry about that mess two years ago."

"You sold me out to fucking HBO. We had a deal."

Let me interrupt for a moment. First, I seriously considered teaching a parrot to say, "We had a deal," and sending it to Felicia as a Christmas present. Emma talked me out of it. Second, Felicia and I did *not* have a deal. What we had was a general discussion of price. We had no agreement, no handshake, no air kiss, no contract, no signature. Felicia wanted to get her hands on the movie rights for a bestselling mystery set in Las Vegas that featured a transsexual detective. She was thinking breakout role for one of her up-and-coming clients, who had been a supporting actress in a couple of midsized hits. So far, so good. Then HBO came calling with a series buy. The cable networks in America do shows about lesbians, polygamists, morticians, serial killers, and gangsters, so making a hero out of a Vegas chick cop with a penis doesn't seem like a stretch. So to speak. Anyway, HBO doubled the offer, and, I admit, I didn't go back to Felicia to tell her she had lost out before I went ahead and signed the contract.

In retrospect, big mistake.

Not that signing with HBO was a blunder. I'd do it again in a minute. But I should have handled Felicia with kid gloves. Back then, I really didn't care about having enemies.

"I should have called you," I admitted. "That was completely inappropriate. I should have let you match the offer."

"Fuck that. I didn't have to match anything. We had already nailed down the price."

The only thing we had nailed down that evening was a bottle of cabernet that cost more than my television, which Felicia was happy to swig down at my expense. However, I figured this wasn't the time to remind her of that.

"I know you feel that way. I do. We just came away from that dinner with two different ideas of where we were. If I had thought back then that we had finalized the deal, I never would have taken HBO's call." I heard myself say that and sighed. "Okay, who am I kidding, that's a lie. We both know I would still have signed with HBO. If you were in my shoes, you would have done the same thing. We're both out to get the best deal for our clients, and that was the best deal. You wouldn't believe me if I said anything else, so all I can say is, I never meant to piss you off. I apologize. I was insensitive. I deserved the frozen treatment from you, and I should have had this conversation with you a long time ago."

I was hoping she wouldn't have anywhere else to go if I voluntarily took all the blame she could possibly hurl at me. Throw myself on the sword. After all, it's not like I slept with her fiancé (see Saleema) or her husband (see Cosima). This was one of the rare moments when my sex life had nothing to do with the disintegration of one of my relationships. This was business, pure and simple.

However, women cling to grudges like barnacles to the belly of a ship.

Maybe it's Felicia's Catalonian temperament. When she was thirty, she moved to London from Barcelona, which is a move that most Londoners would find impossible to fathom. Give up sun and shore for rain and fog? Not so much. Most of us would retire to Barcelona if we had the chance. Felicia is forty now, still skinny the way Spanish women always seem to be. She has streaky brown hair and a petite mole on her upper lip that counts as a beauty mark. She smokes thirty packs a day. No, not really, but I have never seen her without a cigarette as dark as molasses dangling from her mouth. Felicia gets a bad rap for nepotism, because she is where she is in the industry thanks to her father, who became a power broker in Hollywood in the 1960s and 1970s before retiring to his native village in Spain. She used his contacts to make inroads in Hollywood, Bollywood, Cannes, and New York and to party her way to the inner circle of marquee celebs. On any given day, she can be anywhere in the world. Make no mistake, though. Felicia is good at what she does. Cruise works only with the best.

She wasn't crazy about accepting my apology.

"Do you think I believe a word of this crap?" Felicia asked me. "The only reason you're calling is because you want me to push *Singularity*. Like I'm going to put Tom in a Dungeons and Dragons movie."

"It's not like that at all," I said. "Have you read it? *Singularity* is a moral epic. It's a classic."

"So why don't we gather all the people who bought it and put them in a phone booth and talk about what a hit this movie is going to be."

Ouch. She was right about that.

"Yes, okay, it was a bust. We've all had great books go south. The publisher didn't know what to do with it. We didn't get reviewed. All I'm telling you is that, as Cruise's agent, you really ought to give him this book. He's going to love it. He's going to want to do it."

"Pass. Try Rowan Atkinson."

This was the point in the conversation when I would usually scream an obscenity and hang up. I took a deep breath. I counted to ten.

"Look, Felicia, I may be the biggest bitch that ever walked the planet. You wouldn't be the first to say so. I don't really care. This isn't about me. This isn't about you. It's not even about Oliver Howard. This is about a project that's great for your client. I know you. You wouldn't shortchange him because you hate me."

Actually, she would do exactly that.

"I read *Singularity*," she snapped. "It's bullshit."

"You can't possibly mean that."

"Like hell I can't. The book reads like it was written by a drug addict. Which it was, right? It's impossible to adapt. It's too complex."

"The imagery is amazing. So are the characters. It's made for film."

"Face it, you're backing a loser."

"Did you give it to Tom? Has he read it?"

"No way. I'm not wasting his time. I know him. I know what he likes. This isn't the direction he's going."

Okay, Felicia knows Tom, and I've never met him, and I probably never will, but I believed in my heart that she was wrong. Or more to the point, I believed that this had nothing to do with the book. She didn't want to pass it to Tom because I was the one making the pitch. Even so, I kept swinging.

"Come on, we're not talking about Ethan Hunt and *Mission: Impossible. Singularity* is *Born on the Fourth of July*. It's *Vanilla Sky*. It's *Eyes Wide Shut*. This is the stuff he wants to do because it's good, not because it's commercial. He can afford something that's risky business."

"Funny," she said coldly.

"You know what I mean. At least ask him to read it. That's all I'm looking for."

"Good-bye, Tess."

"If you ask him to read it, you're my first call on my next six deals."

"You don't have anything I want. Next you'll tell me I should put Tom in a panda suit and let him do the sequel to *Bamboo Garden*."

"I'd put on a panda suit myself if I thought it would make a difference," I said.

"I told you two years ago that you were persona non grata. No deals. Ever. What part of that don't you understand?"

"Felicia, for what it's worth, I meant what I said. I'm sorry."

Click. End of call.

Okay, my first exercise in tact and humility did not go well. Actually, I was quite restrained, but it's much more satisfying to savage someone with a biting retort rather than hold your tongue, if you're not going to get what you want anyway. The chances of

Felicia Castro passing *Singularity* to Cruise were less than zero, which I suppose I knew before I picked up the phone. That doesn't mean I'm giving up. It just means the direct approach isn't going to work, and I have no idea yet what the indirect approach would be.

Emma hovered in my doorway.

"How did it go?" she asked.

"Send Felicia a cactus dildo, will you?" I said.

"Not good, huh?"

"Not good."

"Dorothy called," Emma said.

I looked up. "What?"

"While you were on the phone, Dorothy called. She wants you to call her back. She said she'd wait by the phone."

I checked my watch. "It's five in the morning in New York. Why on earth is Dorothy calling me now?"

"She wouldn't tell me, but she said it's urgent."

Dorothy? Urgent?

This can't be good.

15

IN LONDON, when someone in publishing talks about "legal problems" for an author, that's usually code for defamation. It's ridiculously easy to get damages for libel over here. If I suggested in print that Elizabeth Hurley has an eating disorder or that she's part of a sex coven in Chelsea or that she's actually a man with the world's most impressive breasts, well, that would probably cost me most of what I'm making by telling you my story.

I said if, Liz. If. Liz is actually a friend of my father's, so I hope she realizes this is just a joke.

Anyway, I didn't know what to think about Dorothy and her legal problems, which were beginning to seem like something more than a rumor. I'm not sure how you can defame someone in an animal fairy tale, but I wouldn't have been shocked to discover that some zoo panda was suing over an unflattering characterization in one of Dorothy's fables. Stranger things have happened in British courts.

The only thing to do was pick up the phone. Dorothy told

Emma she'd be waiting for my call, but I didn't believe it. Dorothy never stays in one place for longer than thirty seconds, so there was no rush. Instead, I called Sally first to see if she had heard any more gossip about Dorothy on the street. I wanted to be prepared for whatever Dorothy might tell me, because part of being a good agent is knowing the answer before your client asks the question. You never, ever want to sound surprised. However, Sally wasn't in her office and wasn't answering her cell phone, so I was on my own.

I called Dorothy. To my surprise, she really was waiting by the phone.

"Dorothy, it's Tess."

I heard Dorothy take a long breath, which is never a good sign. "Oh, Tess, Tess, thank God it's you, I don't know what to do. I really don't. This is the worst thing, just the worst thing. I actually drove all the way to Ithaca yesterday after lunch, because I was so upset, and sometimes when you're upset, all you can do is drive, and it helps to be back in your hometown again. So that's what I did, I went home, but it didn't help at all, and so I drove around the streets and then just turned around and came back to the city. I didn't sleep at all, not at all, I've been up all night, pacing. The dogs are jittery and jumpy, because they know I'm upset, and the kinkajou is running around and pooping everywhere. I can't believe this, I simply can't believe that anyone could say this about me. It's cruel. It's horrible. I may have a heart attack. I was going to call you yesterday, but I was speechless. Speechless. I even thought about driving off a bridge. You have to tell me what to do, Tess. What do we do about this?"

"I need you to slow down for me, Dorothy, because I don't know what happened. Just tell me what's going on."

"What's going on? I could lose everything! Everything! And if this winds up in the papers, people will believe it's true—you know how people are. Of course, it's not true. It's not true at all."

"I'm sure it's not, but you still need to tell me what's going on."

Dorothy sighed into the phone like a bubbling teakettle. "Oh, yes, of course, I keep thinking you were there, but of course, you

weren't—how could you be? I'm so sorry. This thing has me completely beside myself."

I waited. She didn't continue.

"Dorothy?" I asked.

"Yes, dear?"

"What's going on?"

"Oh, haven't I told you yet? I thought I had. I am just so scattered today. It's David Milton, that awful boy. Remember I told
you I was having lunch with him yesterday? He's Tom Milton's
son, and Tom was a gem, so I can't even begin to believe that his
flesh and blood could do something so horrible. To lie like that!
He should be ashamed."

"What did he say?" I asked.

"He's threatening me! Blackmailing me!"

"Over what?"

"He claims that I *stole* the idea for *The Bamboo Garden*! Can
you believe that? Stole it! He says that Tom was the one who
came up with the idea for the book and that when Tom died, I
took it for myself. He says I read Tom's manuscript and then
adapted it and put my name on it. It's absurd! It's ludicrous! I
mean, yes, I knew Tom, and he was an aspiring writer, and I remember him showing me some of his work, but it was nothing
like my stories. Nothing at all, no one would think that. Tom
was a dear, but he was no writer, and I only tried to encourage
him. But now his son says he's going to sue me, and I need to pay
him or he's going to ruin my reputation. He says he has things I
wrote to his father, but he couldn't possibly have that, because
it's not true, none of it is."

I closed my eyes. This was much worse than defamation.

"Did he show you anything?" I asked. "Did he have any of the
documentation with him?"

"He had a note!" Dorothy told me breathlessly. "A note I wrote
Tom! But it wasn't what I meant at all."

"What did the note say?"

"I thanked Tom for letting me read his manuscript, and I
told him he should keep trying and I was sure he would get it

published. Which wasn't true, but you have to be kind to a friend, don't you?"

"So the note was authentic?" I asked.

"Well, yes, I think so, but it was a long time ago. Years! This was back in Ithaca, and it was before Tom died, so it must be twenty or more years ago now. We were both librarians. I don't remember writing the note, but it was my handwriting, so I must have, and it's the kind of thing I would do. To be nice, dear—you know what I'm saying?"

"Did you actually read a manuscript that this Tom Milton gave you?" I asked.

"Yes, I believe I did."

"What was it about? Was it a children's novel?"

"I'm pretty sure it was, yes, because Tom and I were both fans of children's literature. Baum, Milne, Silverstein, and all the others who created such marvelous fantasies, we could read their books over and over."

"What do you remember about Tom's book?"

"Well, nothing at all, really—that's why this is so crazy."

"I understand."

Actually, I was hoping that Dorothy remembered *exactly* what Tom's book was about. If she didn't remember it, there was an outside possibility that she really did take parts of her panda book from an old manuscript written by a friend without ever meaning to do so. I know Dorothy. She has a grasshopper's mind and a memory like a sieve that lets everything but her actual spongy brain matter drain away. I hoped to hell she hadn't accidentally stolen Tom Milton's idea, because it would be the most expensive mistake either one of us had ever made.

But there was no point getting her even more frantic than she was.

"Don't worry, Dorothy, we'll get this sorted out," I assured her.

"This has me scared to death, Tessie, just scared to death."

"I understand, but let me take care of this. Okay? I'll fly to New York tomorrow and see you, and we'll talk over the whole thing."

"Oh, would you do that? I would feel much better if you were here."

"I'll catch a flight tomorrow afternoon and be there for dinner."

"Thank God, that's a huge relief."

"In the meantime, I don't want you worrying, all right? Authors face this kind of nonsense all the time. As soon as they become successful, someone wants to get a piece of the pie."

"I just can't believe it. Tom was a dear, dear friend, and he must be spinning in his grave to have his son doing something like this. I even mentioned Tom in the acknowledgments of my book, that's how close we were!"

That's really not what I wanted to hear.

"Go play with your kinkajou, Dorothy. Or take the girls for a walk. Then pour a glass of wine and get some sleep."

"You're an angel, Tessie. I don't know what I would do without you."

"I'll see you tomorrow."

I hung up the phone.

"Fuck!" I said in an extremely loud voice.

Let me see if I have this right. Yes, Dorothy was a close friend of Tom Milton. Yes, she read a children's book he wrote and sent him a note saying she was sure it would be published. No, she has no recollection of what the book was about. Yes, Dorothy wrote her own children's book after Tom died that has since made her millions of dollars.

I don't see any problem, do you?

Nothing that could implode the career of my principal client just as I'm getting ready to launch my own agency?

I was not looking forward to meeting David Milton.

Of course, every crisis has a silver lining. If I'm on a plane to New York tomorrow afternoon, I can't very well have lunch with Cosima after Lowell's funeral. Not that I plan to tell her why.

On the other hand, if Sally somehow heard rumors on the street about Dorothy's legal problems before I did, then something tells me that Cosima already knows.

I packed a small bag in my apartment that night. Emma booked my flight on Virgin to JFK and arranged one night at the St. Regis. I had a few more days in which I could bill the

Bardwright Agency for my expenses, so I figured I would make the most of it.

My morbid curiosity made me take a copy of *The Bamboo Garden* off the bookshelf in my bedroom and turn to the acknowledgments page at the back. Dorothy writes nine-hundred-page novels and ten-page acknowledgments, so it took me a while to find the reference to Tom Milton sandwiched between mentions of every employee and volunteer at humane societies and animal shelters in the Northeast. I didn't like what I read:

> I have to give special thanks to the late Tom Milton, who worked by my side in the Ithaca library for years and whose passion for children's literature and writing matched my own. I believe that I am here in no small part because of Tom's inspiration.

I suppose it could have been worse. She could have thanked him for writing the first draft of her book.

I dropped a paperback of Dorothy's novel in my purse, along with a copy of Oliver Howard's *Singularity*, which I wanted to re-read on the plane as I considered my strategy in the wake of the latest rejection from Felicia Castro. It was still too early to go to bed, and I didn't think I would sleep much tonight. So I poured myself a glass of sauvignon blanc and sat by the window in my living room, watching the nighttime traffic of pedestrians and black cabs on the street. I left the television, radio, and stereo off. I didn't bother turning on any lights. I was in one of those moods where I could stare into nothingness for hours, and I could drink a lot.

It wasn't Dorothy's problems that had me upset. Or even the agency. If I were honest with myself—and that's a dangerous precedent to set—I would have admitted that the real dread in my heart was because of Darcy. When I got home, I had the idea that there would be a message on my machine. Or an e-mail. Or a text. Or some word from Emma that she had heard from him. Instead, there was nothing. Silence. It's been three days. I told him I loved him and scared him out of my life, and the last thing I wanted was to see his face at the funeral tomorrow and watch him avert his eyes. To see him with his arm around Cosima's shoulders.

All along, I have told myself that my problem is that I listen too much to the hormones originating from that swollen pink bud between my legs, but that's a lie. The problem is that I let myself fall in love. I show the world a tough face and wear a suit of armor, but I'm afraid that everyone will see through the mask and realize that I am a mess of insecurities. When you are neurotic, you believe that you are the only one in the world who feels that way and everyone else you meet is supremely confident and deft in handling life and love. Which is stupid, I know. We all wear our disguises, and behind them, none of us is a superhero.

The phone rang, interrupting my peace and quiet and all my wallowing.

When I picked it up, I thought I would hear Darcy's voice at last, and I wasn't sure if I wanted to know what he would say to me. I was fairly sure it would be one of the many variations of good-bye. Best to make a clean break before he saw my face again.

However, it was not Darcy, and my heart sank to a new low, like a bear market on the LSE.

"I hope I'm not calling too late," Oliver Howard said.

I tried not to sound disappointed. "Not at all, darling. I was just sitting in the dark."

"That's not like you, Tessie."

"I have a lot on my mind."

I felt stupid saying something like that to Oliver. I heard the rattle in his throat, like off-key music from his tar-soaked lungs. I thought about what he had endured in his life. Walking in on the bloody corpse of his mother. Servicing twitch-eyed freaks with his mouth. Falling down with broken-off needles still sticking out of his arm. He had treaded water in a well so deep and black that I prayed I would never know even a glimmer of his despair. It made my own problems seem shallow, and it made me feel guilty for letting my self-pity leak into my voice.

"Never mind me," I added quickly. "How are you, darling?"

"Life goes on."

"How about *Duopoly*?"

He gave me a sour laugh. "Sometimes I hate it so much that I can't be in the same room with the manuscript."

"You felt that way about *Singularity*, and it's brilliant. Every writer hates his book at some point." I felt as if I were trivializing his struggle, but I have never known how to help Oliver wrestle his demons. They are beyond me.

"Well, what does it matter?" he asked. "If I ever get it done, I suppose I'll have to find a vanity press to publish it."

"Don't be ridiculous."

"Malcolm said no, didn't he? He gave up his option?"

I winced. Oliver was always a step ahead of me. "Yes, I'm afraid so. But don't worry, darling, he's a fool. You're better off without him, because he doesn't know what to do with your books. I already have queries out to several other houses. Someone will pick it up."

I hope that I sounded more optimistic than I felt.

"Emma tells me you talked to Felicia Castro again," Oliver said.

"Felicia isn't my biggest fan." Not that there's a lot of competition for that slot these days.

"Well, I appreciate your going into the lion's den on my behalf."

"Tom's not the only actor in the world," I reminded him.

"For this project? I think he is."

"No, we need to forget about Felicia. I'm taking Tom, Katie, and Suri off my Christmas card list. I'll work with a coagent in Hollywood and get the rights sold somewhere else."

"*Singularity* was written for Cruise."

"I know that, but I never thought Matt Damon could pull off Jason Bourne, and look how that turned out."

"Maybe I'd have better luck if I were dead, like Ludlum."

I get nervous when Oliver talks like that.

"Are you staying healthy, darling?" I asked him.

There was a long, uncomfortable silence, as if I had walked into a room marked Private and felt everyone staring at me.

"You mean am I looking for an alley where I can get a hit? Is that what you want to know, Tessie?"

If Oliver wanted cocaine or heroin, it would take him thirty seconds to arrange a buy. The scary thing is that I know the next binge will kill him. It will be suicide. There is no middle ground, just the word "self-control" standing between him and the morgue.

"I know you wouldn't do that," I said. "I just want to make sure you're eating something. Keeping the alcohol to a minimum. Swearing off the death sticks."

"I love it that you think I have any willpower at all."

"Don't take it personally. I'm just protecting my nest egg."

Oliver laughed until he coughed. "Pretend to be hard all you want, Tessie, but I know you're a soft touch. You don't have to worry, though, it will be our secret."

"Thanks."

"Do you want to tell me why you're sitting in the dark?" he asked.

"I won't bother you with my problems."

"Darcy?"

"Yes, he's the tip of the iceberg, but there's plenty more ice under the water, darling. And I'm the *Titanic* sailing cheerily on with the band playing—you know the drill."

"'The Unsinkable Tess Drake.'"

"That's me."

"What about Guy and Dorothy and the rest of your messy life?"

"Still messy."

"Are you going to Lowell's funeral tomorrow?" he asked.

"Yes."

"Would you like some company? We could sit together and vent our sorrow."

"You're going, too?" I asked.

"I thought I'd pay my respects."

"That's kind of you, but you really don't have to do that."

"Lowell was decent to me, at least to my face," Oliver said. "Besides, I find funerals strangely cathartic."

"Shall we meet at the church?"

"Sure."

A funeral date with a gay guy, I said aloud when Oliver hung up. Believe it or not, this is an improvement in my social life.

16

LEAVE IT TO LOWELL to book his funeral in advance at St. Bart's the Great, an historic church in the City that dates all the way back to the days of William the Conqueror. Lowell arranged for the church to be used as a set in several films, which makes for a nice boost to the priory's annual budget, so the rector owed him a place for his last good-bye. I like old churches, with all their stonework and Middle Ages austerity. I wouldn't have wanted to be around back then, but you have to admire the balls of those turn-of-the-first-century priests, who could extort alms from starving peasants in order to build temples of excess in the midst of absolute squalor.

Oliver, with his fists in his baggy black pants, shook his head as he contemplated the statuary. "Artists spent their whole lives carving these stones," he mused. "I wonder if it's worth complete and wretched misery while you're alive to know that your work will survive this long."

"No," I told him.

"Oh, I don't know. No one will be reading *Singularity* in a thousand years."

"Trust me, it's better if you get the fame and money while you're around to enjoy it," I said.

Oliver and I were among the first to arrive, because a funeral is like a sporting event where you want to get there early to get the best seats. It's a see-and-be-seen kind of thing. We draped our raincoats over a pew facing the nave and then made our way toward the altar, where Lowell was waiting for us. The funeral was open casket. Mahogany frame, antique brass trim, bone white velvet.

Lowell was looking better than I'd seen him in some time. A little pasty, maybe, but dying makes you look trim. The tobacco smell was gone. His wild gray hair was combed and coiffed. He wore a Savile Row suit, black and very chic. If you think you might have to answer a few questions before they let you through the pearly gates, you want to look good for the interview.

He wore a red Hermès tie with diagonal yellow stripes. It was knotted firmly around his neck. His shirt had a high collar.

"You don't suppose that's the tie, do you?" I murmured.

"Tess," Oliver chided me.

"Sorry."

I was being sacrilegious, because funerals scare me. Dead people scare me, because they don't look dead. Lowell could easily have opened his eyes, given me a wink, and asked me to climb on board for one last ride. I didn't completely rule out the idea that he had staged his entire death just to scare the shit out of me at his funeral. That would have been just like Lowell.

But, no, he was gone. Peaceful and gone. As we all shall be. He would not bicker with me anymore over deals. He would not grope my arse at the Christmas party. He would not wave a manuscript in my face and shout, "This is bloody crap, Tess! Crap! Bilgewater!" He would not extol the virtues of the Cornish coast. He was done with his body, and it would do nothing but take up space underground.

I was surprised when Oliver looked at me and said, "You're crying."

"No, I'm not."

Except when I touched my cheek, it was wet. I wiped the tears away. I've always believed that we cry at funerals for ourselves, like babies who are left alone.

"Scatter my ashes in the Thames when I go, will you?" I asked.

"Ditto," Oliver said.

I patted the side of the casket with tentative fingers, and then we went back and took our seats and watched the parade. Everyone was there. The whole industry, like a Who's Who of publishing, entertainment, and media. Good for Lowell. Lots of deals would be done right here in the church, and he'd love that. We shall miss him, the poor old sod, and did you happen to take a glance at that debut I sent you last week? I think I shall weep, but before I do, let's say one hundred thousand quid, not seventy-five, okay?

Really, I can't think of a better tribute to Lowell.

You see people you haven't seen in years at funerals. The trouble is you can't exactly get up, smile, hug, tell a joke, admire their clothes. Darling, how *are* you? You look fabulous! You have to be somber and occasionally flick your eyebrows up like a secret message. I nodded at Tina Brown and made a phone gesture with my hand—call me. I got a wink from Richard Madeley. A head shake from Alexandra at *Vogue*, who had seen me in the same black silk top once before. That's a funeral fashion don't.

Rebekah Wade from the *Sun* veered over to our pew after viewing the body. She mouthed in my ear, "So what's the deal, Tessie? Did you kill him?"

I hoped she was making a joke.

"You know me, darling," I said. "If I was going to kill anyone, it would be Cosima."

We whispered to each other, because you have to be careful what you say in churches. The acoustics will surprise you.

"One hears things," Rebekah murmured and then left me to stew.

It didn't help that the next face I saw was the police detective Nicholas Hadley, who had his chocolate Burberry over his arm and eyed me as he stroked his gray beard. I had the uncomfortable feeling that everyone else was watching him watching me. Hadley didn't bother inspecting the corpse (once is enough, I guess), but instead took a seat almost directly opposite Oliver and me. Maybe this was his idea of psychological warfare. Maybe he thought I would break down in tears during the service and confess, and he didn't want to miss it.

"Who's he?" Oliver asked.

"A cop," I told him. "He thinks I helped Lowell strangle himself."

Oliver looked at me. "You're not serious."

"Oh, yes."

"I didn't picture you for the black widow type."

"Now you know."

I tried to ignore Hadley, which wasn't easy with him acting like Inspector Lestrade ten yards away. However, I realized that the woman walking up the nave now was Sally, and I got up and leaned over the pew and took her hand. She smiled at me with more sadness than I expected and squeezed my fingers. I watched her approach Lowell, and she averted her eyes, staring at the floor and not at her ex-husband in the box. I didn't see her cry, but when she returned down the aisle, she didn't look at me, and she didn't come sit by me. Instead, she took a seat at the far back, away from everyone. Death always hits us harder than we expect.

And so does love.

I saw Cosima, and beside her, I saw Jack. Darcy. The man I love, who didn't belong to me. Cosima was regally dressed in a charcoal waistcoat with black buttons, her shoulders squared and her chin lifted toward God. Her three-inch heels tapped like gunfire on the cobbled floor. She was like a fort, built of solid old stone and impenetrable. Jack towered over her and held her elbow delicately in his right hand. My memory caressed his chiseled features, and I could feel my fingers in his swept-back hair. My heart went wobbly. My breathing sped up. I got dizzy and thought I might faint.

"Are you all right?" Oliver asked me.

"Fine."

But I wasn't fine. I sucked in a deep breath of air and tried not to be sick all over the church floor. Cosima turned her head as she passed me and gave me a nod that said everything. Her lips curled into a cruel smile just for me. Somehow, I knew that she knew. Me and Jack. Dorothy and her legal problems. Lowell's death. The agency. I expected her head to do a full circle on her neck, and I would be the only one to see it. I knew that war had been declared.

I wanted to feel Jack's eyes on me. He knew I was there. He could feel me and know what I was thinking. He knew the last words that had been spoken between us, when I told him I loved him. How could he walk by and not even acknowledge me? But he did. His head never turned. He was as impassive as a palace guard. I wanted to scream at him. Cry to him. Run to him.

Oliver took my hand, which was trembling. He's a smart man, and I'm transparent. He shook his head and stared into his lap.

"It's him, isn't it?" he asked me under his breath.

Barely, my chin moved, acknowledging the truth.

"My God, I do love you, but you are such a fool, Tess," he told me.

I tried to say something, but my mouth moved and didn't form words. It didn't matter. Oliver was right. I tried to compose myself, because Marty Goodacre followed the two of them like a tall troll, stooped over, acting as Igor to Cosima's Dr. Frankenstein. He patted his greasy hair and smiled at me with his brown teeth. I looked away. I couldn't summon the will to be civil. I hope he couldn't see behind my mask and realize how distraught I felt.

Nicholas Hadley was staring at me, too. Curiously. Damn him. Damn all of them.

"Shall we go?" Oliver murmured.

"I can't."

Yes, I wanted to get up and run from the church, but instead, all I could do was sit there and hear a roaring in my ears. The service began. There was a man speaking at us, talking about angels and heaven. People stood up and sang. Oliver helped me to my feet, and I pretended to sing, too. Lowell was never a hymn man. We should have been singing Beatles songs. We were all choir members in Sgt. Pepper's Lonely Hearts Club Band.

The service went on forever. The priest spoke again. Cosima spoke, and her haughty voice was like a coronation speech, a new queen smugly bemoaning the death of the king. More speeches. More singing. Plenty of Bible verses for a man who thought Christ was a swear word. I wanted to escape, get on a plane that afternoon, and fly to New York and never come back.

Then it was finally over, and we were left in a churchy silence, where mumbles and footfalls echoed between the stone walls. Everyone stood up, shuffling out in solemn rows. I leaned against Oliver's shoulder, and even his lean, bony frame was a comfort. I felt drained.

"You look like you could use a drink," Oliver said.

"I could use six drinks, but I have to go home and get my bag and grab a cab to Heathrow."

"You'll be late."

"I'm always late, but I get there."

Life goes on. I still needed to sort out Dorothy's troubles. And my own. And start an agency. And ditch the police. The idea of seven or eight hours on a plane where no one could reach me sounded wonderful.

We emerged from the church into the late-morning sun, a rare thing in London. God was apparently smiling on Lowell. Mourners—if you could call them that—gathered in little clusters, where they smoked and laughed and talked about film rights and translation sales.

Life goes on.

I gave Oliver a hug. "Thank you, darling."

"Do you need me?"

"Desperately, but, no, I'll be fine."

He kissed the top of my head. Oliver is a truly decent man, and I felt guilty again that I had done so little to help him. He headed for the iron gates without looking back, and I thought about his tiny flat and his demons and the empty pages staring at him and the temptation of the street. I thought about *Singularity* in my purse. If we are measured by our ability to lift one person up, then Oliver did that for me by giving me a book I truly believed in. So what had I done to lift him up in return?

I checked my watch. My flight left in three hours. I was late.

I thought I was free, but then from behind me, a hand clutched my shoulder with a tight, skeletal grip. When I turned, I saw Cosima's gray eyes and jutting cheekbones and inhaled the smoke from her cigarette. Her hair was ebony against her drawn ivory skin, and the wind was no match for her hair spray. When she took the fag out of her mouth to speak, I saw a bloodred circle on the white paper from her lipstick.

"It was a lovely service," she said.

"Lowell would have been pleased."

"I'm sure he was," Cosima announced. "The dead watch over us, don't you think?"

"No, I don't," I said.

"You're not religious, are you? I understand. Well, it gives comfort. Walk with me for a moment, will you, Tess?"

She sounded as if she planned to make me an offer I couldn't refuse. Maybe she thought she was Marlon Brando. We strolled into the garden, and I made a point of checking my watch again so she could see my impatience.

"I understand you're going to New York," she said.

"Yes, I have a flight to catch."

"To see Dorothy?"

"Yes."

"Don't forget about Guy and the new deal," she reminded me.

"I won't forget."

"I'm sorry you won't be able to join us for lunch. I believe Jack was looking forward to seeing you."

"I'm sure the three of you won't miss me," I said. Did she know? Did she know I had made a fool of myself? Had she already folded Jack back into her wallet and tucked him away?

Cosima exhaled smoke into the trees. She dropped the cigarette into the green lawn and crushed it under her shoe. I didn't think the rector would approve. I have no doubt, though, that Cosima believes herself to be a religious woman and that her schemes are guided by the hand of the Lord.

"Have you thought about what I said, Tess?"

"What was that?" I asked innocently.

"About your future at the agency."

"Yes, I've thought a lot about my future at the agency."

I smiled. She smiled back.

"Good."

"I really need to get to the airport," I said.

"Yes, of course. Do give my best to Dorothy, won't you? Tell her how much we value her at Bardwright. She always has a home with us."

Not if I can help it.

I turned to leave, but Cosima stopped me with her hand on my shoulder again.

"Oh, Tess, one other thing," she told me. "I hate the dance, don't you? The game. The secrecy. Life would be easier if we were all honest with one another, don't you think?"

"Sometimes."

"You're probably wondering if I know, Tess, and I thought I would tell you that I do."

My mind went only one place. Darcy. Jack. Cosima knew about the affair. I wondered if she had known all along, if she had reeled Jack out like a fish on a line and then snapped him back. I glanced at my feet as if there might be a trapdoor ready to swallow me up.

"What is it you know?" I asked.

She took a glance around the garden and leaned close to my ear. "You. Your plans. The agency. I know you're planning to leave us."

I was annoyed that she knew but relieved that she was talking about something else entirely. And not at all surprised that the grapevine had passed along my secret to Cosima. I wondered who had given me up, but it didn't matter. It was inevitable. You talk to clients. You drop hints. You ask for someone's confidence, and he says yes, I won't tell a soul, and then he's on the phone again as soon as you hang up. It was better to have it in the open.

"It's just something I'm thinking about," I said. "I haven't made any final decision."

"No? Well, I'm pleased to hear that, Tess. Loyalty is very important, and the Bardwright Agency gave you your start. You're where you are today because of Lowell and me."

And Dorothy. And my other clients. And ten years of bloody hard work to make her and Lowell even richer.

"I understand that," I said.

Cosima folded her arms over her waistcoat. I caught a whiff of expensive floral perfume. "Then understand this, too. If you follow through with this plan, you will find nothing but misery, Tess. You will be a nonperson in this industry. A nobody. A failure. I will bury you."

17

I'M NOT A BIG FAN of traveling by plane. There's something about paying for the privilege of spending hours shoulder to shoulder and nose to arse with hundreds of strangers that leaves me sick. Plus the unnaturally small food. And the unnaturally small bathrooms. And the turbulence. And the deep vein thrombosis. Oh, and that whole what-if-I-die-in-a-fiery-crash thing, too.

Even so, a Virgin flight from Heathrow to JFK sounded a hell of a lot better than having lunch with Cosima, Jack, and Marty.

I tried to sleep and couldn't. Sleeping on planes isn't my thing, and every time I closed my eyes, I kept seeing Nikita Khrushchev pound his shoe on my armrest and shout, "Ve vill bury you!" Naturally, Khrushchev was bald but had Cosima's face. Talk about a nightmare.

On some level, I was relieved to have everything out in the open. Not to be whispering on the phone and sending secret e-mails anymore. Cosima knew I was going to bolt from Bard-wright and take Dorothy with me. I knew she knew. Let the games begin. I didn't enjoy the idea of a public battle with someone who wielded her kind of power in the industry, but all I could do was hope that my clients were as good as their word. Everyone I had called in the past few days had assured me that they would follow me to a new agency. They were on my side. This business is all about relationships, and my relationships were solid.

Or so I hoped. You never know until you pull the trigger.

It's one thing to have an enemy like Saleema. She may scheme behind my back and win over a client or two, but there's really nothing she can do to ruin me. Cosima is another story. She can pull strings with everyone I know. Spread rumors and lies. Shut doors that used to be open to me. Lean on people to cut me out of their deals. If she really wanted to, if she's not just bluffing, she could make my life extremely difficult.

The question is whether I'm worth the trouble. In her pond, I'm a small fish.

Then again, I'm sleeping with her husband. Not only that, I'm in love with him. Wives get a little funny about that sort of thing.

Jack. Darcy. He was another reason I couldn't sleep. Ever since Saturday, I'd been telling myself I'd gone too far, that I'd let my emotions get the better of me in a moment of sexual afterglow. I'm not the kind of girl to fall madly in love. I'm too smart for that. But you don't have to cluck your tongue at me—I know it doesn't work that way. I thought about calling him to say I had made a mistake, but then I saw him at the funeral, and I knew I couldn't lie. I couldn't go back on what I'd said.

I did love him. Madly.

His silence was eloquent. His refusal to meet my eyes told me everything I needed to know. Darcy had flown from my life. In the battle between love and money, men always choose money. Cosima had it, and I didn't. Simple as that. It didn't matter how he felt about me; he was on the end of a tether, a steel leash hooked to her bank account. I told myself that my relationship with him had been a fantasy, and you shouldn't confuse your fantasies with real life. But sometimes we hold on to our fantasies tighter than what's really in front of us.

No doubt my father would say he told me so. And he did.

My father lives to give me advice and is exasperated when I ignore it. Not that he is a master of relationships himself. My father allowed his heart to run away with him when he married my mum, and, had I been alive then, I would have told him the same thing he regularly tells me. He was being a fool. A thirtysomething political editor for the *Times* marrying a nineteen-year-old Bloomsbury girl from the chorus line of Covent Garden musicals? Anyone could see that was bound for disaster. When I visit my mum in Italy, I try to picture the two of them together, and I simply can't. They are pickles and chocolate. Swimsuits and Alaska. Name any two things that don't go together. You'd think we would learn from our parents, but instead we inherit a road map for making the same mistakes. So if my love life is like the *Lusitania* in the path of a torpedo, well, I blame it on my genes.

My father. Terrence Paul Drake. The starchy old goat. I really need to call him when I get back. Just because I don't follow his advice doesn't mean I don't like to hear it.

I squirmed in my middle row seat and felt claustrophobic. I plucked *Singularity* from my purse to reread it, but after a few pages, all the mutated two-headed ferrets looked like Marty, the bodiless voice in the passage to Nefarious sounded suspiciously like Felicia Castro, and the fat pig turning on the spit for the hobo feast turned out to be Guy. The only hero in this drama was the devil, and no matter who else I pictured in my mind, all I could see was Tom Cruise.

I put away the book.

I stared into space. I played solitaire. I tried to watch a movie. The hours over the Atlantic passed like sand going through an hourglass one grain at a time. The flight attendant asked me if I needed anything, and I told her Tom Cruise. She told me to try first class. I think she was kidding, but Virgin has great amenities, so you never know. I settled for a glass of cognac and another pillow.

When I couldn't stop myself, I began to think about the real reason I was going to New York. Dorothy. I told myself I had nothing to worry about, because successful authors get scammed all the time, and most of the con artists do a quick exit as soon as they get their first threat letter from a lawyer. David Milton wasn't going to be any different. He was a man trying to trade on his father's relationship with a famous author to extort some easy money. End of story.

Except copyright lawsuits are slippery. They drag out. They get bad press. No one wants to be called a cheat or a thief, and certainly not a sweet old lady who writes books about pandas. Milton probably figured that Dorothy would die rather than face public embarrassment, and he was right. The little fucker.

Of course, there was another possibility.

Perhaps Milton was right. The whole panda thing might have been his father's idea.

Don't get me wrong. I don't believe for a minute Dorothy would steal an idea deliberately, but, then again, an awful lot of old family recipes came out of *The Pillsbury Cookbook*. For all I know, Tom Milton's manuscript may have barely resembled the book that became *The Bamboo Garden*, but bare resemblance can still get you in a lot of trouble.

Anyway, I would find out soon enough what this was all about. When the plane lurched, I thought for sure we were heading to a watery grave. That's the way I think on planes. But no. We were finally, blissfully, descending into New York.

My city.

Talk to most people who live in London, and they'll tell you that in their heart of hearts, they'd prefer to live in New York. That's me. Sally's like that, too. She'd sell her soul for a one-way trip to Manhattan. I know it's not going to happen, though. Even with the dollar worth about a nickel against the pound, most Londoners can't afford to live in New York unless they've got family money or two salaries in the banking biz. Publishing won't buy your way to Fifth Avenue.

I'm not sure why we all love New York. London is safer. London is cleaner. London is greener. Londoners know how to queue up and not shove their way to the front of a bus line. The Tube beats the New York subway hands down. And it's not like the weather in either city is anything to brag about. Even so, we're all whores for New York. Stick that on a T-shirt, and you'll make a lot of money.

I could feel it on the cab ride into the city. I don't know what it is, but my adrenaline shoots up like a jolt of cocaine as we cross the river and cruise along the FDR. Cruise being a relative term, because mostly, we sit in traffic and sweat and honk horns and curse in Farsi and flip the bird and smell sewage. Then we push into the concrete canyons, the mile-high buildings funneling hurricane winds through the streets and blocking out the sun. I smell onions. Lebanese sausage. Freshly baked bread. Garbage. There are people everywhere. People hustling across streets against the red lights. People elbowing twenty deep past shop-windows. People in suits. People in saris. People in halters. People on Rollerblades and bicycles. People on balconies, in doorways, in driveways, in alleyways, on steps. People walking, standing, stopping, riding, sitting, and lying drunk and unconscious under moldy blankets. People laughing, shouting, screaming, pointing, and swearing. People from a hundred countries.

God, I love this city.

The cab dropped me off at the St. Regis. Dorothy lives in Tribeca, but I usually stay in midtown, because it's closer to the museums and the theater district. I can get my biannual fix of Steichen and Cezanne. In the evenings, I can go to Broadway and catch up on the shows that I never have time to see in London. Yes, that's a little dig, in case you missed it.

No time for sightseeing today, though. This was going to be a lightning strike in and out of the city. I barely had time to dump my bag in my room before I was back downstairs. The cab line at the hotel was twenty yards long, so I decided to take my chances on the street. I bought a hot dog from a vendor and ate it in large bites as I strolled southward on Fifth. Globs of mustard threatened to squirt over my white blouse, but I managed to remain pristine. There are no hot dogs like New York street dogs. You can taste the soot of a hundred thousand tailpipes mixed in with coarse grindings of mystery meat and cancer-causing nitrites. It is scrumptious.

Half a block down Fifth, as the traffic thinned between red lights, I made my move by leaping into the street. I have a foolproof method for hailing a cab in New York. Don't tell anyone. I stand in the middle of the lane, cock my right knee like a hooker, stick out my left arm, and extend my middle finger.

Then I wait ten minutes, swear, and take the subway.

Flipping the bird to hundreds of Pakistani drivers who still think they're in Islamabad may not get me a cab, but admit it, you can't get one, either. And my way is much more satisfying.

I got off the 1 train at Chambers Street. Dorothy lives a few blocks away on Greenwich, taking up two floors of a renovated brownstone, including the rooftop garden overlooking Washington Market Park. Nice. She's come a long way from her days in a two-bedroom apartment near the Finger Lakes in Icarus. Did I say Icarus again? I mean Ithaca. Dorothy told me that she and her husband always dreamed of a Manhattan condo when they visited the city on weekend trips, but that's like dreaming of a suite in Buck House if you're a small-town librarian. Damn if she didn't do it. And pay cash for the place. Sell enough books about pandas to twelve-year-old girls, and you, too, can snap up a few million dollars' worth of prime New York real estate. Her husband never lived to see the dream come true. He died almost six years ago of a heart attack, and Dorothy didn't move out of Ithaca until four years later.

The merry, lonely, animal-loving widow. She's already a Tribeca fixture, with her street gang of poodles. Everybody loves Dorothy. You can't not love eccentric millionaires.

I was on the steps of her building and getting ready to buzz her apartment when my cell phone rang. The caller ID box told me it was *The New York Times*. I turned around and sat down on the steps.

"Tess Drake," I said.

"This is Wallace Mooney, Ms. Drake," a voice said. "I write for the *Sunday Book Review* at the *Times*."

Mooney sounded like a sad, gray-haired alcoholic in a torn sweater. I heard street noise in the background. He was probably drinking gin and having a slice two blocks away from me.

"What can I do for you, Mr. Mooney?"

"It's about Dorothy Starkwell," he said. "I do have it right, don't I? You're Ms. Starkwell's agent?"

"That's right."

"I heard a rumor about Ms. Starkwell. I'd like to get more details."

With reporters, you never know how much they really know and how much they're bluffing. They like to see if they can make you say something stupid. I say stupid things all the time, but not to the media, not to strangers, and not on the phone. I reserve my worst gaffes for times when I can do the most damage. You know, like telling your married boyfriend you love him.

"A rumor?" I asked.

"Yes."

He didn't rush to fill me in.

"What kind of rumor, Mr. Mooney? I've heard rumors that Dorothy keeps live pandas in her condo. I've heard rumors that Dorothy is a pseudonym used by Nora Roberts. I've heard rumors that the character Filippa was a dead ringer for Camilla Parker Bowles and that Prince Charles called Dorothy personally to get her to rewrite the description. Needless to say, all those rumors were false."

Actually, I've always suspected that Dorothy really did make Filippa a Russian version of Camilla, but I'd rather not know for sure.

"The rumor is that Dorothy Starkwell is the target of a big lawsuit that could cost her millions of dollars," Mooney told me.

Shit.

"Well, I'll add that one to the list, Mr. Mooney."

"Are you saying the rumor is false?"

"Dorothy is not the subject of a lawsuit anywhere by anyone."

Not yet.

"Does Ms. Starkwell face any legal issues that might have caused a rumor like that?" Mooney asked.

"I know she's recently become very interested in kinky behavior, so maybe that's it," I said.

Mooney paused for a long time. "Kinky behavior?"

You could almost hear him salivating over a sex scandal enveloping a noted children's author.

"That's right. Kinky is what she named the kinkajou she's fostering."

I heard him sigh with disgust. Reporters usually don't like me, because I'm not nice to them. "Kinkajou, that's an animal, right?"

"Your guess is as good as mine."

"Good-bye, Ms. Drake."

"Good-bye, Mr. Mooney."

I kept sitting on the steps. My stomach churned with acid, and I tasted a belch of New York hot dog repeating in my mouth. It tasted better on its way down.

A rumor about a big lawsuit? If I had to guess, the rumor was David Milton sending a shot across my bow.

Welcome to the Big Apple.

18

IF YOU VISIT Dorothy's condo, you must put up with the Thunder. It is the noise made by five giant poodle thugs stampeding across a hardwood floor, toenails scratching, tongues lolling, clipped white fur shedding on your clothes as they swarm around you and bathe you with kisses. They are good girls, but they are taller than Dorothy on their hind legs and could easily trample me, mug me, and leave me for dead. They may look like Barbie doll ballerinas, but they have a New York attitude.

Dorothy clasped her hands together and beamed as I struggled for my life with the poodles jumping around me. They backed me against the door. Shoved their gray snouts in my face. Produced a knife. Demanded my wallet. I was ready to give up and hand it over when the girls decided to hunt for easier prey and took off like a pack for new targets in the condo. If you have never seen cotton balls run, it isn't a pretty sight.

I heaved a sigh of relief at my narrow escape. Dorothy tottered up to me in her heels and threw her tiny arms around me.

"Oh, Tessie, you are my savior," she told me. "Thank God you're here. I don't know what I'd do without you, I really don't."

"It's a treat to see you, Dorothy," I told her, checking to see that my watch and jewelry were intact from the assault by the dogs. I pictured the biggest one hocking my emerald ring in Little Italy. "Sally sends her love and says she misses you."

"Oh, does she? That's so sweet. How is Sally?"

"Same as always. Living for gossip and dreaming about New York."

"Yes, yes, she won't be happy until she's on Park Avenue. Well, the grass is always greener, isn't it? You dream about Manhattan, while we New Yorkers dream about London and Paris and Milan. Did I tell you that Alan and I visited Italy once? We took a holiday there for our twentieth anniversary. Oh, it is so beautiful. I really must go back. Maybe the three of us can do a girls' trip sometime, how would that be?"

"It sounds lovely."

"Well, we'll do it then, it's settled. And how are you, Tessie? You are always so busy, busy, busy. And now this agency, how exciting is that! But I worry about you, so lonely over there, always working. I miss Alan every day. We had thirty-five years together, but it wasn't enough, I would give anything for more time with him. Love is what life is all about, Tessie, so promise me you will find someone and settle down, all right? You shouldn't spend your whole life alone. It's not natural. And you're such a delightful girl, you have so much to give. Don't you worry about getting older, you have plenty of time."

I never really worry about getting older until someone tells me not to worry about getting older. Suddenly, thirty-six felt like fifty-seven.

"I'm still looking," I assured her.

"And what about Emma? How is she? She's coming with you to your new agency, isn't she?"

"Yes, of course. Emma's in love again. An actress. Very pretty."

Dorothy winked. "She hasn't talked you into playing for the other side, has she?"

"No, although there are days when I think it would be easier to be gay."

"I don't believe many gay people would agree with you, my dear."

"No, that's true," I admitted.

"Well, come in, come in, come in, it's so good to have you back here again. I wish you lived in New York. It would be so nice if we could see each other more often. Don't you think? Maybe you and Sally could get an apartment here together. You'd both love that."

Dorothy waved her hand and led the way into her living room, which was vast, in the way that New York lofts are like warehouses. The floor-to-ceiling windows stared west toward the park and the Hudson. Dorothy sat primly on a bone white sofa, where her feet dangled above the floor. She wore a pink cocktail dress that fell below her knees. Her face was narrow and pale with two rosy blooms of rouge on her cheekbones and gaudy diamond-studded hoops glittering on her earlobes. She had a pinched nose with tiny nostrils that always made me wonder how she could breathe. Her gray hair was coiffed and sprayed so heavily that it probably hadn't moved an inch in thirty years. Back in the days when spray cans had fluorocarbons, Dorothy probably launched the earth on its path of global warming.

The big loft and big couch made tiny Dorothy look even smaller than she was, like a child in a castle. She was everyone's little old grandmother, which played well on the morning shows. If you had to build a children's writer from scratch, you'd wind up with Dorothy. Sweet, not New York rough. A blithe innocent in the mean city. The small-town bookworm from Icarus, who never had kids of her own, was now an unofficial grandmother to the world.

Dorothy had already red wine poured into two balloon glasses. Good stuff, expensive stuff. I sat down and took a drink and realized I was exhausted. By my body clock, it was well after midnight, and only the excitement of the city was keeping my eyes open.

"You look tired, dear," Dorothy commented. "How was the flight?"

"Fine. I tried to sleep, but I couldn't."

"You should do what I do. Put on a silk mask and take a whopper of a pill. I sleep like a baby. They have to wheel me off the flight." Dorothy giggled.

"How's the kinkajou?" I asked.

"Kinky? He's a hoot! He runs around like he owns the place, although he can be a teensy bit destructive. We'll have to go downstairs later so you can meet him. Did I tell you he's allergic to strawberries? I just find that so funny, because he eats most other fruit. Especially bananas. He usually sleeps during the day, so we'll have to be careful if we go down there not to wake him up too suddenly."

"Why is that?" I asked.

"Well, kinkajous will scream, charge, and bite viciously if they're startled."

"Let's not startle him," I said.

"Oh, don't be alarmed, he's quite sweet." Dorothy's brow knitted in annoyance, and she put her glass of wine down and folded her matchstick arms across her chest. "To think that poachers hunt them for fur and meat! Little things like Kinky! Is there any animal who is safe from butchery by people? It makes me so mad. I actually volunteered to do one of those ads, you know, where you take your clothes off to protest? They were kind, but they said no. I suppose it's mostly models who do that sort of thing, but I wanted to make a statement."

I figured this was a bad time to ask about good steakhouses nearby.

You have to understand about Dorothy and animals. She's not a Dorothy-come-lately on the subject; this is and has always been her life's passion. When I first met her in Icarus, she was the chair of the board for the local Humane Society, and her walls were already plastered over with awards, letters, citations, and photographs from the work she had done for organizations like PETA, the WWF, and the Nature Conservancy. And that was when she had no money. Since becoming a zillionaire, Dorothy has ramped up her efforts all over the world, and I don't imagine there's a zoologist or animal rights activist anywhere on the planet who doesn't know her name. Even her panda books are thinly disguised morality tales about animal conservation. Scratch the surface, and there are lessons about habitat destruction, climate change, endangered species, and human greed, starting with Filippa, the archnemesis of the pandas, who may as well have been a sister to Cruella de Vil.

I love animals, but it's all a little over the top to me, and I'm not about to give up lamb chops just because the little guys are so cute. You won't hear me saying that to Dorothy, though.

"Maybe you'd better tell me about David Milton," I said.

Dorothy got up and paced, wringing her hands. "Yes, of course, yes. Oh, I just cannot believe this is happening. I can't believe anyone could do this to me."

"Let me worry about it, Dorothy," I told her. "Just tell me who he is. What does he do, where does he work. That sort of thing."

"He's a lawyer," Dorothy said.

Figures.

"He has an office on the Upper East Side. I met him at Tavern on the Green. He seemed like such a nice boy. About your age, I'd say, late thirties, somewhere around there. How old are you now, dear? Thirty-eight? Thirty-nine?"

"Thirty-six," I said. I hope your kinkajou eats a strawberry.

"Oh, dear, I'm so sorry—it's not that you look older, although stress isn't good for people's appearance, you know that, don't you? No, it's me, I get confused when time passes."

"David Milton?" I prompted her.

"Yes, I met him at Tavern. He's nice looking, I suppose, tall, but everyone is tall to me. He has a rather odd nose with a kind of fold in it that makes it point a bit in the wrong direction, like it's making a left turn. And you can't help but stare, even when you try not to—do you know what I mean?"

"Do you have his office phone number? And his address?"

"Oh, yes, of course, I have his card."

"I'll see him tomorrow morning," I said. "Tell me about Tom Milton. His father. Anything you remember."

Dorothy nodded. She stopped long enough to take a sip from

her glass of wine and smiled with a faraway stare. "Oh, Tom, Tom, what a sweet man. Very quiet, didn't say much at all. We both joined the Ithaca library around the same time, when we were in our thirties. He was an animal lover, too, like me, so we had a lot in common from the start. Poor Tom. He had been married for a short time—that was where David came from, but David lived with his mother in Albany back then, so I don't think they saw each other very often. Tom never remarried. If I had to guess, I would say he was one of those men who was gay but had difficulty admitting it to himself. He was very private, very reserved. Liked to wear bow ties all the time. I don't believe he and his son were close; he rarely talked about David, and I only met the boy once or twice in the ten years that Tom and I worked together. Alan and I had Tom over for dinner regularly. At least once a month for ten years, isn't that nice? And always bow ties. A tweed sport coat, like a professor. He was allergic to shellfish, didn't know it until he ate a shrimp at our place and puffed up like a sumo wrestler. Well, it wasn't funny—we rushed him to the hospital, but he was fine."

Never say "anything you remember" to Dorothy.

I'm not a lawyer, but I knew one thing. No lawyer would want to put Dorothy on a witness stand or have her face a deposition. In my occasional dealings with the legal world, I remember being told one thing. Answer the question and stop. Don't elaborate. Don't embellish. Dorothy had never met a question she couldn't embellish for half an hour.

"What about Tom's writing?" I asked.

"Oh, well, I think I told you that Tom and I both loved children's literature. It was our specialty at the library. Isn't that funny? Tom and I had so much in common, whereas Alan and I were like opposites, and yet the heart knows what it wants. I find that interesting, don't you?"

"You said that Tom asked you to read a book he wrote," I nudged her.

"Yes, he did. Tom had aspirations of being a writer, which I never really did back then. It was never my life's ambition. Tom wrote short stories and had me read them. He never published any of them, the poor man. He hated rejection, and when publishers and magazines said no, it crushed him. He couldn't take it. He kept writing, though, which I thought was admirable. I encouraged him to keep trying."

"Were his short stories about animals?" I asked.

Just please tell me they weren't about pandas.

"Not that I recall, not really. I mean, there may have been animals in them, but no, I believe many of his short stories were scary, rather Gothic, with ghosts and monsters. The kind you'd read around a campfire, that sort of thing. Not at all like mine."

Thank God.

"What about his manuscript? You said there was something longer. A novel."

"Yes, as I recall, I read a longer work that Tom wrote years earlier. I believe he told me he had gone back to it off and on over the years. This was not long after I met him, so it was years ago. I'm afraid the book didn't make much of an impression on me, although I would have been kind, because that's the way I am. I have a recollection that the book was in the Gothic vein, too, like his stories, but I don't know that for sure. Anyway, if it had been the slightest bit like my own books, then I would certainly remember, wouldn't I? And I don't."

"Tell me again, when did you start writing? Was Tom still alive then? Did he see any of your books?"

Dorothy laid her index finger over her lips. "Tom died ten years after I met him. Very sudden, very tragic. How terrible that was. I don't recall when I started fooling with *The Bamboo Garden*, but I certainly didn't finish it while he was alive, and I know he never read it. I do credit him for being an inspiration, though, as I said in the acknowledgments, because I'm not sure I would ever have tried my hand at writing if it weren't for Tom and his little stories. It seemed to give him such joy to do, and when I tried it, I understood."

"You're sure you don't remember anything about that original manuscript that Tom wrote?"

"I really don't, my dear, I'm sorry. Is it important?"

"Well, keep thinking about it, and maybe something will come to you. Did David Milton actually show you any portions of his father's manuscript?"

Dorothy shook her head. "No, he just showed me a note I had written to Tom, which I didn't remember, but I'm sure it was my handwriting. My penmanship has always been distinctive, I'm rather proud of that."

Elaborate, embellish, elaborate, embellish. Sigh.

Dorothy sat down on the sofa again. "Tell me honestly, dear, do you think I should be concerned? I've been just frantic since this happened."

I reached over and patted her hand. "I know you have, darling, but I'll get this all straightened out. If David Milton didn't show you this so-called manuscript, then I suspect that means he has something to hide. For all we know, he found your old note to Tom and thought he could use it to scare us into a settlement. That's the way lawyers work, the slimy bastards. I'll be in his office first thing tomorrow morning, and unless he can produce that manuscript, I'll tell him exactly where he can shove his lawsuit. Okay?"

Dorothy's tiny chest heaved. "Oh, that is such a relief."

"I know."

"Well, I'm just so pleased to get this nonsense cleared up. Would you like to have some dinner? My chef prepared a vegetarian lasagna. But maybe we could run downstairs to Starkwell South first and you can meet Kinky."

"Sure," I said, trying to muster appropriate enthusiasm.

"But remember, don't startle him."

Screaming. Charging. Vicious biting.

"No, I definitely won't do that."

19

MIRACULOUSLY, A CAB WAS DEPOSITING a man half a block from Dorothy's building when I left an hour later. I waved at the driver, elbowed a nun who was running in the same direction—okay, I'm kidding about that—and fell into the backseat with a groan. We headed uptown on Sixth. My eyes kept blinking shut, and I propped my chin on my palm as I stared through the dirty cab window. It was eight thirty at night, still daylight in May if you were up in a skyscraper, but gloomy and gray down on the street.

I called David Milton's office. He wasn't in. I left a message that I would be stopping by in the morning and gave him my mobile number. I didn't call him a liar, but you can read between the lines. I gave no hint of being concerned.

Actually, I felt better. Even confident. If Milton showed Dorothy an old note she wrote—but not any portions of the manuscript itself—that smelled to me like a con job. If he thought we would roll over and pay him in order to avoid the time and expense of swatting him down in court, well, he could think again.

No, the only thing that worried me was the timing of it all. Which was curiously coincidental. On the week that I'm planning to launch my own agency—and with Dorothy's next deal waiting in the wings—this man suddenly appears with a nasty charge of copyright infringement? Maybe I'm paranoid, but I can't help wonder if David Milton really came up with this idea on his own.

As if to reinforce my suspicions, I glanced out the right-side window as we crossed West Twenty-second and realized we were near the Flatiron Building, which was home to a gaggle of publishers and agents. Including Saleema. I had been inside with her many times in happier days but not at all since our falling-out. I knew she still worked there. I also knew that Evan, her ex-fiancé who had rocked my world in New York and London, still worked there, too. That must make for interesting agency meetings.

On an impulse, I told the driver to stop at the corner of Twenty-third. I climbed out, hurried down the long block to Fifth, and followed the pointed edge of the building around to Broadway. It was late, but Saleema was notorious for working late. Like me, she never had much of a social life. Even if she was still in the office, I wasn't sure what I hoped to accomplish by seeing her. However, lack of a plan has rarely been an obstacle to my charging ahead.

The security guard inside the lobby looked at me as if I might be a terrorist. It didn't help when I told him I was there to see Saleema Azah. He took my picture and asked for identification, and I was sure the next steps would be a strip search and an FBI background check.

Instead, he called upstairs. Saleema answered. I imagined her at her desk, feet up, wine in hand, reading manuscripts in an otherwise empty office. I wasn't at all sure she would agree to see me, but to my surprise, the guard hung up and directed me to the building's fabulous old elevators.

Just like old times. I felt a little sick and wondered what I would say.

The elevator let me out in a dingy corridor on the sixth floor between two locked doors. I waited. And waited. It occurred to me that Saleema might plan to leave me there until I got bored and left, but then I heard a crash bar and the east door flew open. Saleema stood there, hand on hip, giant brown eyes burning, coffee-colored skin turning pink with rage.

"Hello, Saleema," I said.

She stalked out of the doorway and stood in front of me. She hadn't changed much. Her cascading black hair was even longer than I remembered, practically down to her hips. I saw crow's-feet hiding under the makeup around her eyes. Otherwise, she was petite, beautiful, and fiery, as she always was. An Indian goddess.

I smiled. She didn't. With the speed of a snake, she slapped me so hard I nearly toppled backward.

Okay, now I know why she agreed to see me.

"You slut," Saleema hissed.

Slut, cunt, bitch. My friends have such nice names for me. I massaged my stinging cheek. For a tiny woman, she packed a punch.

"Now that you have that out of your system, can we talk?" I asked.

"About what?"

"I don't know. I was passing the Flatiron, and I stopped for the hell of it. I wanted to see you. I still want to put this behind us."

"You were my best friend, Tess, and you fucked my fiancé. Put that behind you."

"Look, I have no defense. Slap me again for all I care. As long as you've known me, you've known I was an idiot when it comes to sex. I hurt you, and I'm sorry."

Saleema brushed her hair back. "I don't care if you're sorry. It doesn't change what you did."

"I know."

"What do you want, Tess?"

"The truth is, I miss you," I said. And I did.

"Poor Tess. Are you feeling sorry for yourself? Are you feeling lonely? Maybe you should ask yourself why. You think because you're smart and funny, you can be a bitch to the world and get away with it. Well, you can't. And you know what? If you keep it up, you're going to wind up sitting in the rain somewhere wondering how the hell you fucked up your life so badly. When that happens, don't bother calling me. You won't have anyone to blame but yourself."

I didn't know what to say. Maybe because, deep down, I had a feeling she was right.

Saleema waited and watched me flounder, and then, with a fierce smile, she spun around and headed back to the door that led into the agency office. I decided I couldn't let her go without throwing another punch.

"I know you were in London," I called after her.

She stopped with her hand on the doorknob. Slowly, she turned around. "Okay, I was in London. Do I need to clear my itinerary with you?"

"I saw you with Guy."

Saleema shrugged. "So?"

"So what are you up to?" I asked.

"That hardly concerns you."

"No?"

"No. We're both agents, Tess. We both do deals. Guy's in the business."

"I hope to God you're not sleeping with him."

Mistake.

Saleema spontaneously combusted right in front of me. Or that's what I thought was going to happen. I expected to see flames.

"How dare you tell *me* who to sleep with!" she screamed. Her voice echoed back and forth in the tiny space.

"You're right," I said quickly. "That was stupid. I apologize. I just meant that you can't trust Guy."

"Oh, and now you're concerned with my welfare? Isn't that sweet. I can take care of myself."

"Be straight with me, Saleema. Were you talking to Guy about Dorothy?"

"Why would I do that?"

"To steal Dorothy as a client," I snapped. "Why else?"

"It's nice to see you're still paranoid," she said, smiling at me.

"Dorothy tells me you ran into her at a dinner over the weekend. I suppose that's just a coincidence."

"She was at a party. I was at a party."

"You told her you were a friend of mine."

"Would you have preferred I told her you were the whore who slept with my fiancé?"

"Do you really think you can take Dorothy away from me?" I asked.

Saleema shrugged. "Knowing you, Tess, I'm sure that Dorothy will soon find a reason to dump you on her own. In that case, I want her to know that she has options. If Guy puts in a good word for me, so be it."

"Did you hire David Milton? Is that what this is about?"

"Who?"

"You know damn well who he is. You know damn well why I'm in town. I can't believe even you would stoop so low."

"I think you should take a Valium," Saleema said. "You're having a meltdown."

That was true. I had been awake for twenty-four hours, and I was starting to fall apart. I was practically shaking.

"Oh, Christ, Saleema, why are you still holding on to this feud?" I shouted at her. "The thing with Evan was years ago. You're better off without him. You sure as hell know that. He was a cheat and a liar."

"And it was noble of you to prove that by fucking him. Not many friends will sacrifice themselves that way."

"I said I was sorry."

"I said I don't care."

"The David Milton thing is never going to fly. I'm calling your bluff tomorrow morning."

"I have no idea what you're talking about."

"We're going to countersue Milton for fraud. And if I can prove you're in it with him, we'll sue you, too."

"Good-bye, Tess."

Saleema punched in the security code to open the door and disappeared inside, leaving me alone in the corridor.

That went well, don't you think?

I shook my head, trying to calculate if there were any new ways I could find to screw up my life tonight. Nothing leaped to mind.

Saleema's words sounded like an ugly premonition. Me. In the rain. Alone. My life in ruins. It didn't feel like I had a long way to fall from where I was.

I needed a drink. I needed to sleep.

I pushed the elevator button and waited for the car to grind slowly back to me. I put a finger tenderly on my cheek. It was sore where Saleema had slapped me. And, yes, I know I deserved it. The elevator car opened, and I staggered inside and collapsed against the wrought-iron frame and closed my eyes. I couldn't wait to get out of this building.

As I waited for the elevator door to close, I heard the door in the corridor open again with a bang, and then I heard a male voice shout.

"Hold that elevator!"

Oh, no, no, no. Oh, shit.

I recognized the voice. As if the day couldn't get any worse.

I stabbed the button over and over to close the doors, but this was an old elevator, and I wasn't fast enough. The doors began to close with all the speed of a turtle crossing a motorway, but long before they did, the man's hand whisked between them and forced them open again.

I said a quick prayer for God to make me invisible. Not for long. Just for six floors. God didn't listen to me. He usually doesn't.

The man eased inside the claustrophobic car, so close to me that we may as well have been naked, having wild, stand-up-against-the-wall sex. Which was certainly the first thought that crossed my mind when I saw his body and smelled his smell again. I thought I could save time and strip off all my clothes now. The elevator was slow. We could be done by the time we got to the lobby. It wouldn't be the first time.

He saw me, too, and his eyes widened with surprise, and then his lips curled into a wicked smile, as if he already knew what was happening between my legs.

"Tess," he said, drawing out my name and caressing it with that damn honey voice of his.

It was Evan.

20

"I GUESS I SHOULD DO my Bogie impression now," Evan told me, grinning. "You know, of all the gin joints in the world, you walk into mine. I never thought I'd see you again."

"Let's pretend you haven't," I snapped, backing into the corner and staring at the elevator buttons so I didn't have to see his face.

"Don't tell me you're still angry at me."

I whirled around and realized he was teasing me. The bastard.

"Don't talk," I said. "Don't say anything."

"I can't help it. You look great, Tess. You always do. I like the colors in your hair. Very wild. Very sexy."

I bit my lip and squeezed my legs together, because they were trying to spread of their own accord. I was fighting the urge to grab him, kiss him, and mount him.

You have to understand that I've seen Evan only a couple of times in my life, and each time we wound up having sex less than an hour later. Yes, he is handsome, but I don't usually react that way to attractive men. He's my age, absurdly tall and lean, with dirty blond hair below his ears and a permanent scratchy stubble on his face. Blue eyes sporting an X-rated stare. A leering smile. Always relaxed and casual, wearing blue jeans and a worn leather jacket over a white T-shirt. Some men know you want them, and they're so arrogant about it that you want to scream, but you keep running back for more. That was Evan and me.

"So why are you here?" he asked. "To see Saleema?"

"Yes."

"How'd that go? Have you two patched things up?"

"No."

Evan laughed. He swept his shaggy hair away from his eyes. "No, I didn't think so. God, that woman can hold a grudge. She had this strange idea that we should be exclusive just because we were engaged, but I told her from the start that monogamy wasn't my thing. It doesn't mean I didn't love her."

"Take my panties off," I said.

No, I didn't.

"Stop talking," I said, but he knew what I meant.

"Saleema was a firebrand in bed, but not like you, Tess. You were insatiable. I loved that."

"We're done," I said. That was better than saying my nipples were hard and I wanted him to suck them. Although they were, and I did.

I am not known for my willpower, but I was trying hard. Evan was determined to test me. He reached out and stroked my face with the back of his hand, and I slapped it away. With one touch, however, I had vivid flashes of the places and positions in which we had screwed around. Several of them involved defying gravity. My face flushed. He knew I was horny as hell.

"One drink," Evan said.

"No."

"I can get us into the back garden at the Waverly. I have Graydon's number."

"So do I."

"Then let's go. You might get to meet George Clooney."

"Too old."

"Russell Crowe."

"Too scary."

"Are you afraid we'll sleep together again?" Evan asked.

"That's not going to happen."

"Then what's the harm in having a drink?"

"I'm tired. I'm going to bed."

"I'll join you."

"No, you won't."

"Tess, why deny the connection between us? You feel it. I feel it. It's there, so why fight it?"

"Because you're a cheating, soulless bastard who used me, betrayed my best friend and split us up, and because you think after all that, you can toss your hair and I'll sleep with you."

And because you're right.

"Would it make you feel better if I said I've changed? I haven't, but if it makes you feel better, I'll tell you that."

"This is the world's slowest elevator," I said.

For once, God listened to me. The doors opened, and we were in the lobby. I stalked toward the street, my heels tapping on marble. The security guard eyed me suspiciously. Evan strolled beside me, hands in his pockets, amused by my pretense of uninterest. He waved and winked at the guard as we passed.

On Broadway, I tried to hail a cab. No luck.

"Want me to get us a cab?" Evan asked. "We could share."

"No thanks."

I walked to Twenty-third and tried again. Apparently now I really was invisible, at least to all taxi drivers. I practically lay down in front of a cab, but it wheeled around me and shot eastward. Evan stepped into the street next to me and whistled, and a screeching, honking cab cut across four lanes of traffic in its hurry to squeeze his long legs in his backseat. I cursed.

Evan held the door for me. "After you."

"This is my cab," I said.

I climbed inside, but Evan followed me and slammed the door shut.

"Where are you staying?" he asked.

"The St. Regis."

"Nothing but the best for you, Tess."

Evan leaned forward to the driver and gave him an address on Bank in the West Village.

"Hey!" I interjected. "What are you doing? Where are you going?"

"One drink," Evan said.

"This is kidnapping."

"Graydon will want to see you," he told me.

"He knows I love him."

"The waiters look like Italian pool boys, and they pour the best martinis."

"I'm not going in." But I was getting weak.

"Okay, we won't go in."

"As soon as the cab stops, I'm leaving."

"Whatever you want."

Evan smiled. He knew he had won. I folded my arms over my chest in mock annoyance and didn't look at him, but we all know how this evening goes from here. Martini. Celeb gazing. Kissing. Second martini. Groping under the table. Groping in the cab. Reverse cowgirl. I hated myself, but a part of me said, what the hell. Darcy was history, Saleema was history, I was whacking tired, and Evan still looked as hot as ever, so why shouldn't I allow myself a few orgasms as consolation?

We stopped at a red light. Evan put his hand on my knee. I didn't take it off.

As things turned out, I didn't even need the first martini or the celeb gazing. By the time we reached the restaurant, my tongue was in his mouth.

You have to wonder about anyone who will pay fifty-five dollars for macaroni and cheese, but this is New York, after all. We slurped it up at a table for two near the fire and washed it down with ice-cold martinis. The back room at the Waverly features dark wood, dim light, and glowing wall sconces, as if this is Jack the Ripper's idea of a Victorian pub. Not that it matters. You're only there to see who else is there, and when the owner is editor of *Vanity Fair*, you're bound to be surrounded by the A-list.

Graydon himself stopped by to kiss me on the cheek. His slate hair looked windblown, as always, and his round face turned positively cherubic when he saw me. Is it possible for someone to look Canadian? He looks Canadian. God love him, he knows everything, so I wasn't at all surprised when he whispered in my ear, "I hear you're planning to ditch Cosima and set up shop on your own."

I winked, but I didn't deny it.

"Go for it," he told me.

"Will you still take my calls?" I asked.

"I don't take them now."

"That's true, you cad," I said.

We laughed.

While we were talking, a thin and unbelievably luminous blonde appeared at Graydon's side and wrapped her waifish arms around his neck. It took me a moment to realize it was Sienna Miller. Graydon introduced us, and I mentioned that my assistant was in love with her, because Emma would chop off my head if I didn't. I was pretty sure Sienna wasn't going to climb the fence to be with her, but I did my part.

Graydon and Sienna floated off into the crowd. I saw Hilary Swank. Serena Williams. Viggo Mortensen.

Evan leaned forward. "You belong here."

"I'm just a poseur."

"No, you can make it in the big leagues."

"We're eating mac and cheese, for Christ's sake."

I scooped up the last forkful and then finished my martini and waved at the waiter for another. Under the table, Evan's hand was on my thigh and moving northward. I'm so glad basketball players have long arms. It was too dark for anyone to see, and I was drunk and tired enough not to care. There were plenty of real celebrities for people to ogle. The word from Graydon was that there had been a Michael Mann red carpet premiere in midtown, and this was one of the hot spots for Hollywood types spilling over into after parties.

I was practically falling over. I can't handle all-nighters like I could in the old days. I felt buzzed as I sipped vodka and chewed an olive. I tried not to think about sleep or Dorothy or David Milton or Cosima or Saleema or Darcy. I spread my legs a little to give Evan better access and was happy to let him feel me up. The room did a pirouette. I knew I would be bloodshot tomorrow, moonwalking on caffeine, but tomorrow was tomorrow, and tonight was for me. Screw everything else. I was in no condition to worry about anything except getting hammered and getting laid. Same thing.

Needless to say, God likes messing with me, because He picked that ridiculous moment for Evan to announce, "Tom's here."

"Who?"

"Tom."

"Who?"

"Tom. Tom Cruise."

I blinked. I shook my head. I had an out-of-body experience. "Did you say Tom Cruise?"

"Yeah."

"WHERE?"

That probably came out a lot louder than I intended.

"Like ten feet behind you."

Evan probably thought I was insane, because I dove under the table, dislodged his talented hand from my crotch, and retrieved my huge purse from the floor. My fingers shivered as I unzipped it and spilled lipstick, coins, pens, cell phone, BlackBerry, granola bars, hairbrush, iPod, and condoms onto the table before emerging with the prize.

A dog-eared copy of *Singularity*.

I swayed to my feet. "Be right back."

"Are you sure you're all right?" Evan asked.

"Perfect."

In fact, thanks to the adrenaline, I was suddenly wide-awake. Through the darkness and crowds of the garden room, I examined each face until I spotted the biggest crowd, and at the center of it, I spied the Man himself. He was unmistakable. Smaller than life. Wavy hair. Trademark grin. I didn't hesitate but dove into the melee.

I was so close. So close. I nudged and pushed and elbowed and shouldered and tripped until I lunged past the outer circle, and then past the inner circle, until there were only a handful of faces between Cruise and me. He could see me. He looked right at me. Our eyes met. He smiled. I smiled. No, Katie, I'm not a stalker, but Tom, you have to read this book. It was written for you. I was hearing the words in my head and rehearsing them as I tried to breathe. In. Out. In. Out.

There was only one face left between him and me.

But that face belonged to Felicia Castro.

"SHIT!" she bellowed, loud enough to be heard in Times Square. "What are YOU doing here?"

"Felicia, let me have ten seconds with him."

"SECURITY!"

Felicia clapped her hands over her head, which was obviously some kind of emergency signal, because two of the largest men I have ever seen in my life appeared out of nowhere and stood in front of me like a beefcake version of the Berlin Wall. I tried to maneuver around them, but they had already grown roots. People were looking at us. Beautiful people were whispering. I was going to see myself on the front page of the *Post*.

Felicia popped underneath the hulking shoulder of one of the bodyguards and then straightened up and extended a long, bony finger at me. "Get her the hell out of here!"

One of the apes grunted and nodded. I hoped it wasn't feeding time at the zoo.

"Felicia, come on, let's be reasonable about this," I said.

Someone put a hand on my shoulder, and I realized it was Evan. "What's going on here?" he demanded. "Who are these guys?"

"This woman is leaving." Felicia sneered.

"Like hell," Evan said.

I was beginning to like him more and more.

The bodyguards realized they had a new foe, who was more formidable than I, but they didn't look worried. Evan was still a boy toy compared to the Incredible Hulk twins. I had visions of a fight breaking out. An A-list brawl. Graydon would blacklist me forever. I would never pay fifty-five dollars for mac and cheese again.

Then the bodyguards stepped aside as if Moses had parted them, and a familiar Hollywood voice said, "Calm down, everybody. What's this all about?"

Felicia and I both tried to talk first, and Felicia won.

"Tom, it's nothing. This woman is trouble, and I've asked her to leave. Don't worry about it."

Cruise looked right at me, and his eyes twinkled, and he gave me one of those boyish smiles. I've never understood charisma, but you know it when you see it. "Is that right? Are you trouble?"

I took a breath. I hoped I could talk.

"Mr. Cruise, my name is Tess Drake. I know I look like hell, and I look drunk, and I probably am drunk. But I have a client named Oliver Howard who wrote an amazing book called *Singularity*. And I think if you read it, you'll think what I think, which is that this book should be a movie, and you should star in it."

Behind me, I heard Evan laugh and say, "My God, Tess, you've got balls."

Cruise laughed, too.

I held out my hand, which had the book in it. I tried not to drop it.

Felicia reached out to snatch it from me.

"It's okay," Cruise said, and Felicia yanked back her hand.

Cruise took the copy of *Singularity*, glanced at the cover, glanced at the back, flipped through some of the pages, and nodded at me.

"I'll take a look," he said.

Hallelujah.

21

I WAITED IN THE LOBBY of David Milton's office the next morning and tried to stay awake. I felt triumphant after my meeting with Tom Cruise, and I celebrated by taking Evan back to the St. Regis and experimenting with several new positions. Evan hadn't lost any of his stamina. We didn't get to sleep until nearly 5:00 A.M., and when my alarm went off two hours later, Evan was gone, but he had made coffee and left me a note that said, See you in London?

A few weeks ago, I would have set fire to the note and beat my head against the wall. Now I realized I was actually looking forward to the idea of seeing him again. I never learn.

The coffee helped. A little. I used Visine in my eyes, and I needed a lot of makeup. The results were passable. I visited the hotel restaurant for a real breakfast and then took a cab to Milton's office at Seventy-seventh and Third. It was nine thirty. I don't know why I expected Milton to be an intellectual property lawyer, but instead, the brochure in his lobby indicated that he was a solo practitioner specializing in trusts and estates. I was hoping he was a graduate of Bwana Bob's Harbor Tours and Law School in the Bahamas, but the framed diplomas on the wall were from NYU and Columbia. Milton was no dummy. Too bad.

He made me cool my heels for half an hour. When he came out finally and shook my hand, he smiled at me pleasantly, and I smiled back, which is a polite American ritual before you take out your knives and start carving each other up. Despite the odd little angle in his nose, Milton was not completely horrible to look at. He was not tall but solidly built, wearing a dark suit that fit snugly across his shoulders. His black hair was thick and shiny with gel. He had bushy eyebrows.

We sat on opposite sides of his desk in the small office. Through the open window, I heard street noise a few floors below us. He offered me coffee, and I declined. He had a half-eaten bran muffin on a piece of wax paper in front of him, and he pulled off chunks and ate them between slurps of Starbucks.

Milton leaned back in his reclining chair. "I assume Dorothy has told you about our little problem," he said.

"She has."

Milton chewed a piece of muffin thoughtfully. "I want you to know that I realize how awkward this is, and I really don't want to cause problems for Dorothy. She's a sweet old lady. I'm sure we can find an amicable resolution."

"That's why I'm here," I said. Except for the amicable resolution part.

"Good."

"Maybe you should tell me what you believe happened between your father and Dorothy Starkwell."

An ambulance passed on the street with its siren screaming. Milton got up and closed the window. He came back and leaned on the corner of his desk, looking down at me. "My father was a writer his whole life. He loved children's books. He wrote many, many stories, and as I recently discovered, he wrote a novel. Unfortunately, he never broke through in the publishing industry during his lifetime. You're an agent, so you know how hard that is.

I know it was one of his great disappointments. Imagine my surprise and dismay, however, to find that the original idea for Dorothy's panda series, which has made her a great deal of money, actually came from my father. I'm not saying she necessarily stole it consciously or deliberately, although I don't know that for sure. She did steal it, however, and I think my father deserves credit, and his estate deserves compensation. Significant compensation."

"When did your father pass away?" I asked.

"About fifteen years ago."

"So how is it possible that you've only made this remarkable discovery now?"

Milton sat down again. He finished his muffin and drained the dregs of his latte. "I live in a small house in New Jersey, Ms. Drake. I've lived there ever since I launched my legal practice in my early twenties. When my father died, it was a busy time in my career, and so I took many boxes with my father's personal effects and stashed them in my attic. I always intended to go through them in detail, but I never did. Until last month. I'm planning to sell my house and find an apartment, and I needed to clean out the attic. So I spent a weekend going through my father's materials. Frankly, I knew I would have to throw most of them out, but I wanted to spend a little time with them before I did. I'm sure you understand."

"What did you find?"

"Among other things, this note," Milton said.

He reached inside a manila folder and withdrew a photocopied sheet. The original had obviously been written on a small notecard. He handed it over, and I studied it carefully. If the handwriting was not Dorothy's, it was a perfect likeness. The language sounded like her, too.

> *My dear Tom,*
> *   I love it! You are so inventive. If this manuscript does not make you the next star in children's writing, then something is surely wrong with the world. I'm honored that you chose me to be your first reader. I*

really believe you have created the kind of lush, charm-
ing universe that children will find irresistible. How
exciting this all is! I am hugely proud of you!

With warmest wishes,
Dorothy

Maybe Dorothy didn't write this. Maybe it was a fake. But I didn't think so. This was exactly the kind of note she would write. Of course, I wasn't going to give Milton the satisfaction of saying so.

"Interesting," I said.

"I thought so. I'm sure you're also aware that Dorothy mentions my father in the acknowledgments in *The Bamboo Garden.*"

"Yes."

"So you see that we have a problem."

"I'm afraid I don't. From what I hear, your father wrote Gothic tales for young adults. Ghost stories. You won't find any ghosts in Dorothy's books. Just pandas and poachers. The fact that Dorothy may have read an unpublished manuscript that your father wrote years ago is meaningless."

Milton got a tiny smile on his face, and he laughed, not in a nice way. "There's more," he said.

"Oh?"

He pulled another sheet from the manila folder and handed it to me. This page was also photocopied, and the original was smudged and difficult to read. The typing on the page was faint and old.

"What is this?" I asked.

"The first page of my father's manuscript."

I studied it, and I didn't like what I saw. The title read, "Butter-ball's Village." The author's name was Tom Milton. The first page included the header for the first chapter, which was: "Black and White and Red All Over."

I quickly scanned the rest of the double-spaced page. There were only a few paragraphs, but it was obvious that Dorothy and I had big problems. I tried to keep my reaction off my face, but Milton was a lawyer, and I'm sure he could spot my dismay. Butter-ball, of course, is the hero of Dorothy's series. The mayor of the panda village, or what Dorothy calls the Bamboo Garden. The first chapter of the first book sets the tone for the entire series— sweet, funny, with a serious message underneath. It's a lovely little fable about Butterball and the flowering of the bamboo, which leaves the community struggling to find enough food. It sounds dark, but in Dorothy's hands, it's not. Kids learn about leadership. Conservation. Working together. When I first read it, I knew she had created something special.

Or maybe it was Tom Milton who had created something special.

The page in my hand used different language and a different style. I could practically recite the first page of Dorothy's book from memory, and this was not at all like her work. But that made it even worse. David Milton hadn't simply taken Dorothy's book and retyped it and changed a few words. If this was a forgery, it was subtle and effective, because it was in fact so different from Dorothy's novel. But the heart of it was the same. The same characters. The same setting. The same action. The same names. If it was real, then Dorothy's book was plagiarism of the first order.

This was a disaster in the making.

"Now you see the problem," Milton said, smirking.

"One page?"

"I have the rest of the manuscript, too. My father wrote a novella. Around twenty thousand words. Dorothy obviously took it and expanded it, but anyone can see that the kernel of the entire series was my father's. He created it. He created the characters, the plot, the setting. The idea was his. After my father died, Dorothy took it for herself."

"I'll need to see the entire manuscript."

"In due time."

"Exactly what are you looking for?" I asked.

Milton reached behind himself and extracted a copy of the American edition of *The Bamboo Garden* from the bookshelf. He opened it and turned the pages delicately. "My father would be very pleased to know that his work has been embraced by so many children. That was what he always wanted, but success was elusive, not through any fault of his own. Obviously, I would like to see him get the public recognition he deserves, even posthumously."

I didn't say anything.

Milton closed the book and put his hand over the cover. "However, I am cognizant of the fact that this revelation would be extremely embarrassing to Dorothy. I have to weigh the pros and cons. On one hand, I want my father to receive credit for having created a series that has garnered worldwide acclaim. On the other hand, I wouldn't want to make it impossible for the series to continue by leaving Dorothy disgraced by these revelations. That would be unfair to the children who love my father's creations."

"Meaning?"

"Meaning perhaps we can negotiate a financial settlement that will honor my father's work without sacrificing Dorothy's reputation. That's certainly my goal. However, if we can't do so, then I'm afraid we face a messy and protracted court battle, charges played out in the press, all those ugly things we both want to avoid. And the end result will still be a large financial settlement but without the confidentiality and discretion. I fear that Dorothy would be ruined, and I really would hate to see that."

"You realize we need to do a lot of research on this issue," I said, which is what you say when you have no idea what to say. "I'll be hiring the finest copyright attorney in New York."

"No doubt."

"Do you have any other evidence to support the validity of this manuscript? Copies of submissions to publishers? Agent queries? Rejection letters?" I wasn't sure what I would do if he said yes.

"Let's leave all that for the lawyers, shall we? I'll give you and Dorothy some time to think about this. But not much time. My father's recognition is already long overdue. If I feel this negotiation is dragging out unnecessarily, then I may have to sit down and have a long chat with *The New York Times*."

"I'll be in touch," I said.

"I'm sure you will. In the meantime, you may want to start gathering financial records. They'll all be discoverable, you realize. And I'll want to know the status of any pending contracts."

"As you said, we'll leave that to the lawyers," I replied. Pending contracts? That made me suspicious.

"Are you going back to London today?" Milton asked.

"Yes, I have a flight tonight."

"Well, take a little more reading material with you," he told me, extracting several more pages from the dreaded manila folder on his desk. "Here's the rest of the first chapter of the manuscript. I think much of it will sound familiar."

I took the pages without looking at them and slid them into my purse.

"Good-bye, Mr. Milton."

"Good-bye, Ms. Drake."

We shook hands. I'd like to say I gave him a firm, confident grip, like someone who saw through his little game and was prepared to body slam him to the mat. But I didn't. The fact is, I had a hard time not peeing on the carpet as I left.

22

I SPENT THE REST OF THE DAY wandering through Central Park with my cell phone turned off. I arrived at JFK three hours early and almost missed my flight because I fell asleep at the gate. No one nudged me when the plane started boarding. Maybe they figured I was dead. When I finally dragged myself on the plane, I fell asleep again, which almost never happens. When I woke up, we were out over the middle of the Atlantic, the droning hum of the plane's engine in my ears. I wondered if anyone would mind if I popped open the door and jumped out.

The pages from Tom Milton's supposed manuscript were still in my purse. I hadn't looked at them yet, and I really didn't want to. I was worried they would be just as convincing as what I had already seen. I actually had a glimmer of doubt that this wasn't just a confidence game.

Dorothy, Dorothy, what did you do?

It's amazing how your mood can swing from peaks to valleys in the blink of an eye. The whole Tom Cruise thing at the Waverly left me feeling on top of the world. Then I met David Milton, and I crashed. It didn't help that I was riding on fumes with no energy other than a guilty, satisfied, postsex high. I was now feeling bleak about my prospects. Cruise would never read the book. Milton would tie me up in knots for months. How do you launch your own agency with your most important client in the midst of a career-threatening scandal?

Maybe that was the point. Or maybe I'm letting my ego carry me away. Not everything is about me. Just most things.

Rather than think about stolen pandas, I thought about Evan. It was silly to feel that I was cheating on Darcy, who was already cheating on Cosima by cheating with me. Darcy had his chance. If he had so much as looked at me at the funeral, or sent me a message after our latest rendezvous, I would have kept my knees shut. Or at least I would have put up more of a fight. However, the reality is that Evan makes me weak in a way that few men do. I loathe him, and yet I can't stay away from him. I don't want a relationship with him, but if he comes to London, God knows I'll sleep with him again. I'll protest that I won't, and I'll tell him to go to hell, even as I start getting the two of us undressed. That's just how it goes between him and me.

I'd be the last to tell you I didn't enjoy it. I did. I also know that I slept with Evan out of anger. I was angry at myself for letting my emotions carry me away with Darcy and angry at Darcy for treating my emotions as if they didn't exist. If I was nothing but meaningless sex to him, well, I could have meaningless sex, too. Meaningless, really great sex.

Anyway, going out with Evan gave me a chance to meet Cruise. To hand him *Singularity* personally. Okay, I know it will probably go nowhere, but a girl can dream. It's not like I'm looking to sleep with him or marry him or bear his love child. All I want is a film deal. That's not asking so much, is it?

Somewhere south of Iceland, I decided I couldn't put it off any longer, so I took the chapter that David Milton had given me out of my purse. I quashed all my doubts and told myself that Dorothy might be scattered and infuriating at times, but she was a sweet soul and a terrific writer, and it was inconceivable to me that she had deliberately stolen another man's idea. David Milton could sugarcoat it, but if his father's manuscript was genuine, then Dorothy set out to steal that book for herself, with malice aforethought, and she was still covering it up now. It wasn't the kind of thing that would slip your mind or happen by accident. Oh my goodness, I wrote a book about a lost girl, a tin man, a scarecrow, and a lion, and now I find out some man named Baum did the same thing! I don't think so. If she did it, she did it as an out-and-out thief. And that's not Dorothy.

So it's a fake. It has to be a fake. The question is how to prove it.

I drank wine as I read the chapter, and I ordered more wine from the flight attendant when I was done. Then I read it again, looking for obvious flaws and not finding any. When you think about it, how do you prove a negative? If someone types a manuscript and claims that he wrote it before you did, how do you prove him wrong just by reading the text? Answer—you don't. You prove it through the laborious process of unearthing notes and gathering depositions and weathering nasty media articles that call you a cheat. It's slow, it's expensive. Most authors don't keep research notes on paper anymore. They toss early drafts. They clean out their files. They keep their ideas to themselves until they're done. What counts is the final electronic version, but by then, who's to say exactly where you got all those words?

David Milton was no fool. He knew all that.

I bet he really was going through old boxes in his attic when he found samples of his father's writing. And the note from Dorothy? I bet that's genuine, too. If you're a lawyer with a hunger for a big score, your mind starts working. You've got a note from a multimillionaire author. Your father is gone. Years have passed. No one would expect you to have electronic records from back then, so all you really need to make your case is a manuscript. One copy you can pass off as the real thing.

I wondered if he really did find his father's book. If he did, he probably burned it. Or hid it away where it would never see the light of day. Then he faced the challenge of creating a new manuscript, something that would stand up to the scrutiny of experts, something that would convince a jury. Or maybe he just figured it needed to be convincing enough to scare Dorothy into settling.

And, yes, it was convincing.

From the photocopy, I could tell that it *looked* old. The manuscript was printed on what appeared to be an old dot-matrix printer with an ink cartridge that smeared and stuttered and made the text hard to read. It was probably printed on yellowed paper that had been sitting in the attic for years, too. It looked like the kind of draft copy an author would have kept some twenty years ago. Smart. If the package feels authentic, what's inside must be genuine, too.

I wondered how Milton had gone about creating the manuscript itself. I didn't think he was the one who wrote it. You'd have to be a writer to pull off something like that. A ghost. Someone who's used to writing in someone else's style and can shed skins like a chameleon. Maybe a talented but unsuccessful novelist who was willing to sell his soul to get a percentage of the fortune that Milton promised would be coming their way. It's not an easy job. You have to make it close but not too close. You have to make it sound like the other stories that Tom Milton wrote, so anyone who read it would believe it was by the same hand. You have to deconstruct what Dorothy did and rebuild it as an earlier, rougher draft. Definitely not easy. Milton needed someone who knew what he was doing and had no integrity at all.

But, hey, he lives in New York. No problem.

We could subpoena bank records to see if Milton made a payoff, but I had a feeling he was too smart to be caught that way. I also wondered if we could subpoena his telephone records and find calls back and forth between him and Saleema. This had her fingerprints all over it. Not that I'd ever be able to prove it.

I knew who I needed to call. My father. If you're on the losing end of a campaign of dirty tricks, the best person to ask for advice is someone who's spent his whole life in politics. Dad has seen it all. Sex scandals. Money scandals. Vice, betrayal, perjury, deception, everything you'd expect from our governing bodies. He is the ultimate insider and the ultimate cynic, but as a result, he knows everyone and trusts no one. If I turn him loose on David Milton, he'll find something. I hate to ask him for help, though, because every meeting with my father is a chance to review the laundry list of my failures and disappointments. He does it so smoothly that you don't feel like shit until later, but when it hits you just how badly you've turned out, you wind up eating chocolate for a week.

I decided to call him anyway.

That was the first item on my mental to-do list as I got off the plane at Heathrow. Emma tells me I'm in a world of my own sometimes, thinking about what I have to do. I would have to check in with Oliver Howard and tell him about Cruise and *Singularity*. Neither Oliver nor I is particularly religious, but if we both start praying, perhaps it will help. I also have to give Dorothy an update about David Milton, which won't be much of an update, because the only things I know now are things I wish I didn't know at all. I have to talk to my accountant. My lawyer. People I hate talking to unless I'm broke or under arrest, and, who knows, by next week I may be both.

I also have to decide if I'm going to pull the trigger. Leave the agency.

So really, there wasn't much at all on my mind as I retrieved my bags and took the green line at customs. All I was expecting was a typical drizzly London morning, take a shower, go to the office, make some calls, do my thing.

Then I saw a face in the waiting crowd, and I told myself I really needed to stop making jokes, even in my head, because lately, they've had a way of coming true. First the corset and heels thing with Lowell. And now the idea of being arrested. The face I saw belonged to Nicholas Hadley, the detective with the gray beard and the muddy Burberry. He saw me and pushed his way toward me, and I knew the day wasn't going to go as I had hoped.

"You really didn't need to come all this way to greet me, Inspector," I told him sweetly. "I was just going to hop the Piccadilly Line into the city." I gave him my most winning smile, which wasn't returned.

"I need to ask you some questions, Ms. Drake," Hadley replied.

"About what?"

People really do say stupid things like that. About what? Oh, hell, maybe he wants to talk about the weather.

"About you and Lowell Bardwright," he said.

"I think we've already talked about that, haven't we?"

"Something else has come up," Hadley told me.

"Such as?"

"Such as your fingerprints. In Mr. Bardwright's apartment."

23

I'M HOOKED ON TV cop shows. I make sure my DVR never misses *CSI* or any of the eighteen million variations of *Law & Order*. So after years of watching Lenny Briscoe and Ed Green and Ray Curtis (thump, thump goes my heart), I know that the police like psychological warfare. You know, good cop, bad cop—that sort of thing. Lie to a suspect. Make friends with a suspect. And sooner or later, the bad guys break down and sob and confess.

For me, it started with coffee. Really bad coffee. I'm sort of a coffee snob about my Caffè Nero dark roast, and the toilet water that Nicholas Hadley poured in a white paper cup made me want to tell him I shot Kennedy. Hadley drank two cups himself without flinching.

At least he didn't put me in a windowless room with a bare bulb dangling over my head. We sat in his office, which had a door and a window and a thousand file folders on his desk. The walls were littered with terrorist alerts and pictures of his wife and two kids.

His wife didn't look like any of the terrorist photos. I'm not sure about his oldest kid.

If I sound cavalier and sarcastic, there's a reason for it. I'm innocent. I never slept with Lowell, I never went to his apartment, and I certainly never helped him play a game of hangman's fellatio. I didn't do a damn thing, so when Hadley tells me he found my fingerprints in Lowell's apartment, I know he's lying. Rule number one: Never believe a word that comes out of a cop's mouth.

I told him all that before he could start with his questions. Hadley just sat there while I protested. You're wrong. I was never there. No way you found my fingerprints. And then something occurred to me.

"How'd you get my fingerprints anyway?" I asked.

Hadley shrugged, as if it were so easy it was hardly worth telling me how he did it. "Remember that woman in the park who asked you for directions? She was one of mine."

"Her map was sticky," I remembered.

"So we had a very nice fingerprint sample," Hadley said, a tiny smug smile under his mustache.

"Okay," I told him. "But that doesn't change the fact that I was never in Lowell's apartment."

Hadley sighed loudly. The kind of sigh that says you're a liar and you know it and I know it, so why keep playing games? Except I wasn't lying.

"There were two glasses of wine on the coffee table," Hadley told me. "One had Lowell's prints on it. The other had yours."

"No way."

"I can show you the lab report if you'd like."

I thought about saying yes, but I don't read enough Jeffery Deaver novels to understand all this stuff. I tried to make sense of this. Either he was lying, or I was being set up.

"Look, Inspector, I was never there, but I've drunk a lot of wine in my life, so maybe someone put it there. And, besides, would I be stupid enough to leave my fingerprints sitting there for you to find?"

"You'd be surprised how stupid people can be."

Well, that's true.

"So, what, I panicked while giving him a midair blow job?" I asked. "Is that what you think? He kicked the bucket, and I ran?"

"Is that what happened?"

"No."

"Are you saying it was an accident?"

"I'm saying I wasn't there."

"It's funny you should mention oral sex," Hadley said. "Exactly how did you know that Mr. Bardwright had been receiving oral sex prior to his death?"

Shit!

"It was a figure of speech," I said.

"Like the corset and high heels joke? That was just a figure of speech, too?"

I felt my face getting hot. "Yes."

"Interesting," Hadley said. Then he added, "Tell me about your dealings with the Santelli Agency in Milan."

"Excuse me?"

"I believe there were allegations that you were rigging deals for Italian publishing rights and getting kickbacks," Hadley said. "This was about two months ago."

"Yes, and it was bullshit," I snapped. "Complete crap."

And it was. An Italian publisher in Rome raised a stink when he lost three deals in a row to a competitor, and Leonardo Santelli and I got caught in a nasty war of accusations and threats between the two archrivals. Sally had warned me about these guys, but I hadn't listened. You shouldn't get caught between two pit bulls in a fight, and you never want to land in the middle of an Italian blood feud. These guys fight dirty. Filing pointless lawsuits. Buying off each other's corrupt politicians. Sleeping with each other's mistresses.

I told Hadley all about it.

"How was it resolved?" he asked.

"I finally said a pox on both your houses. I don't deal with either of them anymore."

"Did Mr. Bardwright know about the allegation of kickbacks?"

"Yes."

"Did he speak to you about it?"

"Yes, of course. I told him what I told you. There was no truth to it. It was complete fabrication."

"So the matter was closed?"

"Yes."

Hadley nodded. "Why would Mr. Bardwright have an e-mail about this issue open on the laptop computer in his home office?"

"What?"

"He had an e-mail about you and the alleged Italian kickbacks on his machine. It was on the screen when we booted it up."

"That doesn't make any sense. We put that issue to bed weeks ago."

"If the allegation of kickbacks were true, what would that mean for your reputation in the industry? It would be devastating, wouldn't it?"

"The allegations weren't true," I told him.

"If they were true, or if people thought they were true, that would give Mr. Bardwright rather a lot of leverage over you, I should think."

"They weren't true," I repeated.

"Would you sleep with your boss to keep something like that quiet? Is that worthy of blackmail?"

"Fuck you," I snapped.

This was probably the point where he expected me to break down and sob and confess. Except I had nothing to confess. Well, not about Lowell, anyway. My list of sins would keep a priest busy for hours, but murder, kickbacks, and erotic asphyxia are not among them.

Hadley smoothed his thinning gray hair. He sipped his god-awful coffee and slowly turned pages in a file folder on his desk. He had an aura of serene calm. I hate people who are calm. If you don't wear your heart on your sleeve, I'm not sure you're really alive.

"Remember that dress you said you lost at the cleaners?" Hadley asked. "The one you wore to the Christmas party where Lowell had his arm around your waist in that photograph in the *Bookseller*?"

"Yes," I repeated. "What about it?"

"We found it in Lowell's closet."

"Get the fuck out of here!" I said in a voice that was way too loud. I'm not averse to the *F* word, but you can tell I'm riled if I use it twice in less than a minute.

Once again, Hadley ignored my outburst. "This, again, is interesting, because you say you've never been in his apartment."

"I haven't."

"So your dress and your fingerprints went there without you?" Hadley asked.

"You did not find that dress. You are lying to me, Inspector, and I'm tired of it. Quit trying to play head games with me."

He passed me a photo of the dress without saying a word. It was definitely mine. I thought about asking to get it back, because I missed that dress, and I was really pissed that the cleaners had lost it. But I figured I would be pushing my luck.

"Okay, someone is setting me up," I said.

"Really?"

"Really."

Really. That was when it hit me. This wasn't a game. This was dead serious, and Lowell was the one who was dead. Someone had killed him, and whoever did it wanted me to take the fall. Someone had given me a motive and put in a lot of effort to make it appear that I was inside Lowell's apartment. I realized that Hadley was right. Lowell ran an agency that made deals worth millions of pounds. For some people, that was worth killing over.

I could think of only one person who would stand to gain from this kind of conspiracy. Cosima.

Cosima, who had bought her way into Lowell's agency and was tired of waiting for him to step down. Cosima, who had plans of world domination that didn't mesh with Lowell's laissez-faire attitude of keeping the agency just the way it had been for forty years.

Cosima, who said she would bury me if I dared to leave Bardwright and go out on my own.

Maybe her threat was more real than I imagined.

I realized I was sitting there like a deer frozen on the highway, about to get flattened by a lorry, and Hadley was watching me.

"Who would want to set you up?" he asked me.

Just tell him, I thought to myself. Give him Cosima's name. Except if I knew Cosima, she had covered her tracks from here to Canterbury, and she had probably already told Hadley to expect that I would point the finger in her direction. And who knows, maybe I was wrong.

But I wasn't wrong. Not a chance.

"I have no idea, but I've told you the truth, Inspector. I was never in Lowell's apartment." I tried to sound sincere. I hope I pulled it off.

"The strange thing is, I believe you," Hadley said.

"You do?"

"I do."

I felt a surge of relief, but I reminded myself of rule number one: Never believe anything the police tell you.

"There's a way we can clear this up," Hadley continued.

"Oh?" I was suspicious.

"Give us a DNA sample."

"DNA? Why?"

"We found DNA in Mr. Bardwright's apartment. We'd like to compare it to yours."

I didn't like the sound of that. "Well, no offense, Inspector, but if someone was able to plant a wineglass with my fingerprints and a stolen dress, why couldn't they find a way to plant my DNA, too?"

Hadley's lips curled into something like a smile again. "This DNA would have been exceptionally difficult to plant."

"Oh?"

"It was saliva."

Okay, well, I didn't know how Cosima would have gotten her claws on my saliva, unless she followed me on a jog through the park and caught me when I swallowed wrong and had to spit. Even so.

"You can get saliva from lots of places, can't you?" I asked.

"The issue is more where we found the saliva," Hadley told me.

"Where was that?"

"On Mr. Bardwright's penis," he said.

Thank God I wasn't drinking coffee. I would have spit it out. "Are you kidding me?"

"No."

"Well, I was never in Lowell's apartment, and I *never* had my lips around his dick, I'll tell you that." I'm not at all averse to oral sex, but Lowell? God, no.

"So let us sample your DNA," Hadley said.

"How do you do that? Do I pee in a cup or something?"

"Nothing like that. It's a simple matter of a cotton swab on the inside of your mouth."

"Will you buy me dinner first?" I asked.

Hadley actually smiled.

"Okay," I said. "Sure. Swab away."

I knew I was going to tell my father about all this tonight, and he was probably going to tell me I had made some serious mistakes. It wouldn't be the first time he had told me that, and it wouldn't be the first time he was right.

I was still innocent, but I wasn't feeling very cavalier anymore.

24

I FINALLY MADE IT to my office in the middle of Friday afternoon. I was seriously sleep deprived. I read once that sleep is a major physiological and psychological function in many if not all mammals, and the more you run away from it, the more it catches up with you. Even so, I had miles to go before I could sleep. More miles than I even realized at the time, but I don't want to get ahead of myself.

My day, which had started out poorly, did not get better in the office. The first voice mail message on my phone was from Felicia Castro.

"Don't think you've won, you cunt," she told me. I could hear the clinking of glasses and party conversations in the background, and so I figured she was still at the Waverly when she left me the message. "I talked to Tom. I told him what a lying bitch you are. I told him what a piece of shit the book is. I told him not to waste his time. He's going to throw it away."

Click.

Felicia sounded angry and drunk. I hoped that she was just messing with me and that she wouldn't risk her relationship with Cruise by arguing over *Singularity*. If you're a smart manager, you drop it when your client overrules you. Even so, Felicia hates me, and I've begun to realize that people who hate me do so with unusual ferocity. So I was depressed to think that she might really have found a way to get Tom to ignore the book.

I wasn't sure now whether to tell Oliver and get his hopes up by giving him the story about Cruise. I decided not to call him right away.

Big mistake.

The next message was from Dorothy. She wanted an update. I called her back, and for the first time, I was pleased when she didn't answer and there was no way for me to leave a message. What could I tell her? Dorothy, it's Tess. Say, there's no way you *might* have plagiarized that million-selling book of yours, is there? Call me. No, I wasn't eager to ask my best client if she was a fraud. I still thought the Milton manuscript was a fake, but I was seriously out of my league and needed help. It was time to bring in the cavalry. I called a copyright lawyer I know at an intellectual property boutique and told him we needed to meet. Soon.

Next I called my father. Suggested dinner. He's part journalist, part politician, which means he never gives away any secrets in his voice. He said yes without letting me hear a hint of surprise or disapproval, but he knows I never call unless I have a problem. I hung up, feeling guilty, as if I had nicked a candy bar from the corner store. I'm thirty-six and felt like I was nine. My father could give Donald Trump pangs of self-doubt.

I looked up and saw Emma in my doorway. Her long bare legs reminded me of New York skyscrapers. She had one pencil behind her ear, sticking out from a sea of red curls, and another pencil in her mouth like a dog bone.

"We're already hearing back on *Duopoly*," Emma told me. She didn't have the look of someone who was about to announce a six-figure offer.

"Let me guess."

"No, no, no, and no. Sorry."

"Fuckers," I snapped. She gave me the names of the editors who had sent their regrets, none of which surprised me. We still had four queries out, but I wasn't holding my breath. People think if you sell your first book, publishers beat a path to your door to buy the next one. Not so much. If the first book is a bomb, you're damaged goods, and people shun you like a coworker with the flu. It's hard enough selling a debut, because publishers worry that it won't sell. It's worse after a flop, because they *know* it won't sell.

"How was New York?" she asked.

I told Emma about meeting Tom Cruise with Evan, and her freckles did a little dance. "Tess, that's wonderful! What a lucky break!"

"Maybe," I said, looking glum.

"Come on, this is what you were hoping for."

"The odds just went from a million to none to a million to one. Let's not book a trip to LA just yet."

"Still."

"Yeah, it's good news, but Felicia swears she'll rip the book out of Tom's hands."

"She won't. She wouldn't dare. Even a bitch like her. Have you talked to Oliver?"

"Not yet. I'm not sure I want to get his hopes up."

Emma closed the door and cast a suspicious glance through the window. She leaned over my desk, giving me a view of her cleavage that Guy would have killed for. When she hits forty and her breasts head for the floor, it will sound like twin meteors striking the earth. "The word is out," she whispered.

"The agency?"

"Yes, everyone knows."

"Who's everyone?"

"Everyone. All the agents and secretaries keep stopping by my desk and asking for details. I think a lot of them would like to go with you."

"Well, don't say anything, okay?"

"No, of course not." Emma chewed her lower lip and studied my face. "Are you having second thoughts?"

"Some." I explained the situation with Dorothy and David Milton, and Emma was aghast.

"Dorothy? No way. This guy must be a crook."

"I agree with you, but crooks sometimes get away with the loot."

"This is terrible."

"It sucks, that's for sure," I agreed.

"But does that really change everything? Does that mean you're not going to resign on Monday?"

"I don't know. I've got to think about it over the weekend. I'm not sure I want to bolt with this cloud over Dorothy."

Emma looked genuinely distressed. "Cosima will make your life miserable if you stay."

"She'll make my life miserable if I leave, so I'm screwed either way," I said.

I didn't tell her about Nicholas Hadley or about my suspicions that Cosima had gone so far as to help Lowell make an orgasmic exit to the afterlife. Not that I think the saliva on Lowell's mushroom really belonged to Cosima herself. I knew from Darcy that Cosima viewed sex as the kind of activity best left to monkeys and cabinet ministers. (Like there's a difference, my father would say.) No, Cosima would sooner let a veterinarian's thermometer inside her mouth as a man's dick. If she really was the mastermind behind this scheme, she'd hired someone else to do the dirty work for her.

I had a fleeting thought that my own life might be in danger. It's hard to take something like that seriously, but then again, Lowell's dead. It made me wonder what bizarre and painful manner of death she might plan for me. After all, one case of erotic asphyxia can seem like carelessness, but two would certainly raise suspicions. Poison would be better. Stick arsenic in a champagne truffle, and I'd eat it even if I knew it was there.

"So what are you going to do?" Emma asked.

"Talk to my father. Talk to a lawyer. Rally the troops. No matter what I do, though, this thing feels like it's going to hang on for months, and I don't really want to close a new deal for Dorothy with some con artist trying to get his hands on her money."

"I'm sorry, Tess."

"Thank you, darling. Don't frown, I'll figure out something. Oh, say, do you remember that box of old crap I gave you last year to put in storage?"

"Yes."

"Get it back for me, will you? I'd like to go through it this weekend."

"Sure. What's in it?"

"Probably nothing."

When Dorothy's original agent died, Dorothy sent me all the woman's files and written materials from the early years of Dorothy's literary career. The box sat in the corner behind my desk for years, serving as a footrest and occasional plant stand, until Emma insisted on cleaning out the hurricane zone that is my office. There was nothing in the box of great value. It was mostly copies of old contracts and correspondence, but since it dated back to the days when Dorothy was first selling *The Bamboo Garden*, I thought there might be a clue that would help me prove that David Milton was a fraud. It was wishful thinking, but I needed a place to start.

I didn't have anything more for Emma, but she sat down and crossed her arms across her ample chest and waited. Her lips folded into a sly smile.

"What?" I asked.

"You left out the best part," she told me.

"About what?"

"You told me you met Cruise while you were having dinner with Evan." She cocked her head, waiting for details. Emma knew all about my sordid past.

"There's nothing to tell," I said, but even I couldn't pull off that line. A furious blush rose like the dawning sun on my face.

"Did you sleep with him?" Emma asked. "Did you really? You naughty girl."

"Look who's talking."

"Was it good?"

"Extremely good." Extremely, as in I'm going to walk bow-legged for a week.

"What about Darcy?"

I shook my head sadly. "I think we may be done."

"No, really?"

"I haven't heard from him since I said the magic words."

"Bastard. I can't believe it."

"The trouble with dating men is that you have to date men," I said. "And they're pigs. You're smart, Emma."

"I thought Darcy was different."

"So did I. At least with Evan, I know what I'm getting. Which is nothing. He makes no bones about being a cad and a cheat."

"If you want to try girls, I can hook you up."

I smiled. "Thanks, but I'm afraid I'm stuck with the opposite sex." I added, "Speaking of which, are you still seeing your new girlfriend? The actress?"

"Jane? Yes! She's amazing. I think I'm in love. I mean, I know I say that a lot, and I just met her, but sometimes everything clicks. It isn't just sex, either, although I can't believe what she knows how to do. Wow."

"Well, learn from my experience, Emmy," I told her. "Don't go blurting out 'I love you' until you're sure you're going to hear it back."

"Yes, I know."

I was a little surprised that the bloom wasn't off the rose yet. This makes almost a week, which is usually enough time for Emma to decide that a girl is not quite right, too clingy, too short, too demanding, too loud.

"Are you two going out tonight?" I asked.

"Yes, and Saturday, too." Emma pouted with her pink lips in a frown. "But Jane's been invited to the BFI gala on Sunday night—very glam, all sorts of stars, TV cameras—and I can't go."

"Why not?"

"Oh, Jane doesn't want it obvious that she's gay. She says the popzees will be staking out the party. She figures if Godfrey Kahn sees her in the tabloids with another girl, he won't cast her in his next boy pic."

"It might help her chances," I said.

"Well, that's what I said. Oh, did you have a chance to put in a good word with Godfrey?"

"I haven't called yet, but I will," I assured her.

"That's very sweet, thank you."

"Don't get your hopes up, though. I know some of his people, but I don't know Godfrey himself."

Emma nodded enthusiastically. "That's okay—anything will help. I really like Jane. I mean, I know I sort of jump from one girl to the next, but this one feels different. You know?"

Yes, I knew what she meant. It's all in how your heart beats. Then again, I thought I was in love with Darcy, and look how that turned out.

25

MY FATHER WAS ALREADY AT THE RESTAURANT and half-way through his glass of Sancerre when I arrived. I'm always late for my father, even when I'm early. It's the first move in our perennial father-daughter chess game. He knows I am habitually late, and he never says anything about it, but invariably I feel like shit for making him wait. Terrence Paul Drake, senior political correspondent for the *Times*, is a busy man, but never too busy for his daughter. Call me crazy, but I have spent my life wishing for him to be something less than perfect, which would at least give me an excuse for falling short of his standards.

Start with the fact that he doesn't smoke. Has never touched a cigarette in his life. He is probably the only journalist whose lungs are as pink and fresh as the day he started using them. Me, I finally quit about five years ago, but I teeter on the edge like a klutzy tightrope artist, always in danger of falling. My father congratulates me on remaining smoke free, which is his way of asking if I really am. He knows me. Damn him.

Then there's my love life. I'm sure he blames my disastrous history of romances on genes from my mother. He never talks about their divorce or how much it hurt him when she ran off to Italy. He acts as if it were just a minor disappointment, like a family cat failing to return home. I don't recall ever seeing him date anyone, and God knows he would never allow himself to be a fool again for a woman. I think that's rather sad. He is always working, always on the phone, always anticipating the next political trend. MPs and cabinet ministers hold their breaths when they read his column. His address book overflows with contacts and friends around the world, but in the thirty years since my mum broke his heart, I don't believe he has ever enjoyed the sheer stupid exhilaration of falling in love. Occasionally, when I visit my mother in Italy, we talk about Dad, and she claims that he never had a heart to break. I don't think that's true. It's just that when you are the soul of a British gentleman, you don't allow your emotions to overrun your decorum.

Unlike me.

It's funny. I obviously take after my mum in so many ways, but the parent I love and whom I long to impress is my father. Not that I'm succeeding.

We met at the Bank Westminster restaurant, where my father keeps a reserved table by the window looking out on the Victorian garden and fountain. Everyone knows him there. Everyone knows him everywhere. We are always interrupted by people stopping by our table, but, bless him, his eyes are always on me, not darting around to observe the comings and goings of Westminster regulars. His cell phone must ring eighty times a day, but not once has it rung during one of our dinners. Not once. Would that I could say the same, because my BlackBerry sits between us and cries for attention every five minutes like an infant. He never says a word when I take calls and post e-mails with my thumbs. He sips his wine and smiles and watches me. I'm sure he wonders how a daughter of his could be such a social misfit.

He gave me a European kiss as I sat down. Both cheeks. I smelled a dab of Clive Christian cologne, just the right amount, hideously expensive without being showy. My dad is a handsome man, no less so for turning seventy this year. He sports a crown of snow-white hair that he gets clipped every other Tuesday; smart baby blue eyes; a long nose like a bumpy ski slope; and a strong, narrow chin. He wears hand-tailored British-made suits—no Euro-zone rubbish for him, thank you. His pocket handkerchief always forms a perfect triangle, in royal blue today to match the silk of his tie. He's tall, a little too skinny, and has big hands and manicured nails.

Somewhere in my head, a little voice tells me that Darcy is like a younger version of my father, but that's the kind of voice that would lead me to a shrink's couch, so I don't listen.

We chatted about politics, which for us is like small talk. My dad is so scrupulously neutral that he doesn't even vote. He is always discreet, because he knows that I'm not. Even so, I tell him everything I've heard on the street, and he is polite about not correcting my gross misperceptions. He has been around long enough to realize that most politicians are either fools or eunuchs, and if you're smart, you'll take a eunuch any day, because they don't mess up the world by accomplishing anything. The fools, well, you know what they say. A fool and my money are soon parted.

I was just postponing the inevitable. My father knew it. When we reached the twenty-minute lull in our conversation, he sat back in his chair and eyed me with a look that said, What are you hiding, Tessie?

"It was very kind of you to invite me to dinner," he said in his Somerset accent.

Translation: You never call unless you have a problem.

"I missed you," I said.

True, but that had nothing to do with why I had called. I smiled and took a long, nervous swallow of a California chardonnay.

"I had an interesting phone call from Gerald at the *Guardian* who had heard that my daughter was starting her own entertainment agency," he told me.

I spit out a little wine on the tablecloth.

"Naturally, I told him that couldn't be the case, because I was certain I would already have heard about those plans from my daughter," he went on. "I would have heard about those plans from my daughter, wouldn't I?"

"Look, Dad," I began.

He scratched an itch on his long nose with his index finger. His eyes twinkled. "Never mind, Tessie. I couldn't be more thrilled for you."

"Really?"

"Of course. I mean, my goodness, you should have done this years ago. I can't think of anyone more suited to running her own show."

"I'm happy to hear you say that."

Stunned is more like it.

"I mean, after all, you never listen to me or take any of my advice, so I can't help think you don't listen to your bosses, either. So you may as well be your own boss."

"Ah."

"I'm kidding, darling."

I glared at him. He laughed. The trouble is, his jokes come with a little drop of poison at the end of the sword point.

"I always thought Lowell would have a heart attack trying to control you, Tessie," he went on. "Of course, his end turned out to be considerably more salacious than I would have imagined. Sexual drive has a way of making us idiots, don't you think?"

Translation: It's made an idiot out of his daughter more than once.

"Yes, about Lowell," I said.

"So when's the big day?" he continued. "When do you strike out to sea like Columbus?"

"Well, I was thinking Monday," I said, "but now I'm not so sure. Some things have come up."

"Is it money? You never ask for my help, but I would be honored to be an investor. You know that, don't you?"

I do, but I would sooner starve than ask my father for help, and we both know it.

"It's not money," I said.

"Then what?"

I finished my wine way too quickly and signaled for another. I leaned back in my chair and stroked the white tablecloth with my fingernails and played with my silverware. I teased the gel in my multicolored hair. Anything so I wouldn't have to talk.

"Tessie?" my father asked, his voice dropping an octave with concern.

"Some bastard is accusing Dorothy of stealing her pandas from his father, Cosima says she'll bury me if I leave, Tom Cruise probably thinks I'm insane, my married boyfriend dumped me, my other boyfriend is a scoundrel, and the police think I killed Lowell."

I ran out of breath and took another.

My father didn't look at all fazed. Jeffrey Archer is a friend of his, so my tale of woe probably doesn't even crack the top ten.

"I could use your contacts on the Dorothy thing," I told him.

He nodded and pursed his lips. "I wonder if we could start with the question of your murdering your boss."

"I didn't."

"I was hoping not. Why does anyone think you did?"

"Oh, something about my fingerprints on a wineglass in his apartment, my dress in his closet, and his trying to blackmail me for sex over my taking kickbacks on Italian publishing deals."

Still not fazed. "Is any of that true?"

"No."

"I don't need to tell you that this is serious, do I?"

"I understand that. All I can tell you is that whoever dispatched Lowell obviously decided that I made a convenient target. I didn't do it."

"Did you ever have sex with Lowell?"

"Dad!"

He raised his hands in surrender. "I'm sorry, it's just that—well, you and your romantic choices, Tessie."

"Give me credit for having at least some taste," I protested.

"I'm sorry."

"I know it wouldn't be the first time I slept with the wrong man, but in this case, I am innocent."

"You realize the police are likely to find out about some of your past indiscretions," he reminded me.

"It's not like I was spectacularly successful in keeping them secret," I said.

"So what's next?" he asked.

"Apparently whoever was with Lowell that night left behind a little spit in a very inconvenient place, if you catch my drift. Again, needless to say, it wasn't me. I gave the police a swab of my DNA so they could prove that."

My father winced. "I wish you'd called me first. Or called a solicitor."

"I'm telling you, it wasn't me."

"Even so."

I sighed. He sighed.

"I'll make some calls," he went on.

"You don't need to do that."

"I'm going to, anyway."

I didn't try to dissuade him. He saw in my face that I was grateful. I reached out and squeezed his hand, which is as physical as we get. While we were sharing that magic moment, my BlackBerry began ringing. My ring tone is some song with a chorus like, "Whoomp! There it is!" Not exactly right for the circumstances. I allowed my eyes to drift to the caller ID and saw that Oliver was trying to reach me.

Normally I would take the call, but not now, not tonight.

Big mistake.

"So what's up with Dorothy Starkwell?" my father asked me.

I gave him the whole story. David Milton. Tom Milton. The manuscript in the attic. The note from Dorothy to Tom. I told him what I suspected—that this was all an elaborate fraud—but that I wasn't sure how to prove it.

"You've talked to an IP lawyer?"

I nodded and gave him the name.

"Well, he's the best," my father said. "Honestly, Tessie, you can find time to call a lawyer over a squabble about a children's book, and you can't figure out how to call a lawyer when the police are accusing you of murder?"

"It's more than a squabble," I retorted. "Dorothy's a client, millions of dollars are at stake, and I can't launch my agency without her."

"You can't very well launch it from prison, either."

"I didn't do anything, so I'm not going to prison."

He harrumphed. "It's not quite so simple, darling."

"I know."

"Anyway, you realize that your lawyer may tell you to settle to get rid of this thing with Dorothy."

"No way."

"Tessie, you are making the classic mistake of everyone involved in litigation, which is to think with your heart and not your head. It doesn't matter whether Dorothy is innocent or guilty."

"She's innocent."

"No doubt she is, but you and Dorothy will have to decide whether the time, expense, and publicity associated with defeating these charges are worth it. People settle bogus charges all the time because it's the best business decision. All I can tell you is, listen to your lawyer and do what he tells you."

"I always do."

He actually laughed. "Yes, what on earth was I thinking?"

"I'll listen, I promise, but can you do me a favor?"

"What?"

"You have investigators in New York, right? People who can find out things?"

He nodded.

"I'd like to know more about David Milton," I told him. "I'd love to find out if he's doing this on his own or whether he has help. Anything that will give me some ammunition when I talk to him."

"Let your lawyer do the talking."

"I will, but the more I know about how all this happened, the better."

"Tessie, you don't have to fight every battle yourself."

"I feel better when I do."

"All right, all right, I'll see what I can find."

"Thank you, Dad."

"Now what's all this about your boyfriends?" he asked. "Married or otherwise. And why does Tom Cruise think you're insane?"

"Oh, God, I don't even want to talk about it."

"I gather you've been making good use of my flat on the weekends," he said.

"Not as good as I'd like. Anyway, it's old news. My relationships are a thing of the past. I'm unattached and planning to stay that way."

"You?"

"Really. I'm considering celibacy."

"Don't take your vows just yet."

I smiled, then screwed my courage up again. "Tell me something honestly, Dad. No kidding around. Do you think I'm up to this whole thing? Do you think I can make it work on my own? With everything going on, I'm wondering if God is sending me a message: Stay where you are. Don't rock the boat."

Dad steepled his hands and leaned forward with his long chin balanced on his fingertips. "You, Tessie? Please. You were born to rock the boat."

Leave it to your father to come through for you when you least expect it. Sure, he worked in his share of zingers, but I left the restaurant actually feeling better than when I went in. Like maybe my life was not the complete and utter disappointment to him that I generally believed.

I hailed a cab and literally fell into the backseat. It was Friday night, and I could sleep as late as I wanted on Saturday, and I was hoping the world would look better after an extended communion with my pillow. I still wasn't sure if I had the balls to hand in my resignation on Monday with Dorothy's future up in the air, but like Scarlett O'Hara, I figured I could think about that tomorrow.

I thought about closing my eyes in the cab, but I am a slave to my BlackBerry. We lost out on two more queries on *Duopoly*, which pissed me off. I got a picture message from Emma that showed her and her actress chicky, Jane Parmenter, mugging for the camera on the London Eye. The message reminded me that I still hadn't called my friend at Godfrey Kahn's production company about pushing Jane for the role in Kahn's next flick. Thanks to Emma, I knew more about Jane's gifts in bed than her gifts as an actress, but the acting business isn't really about talent anyway. It's about who you know. I called Kahn's offices. Got voice mail. Left a message.

When I was done with e-mail, I checked my own voice mail. Sally called, wondering about my plans, asking what was up with Dorothy. Marty Goodacre called, looking to schedule a meeting for me with Cosima for eleven o'clock on Monday morning. No doubt she wanted to talk about Dorothy's contract again. Maybe I'd have a surprise for her. Guy called, asking if I was heading to the premiere of the newest Boublil and Schönberg musical on Saturday night. I wondered if Dorothy had told Guy about David Milton. That would be stupid, but it would be just like Dorothy to confide in Guy. Anyway, yes, I was going to the premiere, so I'd see him there.

The last message was from Oliver, time-stamped two hours ago. Hearing his voice, I realized that I should tell him about Cruise, even if it came to nothing. Oliver needed a pick-me-up. Something to lift the cloud.

And then I realized, as I listened, that he needed much more.

"Tessie, it's Oliver, I'm sorry I missed you," he said. He sounded drunk but not an ordinary kind of drunk. He sounded depressed, but not an ordinary kind of depressed. "Look, thanks for everything, okay? I just wanted to make sure you knew it's not your fault."

That was all.

I hung up and sat there, wondering why my dinner was doing cartwheels in my stomach and why my heart was pounding in my ears. I used my phone and called my voice mail and listened to the message again. And again. Until there was no mistaking what he meant.

"Oh, shit," I said aloud.

I gave the driver a new address and told him to hurry.

26

OLIVER LIVES, if you can call it that, in a basement studio flat not far from King's Cross, in a part of the neighborhood that has stubbornly resisted redevelopment. Drug dealers and whores have to live somewhere, and this is where they call home. No yuppie condos. No quaint boutiques and bistros. I would sooner walk alone after midnight in most areas of London than in New York, but not here. My taxi driver looked at me as if I were crazy when I changed my destination from Putney and he let me off on this garbage-infested street.

It was raining hard. Good thing. Rain keeps the night people inside. I saw silhouettes in doorways and twentysomethings crowded near the lit window of an Indian restaurant. Smelled cigarettes and hash. Heard loud voices and, somewhere, glass breaking. I tugged my trench coat around my shoulders and hurried down the slippery wrought-iron steps to the underground level of Oliver's building. I kept an eye out to make sure no one followed me, and I listened for footsteps in the rain. God knows how I hoped to get a taxi back. This wasn't the area to cruise for fares.

Something brown and quick moved in the shadows under the steps. A rat, nibbling on thrown-away food. Someone told me once that wherever you are in London, there's a rat no more than ten yards away. He wasn't even talking about Parliament or Fleet Street, where it's probably five yards.

I was pissed off, being here. Not at Oliver, but at the world I inhabited, which treated genius so cavalierly. I don't throw that word around lightly, but with Oliver, I do. He has seen and survived things that would have killed me and most of you. He stares at the devil in the open door of his closet every night. He creates worlds of squalor and beauty in his books, worlds that worm their way around your brain, worlds you cannot escape or forget. And no one cares. No one even looks down. We let our geniuses die in the gutter.

I wondered if I was too late. This is the "if only" time when you have a friend in despair. If only I had called him earlier. If only I had answered my damn phone. It was so like Oliver to make sure I didn't blame myself when he committed suicide.

I pounded on his door, making the broken windows rattle. "Oliver!"

I stared through the dirty panes, trying to see inside, but he had a black bedsheet taped on the glass. Around here, you don't want the neighbors having a looky-loo at your TV or your stereo or your food. Assuming you have any of those things to begin with.

"Oliver!"

I pounded again. Rain poured on my head and ran down my face. The rat scampered away in annoyance. I was disturbing his dinner. Somewhere close by, I caught the sweet-sick smell of feces, like perfume from the sewers. I hoped it wasn't coming from inside.

As I waited, and no one answered, I had visions of where I would find him. On the floor. In his bed. On the bathroom tiles. It's selfish, but I was obsessed with my own failure. I had let this happen. Me, the superagent, who couldn't sell the best book I'd ever read. Who couldn't deliver on my promises. Who let this extraordinarily decent and talented man get sucked into a whirlpool rather than lift him up.

I twisted the rattling doorknob, but it was locked. I beat on the door again with my fist. A lake of water slurped around my feet, soaking into my stockings.

"Oliver, damn you, open the door!"

Be alive, damn you. Don't be dead. Don't make me find you.

Finally, I heard something. The jangle of a chain. The door swung open like a creaky closet in a haunted house, and there he was, dark and alive. Eyes like a cave. Skin the color of wallpaper paste. A cigarette between his lips, pointing at the floor, and his fingers twitching as he propped it up.

"You bastard!" I screamed at him.

I shoved him backward into the flat, stormed inside, and slammed the door behind muself. He wore a black T-shirt. Boxers. Bare feet. There was sweat on his forehead.

"Where are they?" I demanded.

Oliver stared at me and didn't say anything. He blew smoke, adding to the pungent cloud in the flat.

"Where are the drugs?" I repeated.

He gave the barest of shrugs. "Bathroom."

I stalked into the loo, which was the size of a phone booth. If you sat down on the toilet, your feet were in the shower. The sink was dirty with hair and dried toothpaste. The mirror showed me my face, my makeup streaked, my hair flat and soaked. Some superagent. I yanked open the medicine cabinet and found two pill bottles inside. One was aspirin. The other was unmarked, with capsules stacked to the lid.

I took them both, opened them, and poured the contents into the toilet bowl. I flushed and watched the water get sucked down, taking the pills with them. I felt as if I had saved him, but I hadn't. He could have taken them anytime before I got here. And he could replace them anytime he felt the need.

When I went back into the other room, Oliver was sitting on a chair, bent over, his elbows on his knees. The cigarette smoldered between his fingers.

"Is there more?" I asked.

He shook his head. I believed him. I took off my wet raincoat and flopped down on the flea market sofa.

"Why?"

"You wouldn't understand," he said.

That was true. I probably wouldn't.

"I want you to see someone, Oliver. A counselor. I'll pay."

"Fuck that, Tessie."

"I'm serious."

"So am I. No shrinks. And not on your dime, either."

I saw an empty bottle of wine on the card table where he ate his meals. "Is there more to drink around here, or did you finish it all yourself?"

"There's more."

I got up and opened the refrigerator in his kitchenette. He didn't have much inside. A brown banana. A box of takeout curry. A pork pie. On the door, I spotted a half-empty bottle of cheap Riesling. I grabbed the bottle, yanked out the cork, and didn't bother looking for a glass. There probably wasn't a clean one anywhere in the flat. I drank from the bottle, kept it in my hand, and went back to the sofa.

"Did you call me so I could stop you?" I asked.

"No."

No, he called to spare my guilt, and I felt guilty anyway.

"So why didn't you go through with it?" I asked. "Or are you going to do it when I leave?"

"You make it sound like a big deal."

"Isn't it?"

Oliver shook his head. "No, it's not a big deal. None of us leaves a ripple, Tessie. Not me. Not you. Not Lowell Bardwright."

"Yeah? How about those guys who did the sculptures in the cathedral?"

"Like I told you, no one will be reading *Singularity* in a thousand years."

"You don't know that. And even if they're not, the point is that people are reading it right now."

"Really? How many? Eleven people isn't a legacy, Tessie."

"How about that note you showed me last year? From the woman who was reading *Singularity* while her father was dying in hospital? Your book comforted her. Your words helped her deal with her pain."

Oliver sighed. "One person."

"Yes, damn it, one person. And you didn't answer my question. Are you going to do it when I leave?"

"No."

"What about tomorrow? Or next week?"

"I'm not going to make promises, Tessie. They're not worth anything."

"Promise me anyway."

"I can't do that. I wish I could, but I can't do it."

"So what do you want? Something to live for?" I swigged more wine. "I met Tom Cruise. I put *Singularity* in his hands."

Oliver's eyebrows arched. "Are you lying to me?"

"No, it's true. I saw him at a restaurant in New York. Don't get me wrong, I'm not saying it will change anything. He may love the book, but the odds are that he won't do a damn thing about it. And I'll tell you something—it doesn't matter, because that one person who wrote to you is already more important than Cruise. She'll remember your book for the rest of her life."

"You're good at this," Oliver said. "But it doesn't change anything."

"How can you say that?"

"Look, Tessie, you're not the kind of person who gets depressed, so you don't know what it's like. I'm not talking sad or blue, I'm talking about fucking empty, paint it black, not caring about a single damn thing. What happens is that you're holding a machine gun and you blow away everything around you, until the barrel suddenly turns around and you see it's pointing at you. And you realize how easy it is to wipe out yourself like everything else."

"You're scaring me," I admitted.

"I'm scared, too. It's not like I want to feel this way. I just do."

I finished the bottle of wine. I was almost as drunk now as he

was. I sank down on my knees in front of Oliver and put my warm
hands on his face. His cheeks were rough.

"You know that I'm a self-obsessed, neurotic egomaniac," I
told him.

"Of course."

"You're also my only real friend."

"Not true."

"Yes, true. I'm telling you this because you seem to think I'm
taking pity on you, and the reality is, you should be pitying me.
The last few days have been like seeing my reflection in a mirror,
and I have to tell you, I haven't liked the view. People hate me. I
used to wear that like a badge of honor, and suddenly I realize it's
not a good thing at all. I'm afraid of losing everything, and if I
have to start over, I'm not sure I can do it on my own. I need someone to believe in me. For whatever reason, no matter how much I
fail you, you still believe in me, Oliver. If I lost you now, I can't tell
you how grotesquely alone I would be."

I wasn't lying. And, yes, pity me that I have to make a friend's
attempted suicide all about me. Oliver smiled, because he is smart
enough to recognize the irony.

"So I should hold off killing myself until your agency is well
established?" he asked.

"That would be more convenient," I agreed.

"Well, anything for you, Tessie."

"Thank you." We both laughed, and I added, "You know, you
can talk to me about why. It doesn't matter if I'm stupid and I don't
get it."

"The 'why' isn't really important. The only thing that matters
is whether you do it or you don't do it."

"Don't do it," I said.

"I told you, the danger has passed for tonight. I wish I could tell
you it would never come again, but chances are, it will."

"If it does, don't be alone. Call me."

"It's not that simple."

"Okay, but call me anyway."

He kissed my forehead. "Poor Tessie, such a little girl lost. I like it better when you're hard as nails."

"I show you my vulnerable side, and this is what I get?"

"Give me your kick-arse side instead. That's what I need. The don't-fuck-with-me-I'm-Tess-Drake side."

"Shut up, you bastard."

"Ah, that's better."

I got off my knees. It's not a place I like to be unless I'm, well, you know. And I don't mean praying. "So tell me about *Duopoly*," I said. "Are you blocked? Is that the problem?"

"Yes, I'm blocked, but that's not the problem."

"Are you afraid it's no good?"

"Yes."

"Are you afraid you can't finish it?"

"Yes."

"Are you afraid I can't sell it?"

"Yes."

"Well, it's fabulous, you *will* finish it, and I *will* sell it."

"Suddenly you ooze self-confidence again," Oliver said.

"Don't fuck with me, I'm Tess Drake."

Now we were being silly. Joking. Teasing. But at least neither one of us was looking to kill ourselves. Oliver stood up and hugged me with surprising tenderness. He pushed away eventually but held on to both my hands.

"Can I tell you something, Tessie? In all seriousness?"

"Of course."

"I know you're scared for me, and scared for you, but there's something you have to remember. If the worst thing you ever face is losing everything and starting over, you will lead a charmed life."

27

SLEEP.

Sleep, sleep, sleep.

I arrived home at nearly three in the morning, thanks to a cab-driver who showed no qualms at the thought of picking me up in the slummy section of King's Cross. He was a veteran of the Afghan theater. There is very little that scares men like that, thank God. He took me out of the mean streets and through the City and across the river, and I closed my eyes and missed most of the drive. It was only the bump as he stopped in front of my building that woke me up.

I tipped him well. He deserved it.

My flat is above the Putney Exchange in a security building, with a view toward the Thames. Easy access to shopping, buses, Tube, etc. Parks nearby. 24/7 lobby guard. Arriving home in the middle of the night isn't an unusual experience for me, so I like the idea of a locked door and a beefy man with a truncheon in the lobby. It is always the same man, an Indian named Samur with a round face and arms the size of tree trunks. Samur moves as slowly as syrup, but he is unfailingly polite and helpful, and his cousin owns the best vindaloo house south of the river. I think I amuse Samur—a frantic woman coming and going at all hours, always on my mobile.

Not tonight, however. Tonight every footstep felt like lead, and the elevators, which were only ten yards away, taunted me from a distance. I wanted nothing other than to unlock my door, strip off my clothes, fall face-first into my pillow, and remain motionless for ten hours.

Samur waved at me. I nodded a greeting and looked at him through slitted eyes.

"Ms. Drake!"

"Hmm?"

"Ms. Drake! I have something for you!"

"Can I pick it up in the morning?"

"Oh, no, no, the man, he said to me, you must have it at once when you come into the building."

The elevators were so close and yet so far. I shifted direction and shuffled to the guard's desk. I expected an envelope. All my deliveries are envelopes. Contracts. Letters. Queries. Someone was sending me something to read and sign. I held out my hand for Samur to put the envelope in my palm.

He grinned at me—big grin, yellow teeth. He reached underneath his desk, squeezing his whole giant torso out of sight, and emerged with the largest rectangular box I had ever seen. It was wrapped in brown paper, and I could see my name neatly lettered on the outside.

"What the hell is that?" I asked.

"I do not know. But the man, he made me sign for it, and he said it is for you as soon as you return."

"Who was the man? What did he look like?"

"Big man, very handsome."

"Hmm."

"Do you need me help you carry it?" Samur asked.

"Is it heavy?"

"Not so heavy but very big."

"I'll be fine."

He maneuvered the box across the desk, and I took it in my arms. It wasn't heavy, but it was like carrying a sandwich board in the wind. I shook it up and down out of curiosity. Whatever was inside didn't move or give me any hints. I held it out and hunted for a return address, but there was nothing on the box but my name.

"You need help?" Samur asked.

"Thanks, no. Good night, Samur."

"You sleep well, ma'am."

"If I'm not awake in five or six days, come get me," I said.

He grinned. I continued to amuse him. I navigated the remaining steps to the elevator and fitted myself and my box inside. I spent five floors leaning against the elevator wall, eyes closed, arms wrapped around my box, hypnotized by the hum of the motor. The doors opened, but I think I was asleep by then. They closed again. When they opened a second time, I peered around the edge of the box and discovered that I was back in the lobby. Samur looked across the tiled floor at me with the same grin he had given me when I left. I woke up and pushed the button again, and this time, I staggered out of the elevator on my floor and made it to my flat.

Inside, I had two choices. Open the box and go to bed. Go to bed and open the box. I chose the latter. I deposited the box on my kitchen table, took ninety seconds to brush my teeth and drain some of the liter of alcohol I had consumed, littered the bedroom floor with my damp clothes, and fell spread-eagled onto my blanket. It was heaven. I felt as if I had not seen my bed in weeks. I felt as if the next twelve hours were my birthday and Christmas rolled into one.

Except for one problem.

I was wide-awake.

My eyes popped open. It works that way sometimes. You're dead on your feet, and then you're on the rocket end of a quadruple espresso. I tossed and turned. I scrunched the pillow over my head. I imagined I was flying with Peter Pan over the streets of London. Nothing worked. I was up.

I knew why, too. It was that damn box. Knowing it was there, unopened. If I ever hoped to sleep, I needed to know what was inside.

I got out of bed and wandered back into the kitchen and flipped on the light. I hadn't even been in the dark long enough for my eyes to squint. I was naked, and the curtains were open, so theoretically there was a pervert insomniac with a telescope somewhere getting a view. Don't get too aroused. I wasn't at my best. Rain, sleep deprivation, alcohol, tears, and stress had worked a curse on my waning beauty. I was having a bad hair day. Bad makeup day. Bags under my eyes. Blanket wrinkles on my breasts. My legs needed a shave.

I grabbed a cleaver from a butcher block near my refrigerator and tore into the brown paper wrapping with the enthusiasm of a serial killer. Inside was, obviously, the box itself, surrounded by more wrapping paper, a ribbon, a pink bow, and a card. There are card-first, gift-second people, but I am not among them. I put the card and its mauve envelope aside and sliced and diced the ribbon and made short work of the metallic silver paper.

Finally, I reached the box itself, which was black. There was a name engraved in small type, as if the name on its own were enough to get my attention. Which it was. Julien Macdonald. If you are a woman in London, the name Julien Macdonald is enough to make your legs go weak and make your husband clutch his wallet. Julien is one of the catwalk glitterati, the kind of designer that A-listers turn to for nights in Cannes and LA. I probably don't make enough money to afford the box, let alone whatever is in it.

I whisked off the lid like I was rubbing a magic lantern. My mouth fell open. I screamed loud enough for Samur to hear me five floors down. I stared into the box and wasn't even sure I dared to touch the fur, which nestled inside on a bed of tissue paper, all white and mink, layered and deep. My eyes caressed fold after delicious fold. I was suddenly hungry for caviar, champagne, white truffles, single malts—anything that was decadent and expensive.

I put my fingertips near it, then pulled them back. When I couldn't resist for another second, I buried my hands in it up to my elbows, and, oh dear Lord, it was the softest, richest, most supple, most lavish, most revoltingly beautiful thing I had ever put my fingers on. I lifted it up by the collar, and it was almost as tall as I was. It was a thing of royalty.

If I wasn't already naked, I would have taken off my clothes. Because this is not a coat you put on to touch anything but bare skin. I didn't even know if I had the courage to slip my arms inside. I rubbed it over myself like a cat rolling on catnip. I inhaled it. I stroked its sleeves. Then I spread it open and eased it over my shoulders, enveloped my arms in its soft tunnels, and closed the forest of fur around my torso. I became an entirely different person. Strangers crowded at the velvet rope to see me. Flashbulbs popped in my face.

Arriving now in the Julien Macdonald mink is London super-agent Tess Drake.

She is a stunner, isn't she, Judy?

Yes, she is, Richard. In that coat you have to wonder why she sells film rights when she should be starring in films herself.

Is that Tom Cruise walking her down the red carpet, Judy?

I believe it is, Richard. And who can blame him when Tess has a coat like that?

Although what's with the skanky hair, Judy?

You're right, Richard, she's having a bad hair day.

And the bags under her eyes?

Yes, a bad makeup day, too. And you can see where the coat ends that her legs need a shave.

Okay, it didn't take long for reality to set in, even in the midst of my fantasy. After pretending to be a princess for about ten seconds or so, I put the coat back in the box, dug expensive mink lint out of my navel, and reached for the card in the mauve envelope. Honestly, my mind wasn't working at all. The only person I could think of with the money to send me something like this was my father, and he would be more likely to send me a signed first edition of Wedgy Benn's diaries.

I recognized the handwriting inside, though, and the emotions I had spent the last several days trying to erase from my mind all came flooding back. I read what he had written and knew that I had begun to climb out of my cave into the sunlight again.

> *Tess,*
> *I love you, too.*
> > *Darcy*

28

I SLEPT UNTIL NOON on Saturday, the sleep of the angels, or at least of the angels who have an unbelievable fur coat.

I took a long, hot shower, washing away the grime and restoring my hair to its full rainbow-streaked beauty. I pulled on sweatpants and a roomy T-shirt. My head ached from the wine, but I took three aspirins to combat the hangover, and then I ate cold Chinese takeaway for lunch. I called Oliver to make sure he was still alive—he was—and then I checked in with Emma, who sounded as if she had just crawled out of bed with Jane to answer the phone. She told me she would deliver the box of papers from Dorothy's old agent to my flat later in the day. She also asked if I had received her text—I hadn't—and told me to check it right away. I heard a giggle in her voice.

When I checked my BlackBerry, I understood why. There was a message from Emma to go along with my Julien Macdonald:

DARCY CALLED! SUNDAY AT HILTON PARK LANE, 10 P.M.!

I felt a flush of anticipation, knowing my life was back on track. It was tinged with a little bit of guilt that I had fallen into bed with Evan after Lowell's funeral, but a date with Darcy would make me forget all about that. Now if only I had something to wear, ha-ha.

Coffee in hand, I sat out on my terrace over the high street in the early afternoon, legs propped on the balcony. It was a beautiful day, warm and sunny to match my mood. I thought about Darcy, and I couldn't help wonder what his declaration meant for the two of us. We were in love. Scary thought. I live in the present, and I let the future take care of itself, which is one reason I have procrastinated for so many years about going out on my own. Darcy and I made an unspoken promise in the beginning never to look beyond our nights together. Now we've both broken that promise. So what comes next? I am not a marriage, white dress, fairy tale kind of girl. Darcy is not the kind of man who is ready to give up the lifestyle Cosima's money affords him. People like us don't change because Cupid shoots them in the arse.

Or do we?

Part of me wonders if I could tame my independence enough to really let a man in my life. There's security in meaningless affairs, because you never put yourself at risk. I think of myself as strong, but here comes the real test. The agency. And Darcy.

Maybe I need to ask the wizard for some courage.

This would be easier, I admit, if it weren't for Evan. Not that I'm in love with him. God, no. I just wonder why it was so easy to let him ravish me. I tell myself that he was a consolation prize, that I was hurt and angered by Darcy's rejection. Screw love, give me a one-night stand. That was the old Tess, and the note from Darcy changed everything. Right? If Evan were here right now, I would not have sex with him. Not standing up. Not lying down. Absolutely not. No way.

Except there was a devil Tess at my shoulder who whispered, "You're lying."

I drank my coffee and watched the traffic on the street and smelled bread baking and realized that life is complicated. Messy.

I thought about Oliver next. I was relieved that he had backed

away from the precipice, although with Oliver, sanity is a tempo-
rary reprieve. He might face another crippling episode of depression at any time. In my gut, I knew that his thoughts of suicide had
nothing to do with his books and everything to do with the night-
mares from his past. I also knew that I could extend a hand to help
him, but that he would have to do the hard work himself. I don't
like to think that way, because I'm a fixer, and my habit is to rush
in, believing I can solve any problem. But not all problems have
solutions.

Complicated. Messy.

Inside my flat, someone knocked on the door. That's a rare
event in a security building. I climbed out of the chair and padded
across the carpet to the door, where I checked the eyehole. My
father waved back at me. Naturally. He has made friends with
the guards in my building, and you don't say no to Terrence Paul
Drake when he says he is going upstairs to visit his daughter. You
just buzz him up.

"One minute, Dad."

I made him wait, as I usually do. My Julien Macdonald was still
on the dining room table, and I didn't want to explain it to my father. I put the lid back on the box and tucked the box away in the
back of my bedroom closet. Then I let him in.

We kissed.

"What are you hiding, Tessie?" he asked me, with a glance at
his watch. "A buff young gentleman? Is he hiding under the bed?"

"I slept late. I wasn't dressed." A little white lie.

He eyed me in the way that fathers do when they know their
daughter is keeping secrets, but he didn't press me for the truth.

"I understand there's a gala premiere tonight," he said. "Are you
going?"

"Yes, why not come with me?"

The big new musical from the *Les Miz* guys was opening at the
Garrick. The play was adapted from a bestselling novel published
by Random House, which was boasting of its success by sprinkling
free tickets among industry insiders. The story involved a romantic triangle in the midst of a religious civil war, sort of *Dr. Zhivago*

meets Khaled Hosseini. I'm not a big fan of musicals. I rarely break into song spontaneously. Even so, it's a chance to see and be seen.

My father shook his head. "No, thank you, dear."

"You could be my date."

"A lovely offer, but I'm having dinner with someone from the Ministry of Defense tonight. That's why I stayed in the city this weekend."

He gave me another one of those looks when he said this. As if he knew that I might have had plans to borrow the flat in Mayfair again if he weren't in it. Which was true.

He handed me an oversized white envelope. "Here. Ask and ye shall receive."

"What's this?"

"Dirt on David Milton."

My eyebrows went up. "That was quick. How did you get this so fast?"

"Never ask a journalist his sources, darling, you know that. Anyway, my daughter rarely asks for my help, so when she does, I make it a priority. I have a good friend in New York who can pretty much assemble anyone's life story in a few hours just by retrieving bits and bytes from cyberspace."

I hope no one ever does that to me.

"Brilliant. Dad, you're amazing."

"There's more to come, but I figured you'd want the first pass as soon as possible."

"Absolutely. Did you look at it?"

"I did."

I waved my father into the living room, where he sat uncomfortably on my modern pastel sofa. I usually put my feet up on the glass-and-metal table, but Dad never does. I went to the kitchen and got us both cups of coffee, then sat down in the recliner opposite him and extracted the sheaf of papers from the envelope.

"So what is all this?" I asked.

"Educational background. School records. Housing records. Legal actions in which he's been involved. Where he shops. Where he eats. What videos he rents. When his automobile warranty expires. What type of pornography he prefers. That sort of thing."

"Jesus. Is this legal?"

"I'm sorry, what?"

"Never mind. I don't want to know. Did you see anything that might help me?"

"Nothing jumped out at me, I'm afraid, but I'm not sure it would. This is your world, Tessie, not mine."

I began skimming through the materials. "Does this include financial information? Bank records, that sort of thing?"

"No."

"So we can't figure out if he's been making payoffs?"

"If you want that kind of detail, you're going to need to sue him in a U.S. court and file a discovery motion. Which I imagine you don't want to do."

"It wouldn't be my first choice," I said.

"What exactly are you trying to find out?" he asked.

"I'm not sure," I admitted. "Anything that would help me prove he's a fraud. Some clue as to who he might have used to write the phony manuscript. It's a long shot, but I really appreciate your getting this to me so quickly. You won't wind up in jail over this, will you?"

"I trust you'd visit me."

"Remember, I might be there, too," I said. "That whole murder-the-boss thing."

"I'm still making calls on that."

"I'll be fine, Dad."

I continued reading about David Milton. His educational credentials matched the diplomas I saw on his wall from NYU and Columbia. He was an average student. You'd think that a lawyer would have all the money he needed without fleecing an old woman, but you'd be wrong. Law is a tough racket these days unless you're a corporate partner billing at eight hundred dollars an hour. Personal injury attorneys, divorce lawyers, estate lawyers, they all scramble in the mud for clients. And a New York lifestyle isn't cheap.

"Oh, interesting," I murmured.

"What?"

"Milton got divorced recently."

"Are you planning to add him to your list of available men?"

I looked up with annoyance to find my father smiling at me.

"It looks like his wife won everything but the clothes I saw him wearing," I continued. "Apparently it's not just online pornography that Mr. Milton enjoys patronizing. The divorce filing talks about hookers, too. Oh dear, and not female hookers, either. Naughty boy."

"So he needs money," my father concluded.

"Yes, he does. He mentioned that he was selling his house, proceeds of which go to the ex-wife, apparently. David Milton could use a large cash infusion."

"Enter Dorothy and her pandas."

"Exactly."

I was feeling better. Not that I was any closer to proving that the manuscript was fake or to figuring out how an estate lawyer who got low grades in his NYU literature class had managed to write a credible forgery. However, you know what the crime shows always say: Motive, means, and opportunity are what you need to prove guilt. His father's relationship with Dorothy gave David Milton the opportunity, and his wallet-sucking divorce sure gave him the motive. Now I needed to know the means.

At least I was more and more confident that Dorothy was a victim here and not a poodle-walking plagiarist. It was an awfully big coincidence to believe that David Milton had stumbled onto a twenty-year-old literary crime just as he was about to lose his shirt.

"You'll need more than his divorce," my father told me, reading my mind.

"I know."

I was deep in thought, because I was staring at the list of social and professional activities in David Milton's file. Something in there was triggering a memory, but it was just out of my reach. What was it?

"He served on the New York bar's pro bono estate counsel committee after 9/11," I said.

"Laudable."

"Yes."

"Is that meaningful somehow?" my father asked.

"I don't know."

But something about it rang an alarm bell in my head. Why? The more I tried to remember, the more it slipped away.

Maybe it didn't mean anything. And yet.

"Tessie?" my father asked, watching my face.

"Hang on."

And then I knew.

"One of the secretaries at the Robinson Foote agency lost her daughter and her son-in-law in the attacks," I said. "I remember there was some weird testamentary problem. A big life insurance policy. The daughter was in the tower that went down first, but the son-in-law worked near the floor where the first plane hit. So there was a bizarre argument about who died first and where the money would go. The secretary, the mother, didn't have the money for a lawyer. They were all talking about how to find someone to represent her."

"How do you know all this?" my father asked.

"I know all this because Robinson Foote is where Saleema works," I said. "It was her secretary."

29

IF DAVID MILTON HAD REPRESENTED Saleema's secretary as part of his pro bono work after 9/11, the case wasn't included in the materials about him. However, that didn't mean anything. It could easily have been overlooked in a search of legal records. Or perhaps Milton and Saleema met during the legal process even though Milton was not the attorney on the case.

Or perhaps they never met at all.

Was I being oversuspicious? I didn't think so. In a city of eight million people, what are the odds of an innocent connection between the man blackmailing Dorothy and the agent who has made it her life's work to sink me? It wasn't hard to imagine how a conspiracy could be born. Milton wants money. Saleema wants revenge. He's got an innocent note written by Dorothy, and she's got a farm team of frustrated writers looking for a break. Left hand, meet right hand.

I went through the rest of the materials my father had given me, but I didn't find anything else that made a blip on my mental radar. Not that I would. Saleema and Milton were both smart. It was a shot in the dark that I spotted something to tie them together, and if I really wanted to prove it, we'd need to do a lot of digging.

I'd like to say that this changed everything, but it didn't change a thing. I was still between a rock and a hard place. More than anything, I wanted to show up for my Monday meeting with Cosima and tell her to shove the job and the agency up her arse. Bury me if you like, but I'm out of here. Give her a long list of the clients who were going with me. With Dorothy's future hanging in the balance, though, I wasn't sure I was ready to make my move.

I needed to be patient for a few more days. Maybe a few more weeks. The trouble is that I'm not exactly long on patience. I also didn't want to see my opportunity slip through my fingers.

After my dad left, I caught up on my reading and wore out my thumbs sending e-mails to a few more clients. Basically, I told them I was in a holding pattern but that I hoped they would be with me when I made the move. No one wrote back. It was Saturday, and not everyone is as anal as I when it comes to e-mail.

Emma arrived around four o'clock, carrying a battered old box of papers from Dorothy's first agent. Her strawberry hair was tied behind her head in a furry ponytail. She wore a sleeveless pink T-shirt, short shorts, and fluorescent white tennis shoes, looking annoyingly youthful and fit. For years, I was the young agent, the upstart, and somehow this whole generation of children sneaked up behind me and became adults. Where did they come from?

I flipped the lid off the box. It smelled musty and made me want to sneeze. The contents included bulging file folders of letters and contracts, old manuscripts, and advance reading copies of *The Bamboo Garden*. None of it was organized in any coherent fashion; it would take me hours to go through it.

"What are you looking for?" Emma asked me.

"Haven't a clue," I admitted.

I'm not one to live in the past. I barely looked at the box when Dorothy sent it to me. Even so, David Milton's little plot is all about the early days of Dorothy's career, and this box may as well have been the archives from the Starkwell Museum. Someday my heirs will sell it for a fortune to some obsessive collector on eBay. Assuming I have heirs, which doesn't look too likely right now.

The box could wait until tomorrow.

"Want to see something?" I asked Emma.

"Sure, what?"

"It's a surprise."

There is no point in having something extravagant like a Julien Macdonald fur coat unless you can show it off to another woman. Men buy these things for their wives and mistresses, but they don't appreciate them. It is the kind of thing that only a woman can truly scream about, lust over, and envy.

I went to the bedroom and retrieved the box.

"Close your eyes," I said.

Emma did so and wobbled a little on her feet. I think her breasts are so big they leave her a bit off balance.

I opened the box and slipped the coat over my T-shirt and sweats. Yes, I am oh so chic. I admit this wasn't the first time today I had worn the coat. I put it on when I got out of bed. And again after my shower. And again after my lunch. If you are going to look this beautiful, you want to admire your beauty every fifteen minutes or so.

"Now," I said.

Emma opened her eyes. "OH MY GOD!"

"Nice, huh?"

"OH MY GOD! Where did that come from? Where did you get it?"

"Darcy," I said.

Emma panted. "I have never seen anything so gorgeous in my life. Never. Ever. You look like a movie star."

"Lana Turner, eat your heart out," I said.

"Who?"

"Never mind," I said.

Damn, I am so old.

"Could I, like, try it on maybe?" Emma asked. "Just for a second? Please?"

"Sure."

I eased the coat off my shoulders and handed it to Emma, who put it on with the gravity reserved for a coronation. Her eyes went back in her head. Her freckled face lit up. "Do I even want to know what something like this costs?" she asked.

"No."

"I can't imagine anything sexier than being naked in this coat."

"I can vouch for that," I said.

Emma spun with her arms straight out. Her ponytail bounced.

"So I guess that answers the question of whether Darcy loves you back," she said.

"Well, he said the three little words." I showed her the note.

"I am *so* happy for you, Tess."

"Thank you, darling, but don't hire a band and print invitations. It's not like he's going to dump Cosima and get down on one knee."

"You don't know that," Emma said.

Yes, I do. To Emma, in her twenties, love is a fantasy. To me, in my thirties, love is an awkward reality you try to squeeze in around the complications in your life. Somewhere along the way, you have to decide if it's worth it.

I held out my hands to reclaim the coat from Emma, who reluctantly slipped it off. I knew how she felt. It's like taking off your superhero costume and becoming an ordinary human being again. She bit her lip with undisguised jealousy and desire as I folded it and returned it to the box. I was pleased.

"Are you going to wear it for your date at the Hilton?" Emma asked.

"Absolutely."

"Oh, wow," she said. "This is so romantic."

"No, no, romance is dead," I informed her, which is my way of controlling my expectations. It's easier than being wildly disappointed.

"You should let herself be happy once and awhile," Emma told me, shaking her head.

"Maybe tomorrow."

Emma sighed. "Jane's going to be at the Hilton, too. Remember, the BFI gala on Sunday is in the hotel ballroom. There will be stars and popzees all over the place. You can show off."

"Darcy's the only one I'm showing off for," I said.

"Well, everyone will think you're somebody, Tess. I mean, you are, of course, but you know what I mean. Somebody famous. You're going to stop traffic, honestly you will. I'd love to see the looks you get when you stroll into the Hilton lobby wearing that coat."

I could tell you that I don't care about things like that, but I'd be lying. Every woman wants to get the looks.

"Speaking of Jane, I left a message for the guy I know at Godfrey Kahn's production company," I told Emma. "I said he should be taking a close look at Jane for that part in Kahn's next pic."

Emma clasped her hands together. "Did you really? Thank you! Jane will be so pleased."

"I don't know if it will help."

"I'm sure it will. That's brilliant, Tess, really. You know, I'm sure Jane would love to meet you. Who knows, maybe she could be a new client for us. She and I are having dinner tonight at Hakkasan. Would you like to join us?"

"Tonight's the premiere for that damn musical at the Garrick," I said.

"Oh, yes, of course."

"Sorry."

Emma headed for the door with one last, longing look at the box on my kitchen table. "I suppose it's because of the premiere tonight," she added. "That makes sense. Everyone is busy getting ready."

"What do you mean?" I asked.

"No one's writing or calling back today. It's weird."

"It's Saturday," I said, but I had noticed the same thing. Fool that I am, I didn't give it a second thought.

The Garrick is one of those classic nineteenth-century London theaters, lavish and Victorian, gold leaf adorning everything inside but the toilet stalls. It's only a few steps from Trafalgar Square, so I walk past it every day to and from the bus stop. I arrived an hour before the curtain, in time for a glass of red wine and some puff pastry snails. The premiere was obviously a hot ticket, attracting snotty City types along with the theater and publishing mafia. The evening was warm, so the glitterati were spilling out onto the sidewalk, where the smokers could get their fixes.

You wouldn't think I would feel underdressed in a shimmery silver cocktail dress, but everything feels shabby after the fur. I air kissed Penelope Keith. I pinky waved at Simon Cowell, who looked unbelievably bored. I pushed my way into the lobby, which was crowded with bejeweled women and gay men bumping drink glasses into each other. Everyone was sweating in the heat. The Random House directors strutted around like they owned the world, but they mostly do, so who can blame them?

I got more wine. Alcohol is the only way to survive these things. I had some pâté smeared on a cracker and threaded my way through the room, stopping to smile and hobnob. Most of the men were in tuxes. The women's breasts were high and outside. Lots of silk and chiffon. Diamonds everywhere.

I spotted Cosima in a corner holding court with three executives from Sony. Tiny Asian men with lots of money. Darcy wasn't with her. I know she saw me, but she declined even to nod her head imperially in my direction.

I didn't care. I wondered how God would score this battle, her plotting to ruin me, my sleeping with her husband. I never claimed to have the moral high ground in this fight. Looking at her, I wondered if it was really possible that she had had something to do with Lowell's death. People cross terrible lines for power all the time, but there's also that biblical admonition about gaining the whole world and losing your immortal soul. Perhaps it doesn't apply if you lack a soul to begin with.

Sally Harlingford appeared at my shoulder. She was dressed the way she always is, elegant and precise in yellow silk, someone who would rather take a little of the best than more of something second-rate. She had worn that same designer dress several times before, but it was beautiful and timeless. I wasn't going to tell her about my fur. I'm sensitive to not making Sally feel at all jealous. I know there are things she would love to do that she can't. It's strange, seeing Cosima and Sally at the same time, two women veterans of the industry with such different paths. One ruthless and successful and enamored of the limelight; one world-weary and private, I wondered if I was staring at my fate in another fifteen years, and I couldn't help ask myself which path I would choose if I could and where I would like to end up.

Like Cosima or like Sally.

"Are you going to smile and make nice with her?" she asked me, following my eyes to Cosima.

"Why spoil a lovely evening?" I said.

Sally shrugged, as if I was being petulant. And maybe I was.

"You don't want Cosima as an enemy," Sally told me.

"I think it's too late for that."

"What do you mean?"

"Lowell," I said.

Sally looked at me sharply. "Excuse me?"

"Someone's trying to make it look like I was at Lowell's place when he died. Cosima's the only one I can think of."

"Don't be ridiculous."

"The police say he wasn't alone when he died," I told her.

"Lowell? That's hardly a surprise."

"Whoever was there planted evidence against me. They made it look like Lowell was trying to pressure me for sex over the Santelli affair."

"I assume that's not true?" Sally said, with a ghost of a smile.

"Sally, please."

"I think you're making too much of this."

"They used a cotton swab to sample my DNA!" I protested. "I'm like a suspect in a damn Patricia Cornwell novel!"

"I love those books," Sally said mildly. She flagged down a waiter with a silver tray of appetizers and studied the bruschetta carefully before selecting one. "Don't worry—you're about fifteen years too old for Lowell's tastes."

"Is that supposed to make me feel better?" I asked.

"Not really."

"The scary thing is that Lowell's death isn't even my biggest problem," I added.

"Oh?"

I gave her the thirty-second synopsis. Dorothy. Milton. Saleema.

"So what do you do now?" Sally asked. "Kill him? Would it be too suspicious if this Milton person died of erotic asphyxia, too?"

"Funny."

"Seriously, what's your next step?"

"Get a lawyer."

"You know this could take months to resolve," she said.

"Maybe years."

"So what happens in the interim? Do you stay put, or do you leave the agency anyway?"

"I'm still deciding," I said.

"I've already told you—it wouldn't be the end of the world to stay with Cosima. You can make a lot of money." Sally stroked blond hair away from her eyes.

"It's not about money."

"Then what?" she asked.

"Oh, come on, Sally, you should know. It's about freedom. It's about doing what the hell I want to do, making choices for myself. Isn't that what you wanted, too?"

Sally smiled. "You can savor all that for a while when you're on your own, and then it becomes about money again."

That's true. We can't all be like Oliver, reveling in our poverty. You can talk about freedom, and you can talk about power, but in the end, you're talking about money.

"The industry is a world of giants these days, Tess," Sally added. "The little people get stepped on. I'm not trying to be the voice of doom, just telling it like it is."

"Well, you're depressing me."

"I know you," she told me. "You're impulsive. Sometimes that works for you, and sometimes it doesn't. This may be a moment in your life when you should listen to the angel that tells you to slow down."

"I'm not sure I have any angels around me," I said. "Just devils."

Sally's eyes flitted over my shoulder. "Shh," she warned me.

I turned around and flinched when I saw that Cosima had swooped down on us, leaving the Japanese men from Sony in the care of a young blond intern from Bardwright. I felt a little like a squirrel that looks up just as the hawk is landing on it. Cosima's nails resembled talons curled around her wineglass, long and sharp enough to cut flesh. Her eyes could spot wounded prey from a thousand feet.

"Sally, Tess, how wonderful to see you both," Cosima said, in a voice loud enough for people near us to hear her.

"Hello, Cosima," Sally murmured.

"Would you mind giving me a moment with Tess?" Cosima asked pointedly.

I wanted Sally to stay, but when the ship hits the iceberg, it's every man for himself.

"Not at all," Sally said and melted into the crowd, leaving Cosima and me alone.

I had the feeling that people were watching us together. Cosima put a hand on my shoulder in what probably looked like a friendly gesture.

"Tell me about your trip to New York," Cosima said.

I sipped my champagne. "It was fine."

"Fine? That's all?"

"That's all."

"I wonder why you were in such a rush to go there. Is anything up with Dorothy?"

"No."

"Oh, please. You think I don't hear rumors?"

"Like what?" I asked.

Cosima's lips hardly moved, as if she were a ventriloquist. I felt like the dummy. "Rumors of big legal problems, Tess. If one of the agency's leading clients is having trouble, then I need to know at once. We have lawyers who can help us in these circumstances. This is not about you. This is about what's best for Dorothy."

"I'll let you know if I need help," I said.

"Do that." Cosima folded her arms and smiled at someone in the crowd. She didn't look at me.

"Marty tells me we have a meeting on Monday," I said to her.

"Yes, we do."

"What about?"

"That's up to you," Cosima informed me.

"Oh?"

"I hope we can talk about your future at Bardwright. It's not too late to stop all this nonsense. We can work together. I can be an ally for you, Tess. A powerful ally."

Or a powerful enemy. The message was clear.

30

I'M A PRACTICAL PERSON when it comes to the theater. I get an aisle seat in a back row, because by the time intermission comes around, I'm dying to pee, and if you don't sprint for the ladies' toilet as the orchestra plays the last trumpet fanfare, you wind up in a queue of ninety women crossing their legs and dancing in place. Theaters are obviously designed by men, who think this is all very funny.

I exited the loo after conducting my business and strolled out to the sidewalk, where the smokers were gathered. The Garrick is not air-conditioned, so I decided that smoky air outside was better than hot air inside. They say that secondhand smoke will kill you, but as an ex-smoker myself I like to take the occasional whiff to remind me of what I'm missing.

Taxis whizzed up and down Charing Cross. Teenagers with punk-spiked hair spilled out of Leicester Square. I was only a block or so from the Bardwright offices, and I thought about bailing on the rest of the musical and heading to the building to get some work done. Maybe pack a box or two. If I did want to resign, there were things inside I'd like to remove before Cosima had a chance to lock me out. But I wasn't ready to do that yet.

Nearby, someone lit up. Smoke greeted my nostrils. God, I want a cigarette. I drifted in the direction of the Benson & Hedges aroma and realized that the smoke trail led to Guy Droste-Chambers, looking like a swollen wine barrel in his tuxedo. His plump cheeks were two rosy spiderwebs of blood vessels, flushed by several ounces of gin. There were crumbs in his beard, and his thinning hair had been mussed by the wind. He stood alone, leaning against the theater's stone wall as if propping it up. When you catch someone like that, before he knows anyone is watching him, you can take a little peek into his soul. Guy looked like a man whom life was passing by too quickly, and he wasn't happy with the course of the river.

"Hello, Guy," I said.

He took the cigarette out of his mouth. His smile bloomed with a sinister delight when he saw me. He made the requisite review of my breasts, to make sure they had accompanied me to the theater.

"Ah, Filippa, darling, what a delight."

"Nice tux," I said.

Guy patted his stomach where the cummerbund labored to cover it. "Thank you for saying so. And you're a vision, as always."

He checked again. My breasts were still there.

"Enjoying the play?" I asked.

Guy shrugged, and his jowls quivered. "You know me. I was probably the only person on the planet who laughed at the end of *Les Miz*. The only damn musical I ever liked was *The Producers*. That 'Springtime for Hitler' number? What a hoot."

"Yes, I loved that."

Guy threw his cigarette on the ground. I thought about picking it up to get a puff or two, but I restrained myself.

"I understand you were in New York," Guy told me.

"Dorothy called you?"

He nodded. "That was why I left a message on your voice mail.

I thought we should talk. She told me all about this con artist and the scam he's trying to run on her."

I needed to tell Dorothy to be more discreet. The more people who knew, the more likely this would wind up in the papers. Guy was a sieve when it came to gossip.

"I don't think it's anything to worry about," I told him.

"No? It sounded bad."

"I'm sure the manuscript is a fake. We just need to prove it."

Guy stroked his beard. "No doubt, but it is a tad inconvenient. The timing and all, I mean. Not just for Dorothy but for you, too. Perhaps we should talk about making it go away."

"You mean pay him off?" I asked. "No way."

First my father, now Guy. Everyone thought I was backing a losing horse.

"Well, you know best, but Dorothy is a wreck. The sooner we get past this, the sooner she can forget this nonsense and get back to her books. Sending a few dollars toward this Milton character wouldn't be the worst thing in the world."

"A few dollars? If he had a legitimate claim, Milton would want millions."

"Not exactly a dent in Dorothy's net worth," Guy said.

"You're crazy."

"Maybe, but this is bad for both of you, darling. You can't exactly waltz away from Cosima if Dorothy's next deal is tied up in court. And, speaking for myself, I don't want to delay our next bestseller any longer than necessary."

"Dorothy would never agree to a settlement," I told him. "You know that. It would be like admitting she's a thief. And if it ever got out, the whole industry would think she stole the idea for the panda books."

"Are you one hundred percent sure she didn't?" Guy asked.

"That's nice, Guy. Very nice. Shall I tell Dorothy you said that?"

"Oh, come now—do you mean to tell me you don't have any doubts? We live in the real world, Filippa. Have you seen the manuscript?"

"Parts of it."

"Well?"

"It's convincing," I acknowledged. "But that doesn't mean a thing."

"If it's convincing to you, what would a jury say? You know as well as I do that proof is a slippery thing in this kind of case. Which is why it might be better for all of us to make this unfortunate allegation disappear as quickly as it came."

Something in Guy's manner made me suspicious. Fat men sweat, but he was sweating more than usual. I thought about seeing him and Saleema together at the restaurant in Mayfair, shortly before David Milton made his move on Dorothy.

Could Guy be a part of the conspiracy?

Who better to coach a writer on imitating Dorothy's style than the man who had been her editor for ten years?

"Have you seen the manuscript?" I asked.

"Me? No."

"So why would you be talking about a settlement without even seeing it?"

"I'm just thinking about the proper strategy," Guy said. "This has to be a legal and business decision, nothing more. Sometimes emotions cloud our judgment in these matters."

In front of the theater, people started to flow back into the lobby. The second act of the musical would be starting soon. Passion and betrayal in the midst of religious strife. My lover is dead—I think I'll sing about it.

"The manuscript is fake," I told Guy.

"And two years from now, maybe a jury will agree with you. Or maybe not. Either way, it's likely to ruin Dorothy, and you'll still be sitting in your little cubicle at Bardwright."

I thought about telling Guy what I suspected—that there was a connection between David Milton and Saleema Azah. If Guy was part of the plot, however, I didn't want to tip them off and give Saleema a way to cover her tracks. Except Guy was right. So was my father. I couldn't let this linger in the hands of dueling lawyers for years. Dorothy wouldn't write a word with this hanging over her head. If someone wanted to target her Achilles' heel, they had found the perfect spot.

Which was something Guy would know better than anyone.

"This is in your hands, Filippa," Guy continued. "You need to do what's right for Dorothy, which is to make this go away as swiftly as possible. If you can prove the manuscript is a fake, so be it. If you can't, then you need to help Dorothy understand the realities of the situation."

There was a smugness in how he said it. As if he knew I would never prove it was a fake. It made me more convinced than ever that Guy's hand was in this. He had his eyes on a retirement home in the Lake District, and this was a way to get the assets he wanted. Maybe it was ego, too. To prove that he could mastermind a literary fraud, like an artist who does a painting that could pass for a van Gogh.

Great, now all I can think about is one-eared pandas.

"Tell me something, Guy. How do you think I should go about exposing this bastard?" I asked. "What should I do?"

Guy picked at his beard. "If the manuscript is as good as you say, then I wouldn't know where to begin."

"Maybe I should send it to you and let you take a look."

"Maybe you should."

"I have Dorothy's old notes. From her first agent. This all goes back more than ten years. I figure maybe there will be something in there."

Guy offered me a sad smile. "Except if I understand the time line, the original idea goes back well before Dorothy's first scribblings, right? This man, this Tom Milton, would have written his book years before Dorothy did. So it doesn't really prove anything to look at her early drafts, does it?"

"Probably not," I agreed.

"There you go. Take my advice, Filippa. Make him an offer, and make this go away. If it's a fake, as you say, then he won't be anxious to take it all the way to court and risk exposure. A modest sum will probably send him back into the closet where he belongs."

"How modest?" I asked.

"Oh, I have no idea. That's for the solicitors to work out."

"I'm surprised you're pushing so hard about this, Guy."

"Like I said, my only interest is in selling more books. The sooner this is all behind us, the sooner we can wrap up that new contract for Dorothy that you want so badly. The first contract for your new agency."

It was tempting, I admit. Tempting to cross David Milton off my list. If I talked to Dorothy, if I explained everything to her, I could make her see the wisdom of settling early. Guy knew it. Hell, I could even argue that it might save her money in the long run, given the legal expenses of a drawn-out investigation and trial. Regardless of whether the book was a fake, there was also no guarantee that we would win in the end.

"I'll think about it," I said.

"You do that. Believe me, I want to see you and Dorothy both out from under Cosima's thumb."

"I'm trying to be patient," I said.

"You?"

"There's always a first time."

"Well, timing is everything, Filippa. I gather the street is way ahead of you in talking about your plans."

"Oh?"

Guy nodded. "Haven't you heard the gossip tonight? I assumed you were the source of it."

"What gossip? About my leaving the agency?"

"In a manner of speaking," Guy said. "Word is that something huge is going be announced at Bardwright next week. An earthquake of some sort. I figured you must know what that is."

You'd think so, wouldn't you? But I don't.

31

AFTER THE MUSICAL WAS OVER, I tried to catch up with Sally in the crowd of glammed-up socialites heading for the exits. If anyone had the dirt about big changes coming at Bardwright, it was she. Sally knows everything. When I finally spotted her from afar, however, she had already been cornered in the Garrick lobby by Cosima, who flashed a barracuda smile and clutched Sally's shoulder with a death grip of red nails. The noble thing would have been to rescue my friend, but I didn't want a rerun with Cosima. That could wait until Monday.

I wasn't feeling particularly sleepy. My body clock was off. Two transatlantic flights in two days, followed by a late-night visit with a suicidal friend, will do that to you. As far as my brain was concerned, it may as well have been noon in the midst of a solar eclipse.

I strolled into Leicester Square, which on Saturday nights is like an outdoor showing of *The Rocky Horror Picture Show*. Hair the color of Easter eggs. Pierced noses, lips, eyebrows, belly buttons, and nipples. Leather and mascara. Black boots with six-inch heels. Gangs of young people swarmed around the Odeon, which is where most of the London movie premieres take place. I had traipsed the red carpet myself a few times, which was when the popzees usually changed the batteries in their cameras. But that was before my Julien Macdonald.

I smelled Chinese food and Lebanese kebabs. I was in the mood for something sweet, so I bought a scoop of Häagen-Dazs ice cream in a cup and ate it slowly as I wandered past the gift shops on the west end of the square. Boys eyed me in my silver dress, and I knew what they were thinking. Hot older chick, mates, bet she could teach us a thing or two. Snotty bastards. Just yesterday I was seventeen, hanging out with bad boys like them on the weekend, inhaling the occasional joint in nightclub doorways. Then the magician waves his magic wand, and I'm thirty-six.

I wandered past the entrance to Chinatown and into the craziness of Piccadilly Circus. Traffic hurtled by in every direction. Laughing young people went up and down the stairs to the Tube. Neon reflected on my glittery dress. I leaned on the railing and stared at the status of Eros across the street and thought about life and love whipping by me as fast as the taxis. Guy probably felt the same way. More often than not, we are spectators at our own lives. I didn't want to end up like him or Cosima or even Sally. I had other plans in mind.

Life in the fast lane was fine. Bring it on. Plane rides and sleepless nights. Good days and bad. Geniuses, fools, and shallow egos. A high-wire act without a net. That was okay. Win or lose, it was okay.

I knew Guy was right. So was my father. Better to settle with David Milton. Better to get it off the table and move on. Better for Dorothy, better for me. The lawyer would tell me the same thing. Except there was no way I was going to give David Milton the satisfaction. Or Saleema. No way I was going to allow myself to be beaten. No way I would roll over and let Dorothy hand her money to blackmailers. My dad calls it pitching a Winnie: when you get the steel in your back like Churchill and choose to fight a battle that everyone tells you you're going to lose.

I wasn't going to lose.

I took out my phone there in the Circus and dialed the United

States, I held my other hand over my ear to block out the noise. When I reached David Milton's voice mail, I left him a message. Short and to the point.

"This is Tess Drake. We both know your manuscript is a fake and a fraud. See you in court."

I hung up and felt better. Maybe I'd have to eat my words, but it was time to put the fear of God into him for a change. When you have a lousy hand, go ahead and put on your game face and double the bet.

Someone was leaning against the railing next to me. You're always surrounded by people here, so I didn't pay any attention to him until he said, "Is that what the life of an agent is like? Leaving crank calls at midnight in Piccadilly Circus?"

I turned and found Nicholas Hadley standing there in his Burberry and gawking at the neon. He was eating chips from a greasy white bag.

"Are you following me, Inspector?" I asked.

Hadley shrugged and offered me a chip, which I accepted. There is nothing better than soggy, yellow-brown, straight-from-the-lard British chips.

"In fact, I am. Your assistant told me you were at the premiere tonight. I saw you come out, and I tracked you here. Sorry for eavesdropping on your call, but that's the kind of thing I do."

"It's late," I said. "Couldn't this wait until tomorrow?"

"It could, but I thought you'd want to know."

"What?"

"The DNA isn't a match," Hadley said.

Hooray. Finally, some good news.

"I don't want to say I told you so, but I told you so," I said. "Never have my lips connected with any of Lowell's private parts."

Hadley cocked his head and nodded. His jaw worked on his chips.

"Does this mean I'm officially cleared?" I asked.

"Well, let's say I'm not as convinced of your guilt as I was a couple of days ago."

"That sounds like you still have a sliver of doubt."

"Yes, but only a sliver."

"Was it the DNA that changed your mind?" I asked.

"Oh, that was a big part of it, but there's more. Actually, my superintendent informed me in a loud voice that I had better make damn sure of the evidence against you before I made an even bigger fool of myself. So with that cheerful advice, I took another look at Mr. Bardwright's apartment."

Hadley didn't look happy as he said this.

"Do I know your superintendent?" I asked, wondering why one of the muckety-mucks among the police would want to do me a favor.

"No, but apparently your father does."

I tried not to laugh. I really owe that lovely, exasperating father of mine a kiss. Every time we try to prove that we can make it on our own, our fathers go and do something to make us realize they are irreplaceable.

"I didn't ask him to interfere," I said.

But I'm glad he did.

"It was just as well," Hadley admitted. "When I took a second look, I realized that things didn't add up quite as neatly as I thought they did."

"Oh?"

"Yes, it was one of those crime scenes where everything makes sense until you realize that nothing makes sense," he explained. "Take the wineglasses. I checked Mr. Bardwright's kitchen cabinets and found that the rest of his crystal set didn't match the two glasses I found on his coffee table. The glasses with your and his prints on them were unique. That seemed very unusual to me."

"Very."

"I also checked with your dry cleaner about that dress."

"Former dry cleaner," I said.

"Indeed. There was still a tag on the dress in Mr. Bardwright's closet. The nice Asian woman who runs the store in Putney had no trouble remembering you or the dress you accused them of losing. Apparently, you used a long list of expletives when you went to pick up the dress and it wasn't there. Including questioning the marital status of her mother and making a few slurs against the Chinese people as a whole."

"That does sound like me," I acknowledged.

"Yes. She seemed hopeful that I was planning to arrest you for something."

"I guess it's not her day."

"Well, I'm a little disappointed, too," Hadley admitted. "Anyway, I also spent a long hour on the phone with an excitable publisher in Italy, who shared the sentiments of your dry cleaner with regard to your imminent incarceration. He swore up and down that you were a liar, a thief, a cheat, and a whore."

"Three out of four ain't bad," I said.

Hadley managed a smile at that one.

"However, the more I talked to him, the more I realized that he had no evidence of any wrongdoing on your part, other than disbelief that his competitor in Milan had outbid him on several successive deals. Also, as you indicated, it appeared to be at least six weeks since he had had any communication with anyone at the Bardwright Agency about your dealings with him and Leonardo Santelli. So I had to wonder why Mr. Bardwright would have an old e-mail open on his computer, since these allegations didn't appear to carry much weight against you anymore."

"I'm feeling vindicated, Inspector."

"And I'm feeling more than a little stupid. Which is not a feeling I enjoy. I'm not in the habit of apologizing to murder suspects, but in this case, I appear to have misjudged your involvement."

"Thanks, but you said you still have a sliver of doubt."

"I always have doubt. I'm a professional cynic."

"Funny, so am I," I said.

"So a little part of me still thinks you could have masterminded all this phony evidence in order to deliberately point suspicion at yourself and then ensure that it all falls apart."

"That seems like an awful lot of trouble," I said.

"It does. Also, you may be smart, but, no offense, you don't strike me as being quite that smart."

"Your apologies need a little work, Inspector."

"That's because I don't get much practice," he said. "I still need to ask you some questions, though. It appears that someone went to a lot of trouble to point a finger in your direction. It makes me wonder who would be so intent on watching you rot in jail."

"It's a long list," I admitted.

"So I gather. Anyone near the top?"

Cosima. C-o-s-i-m-a. Backward? Amisoc. Anagram? Mosaic. Just tell him. TELL HIM.

"I probably shouldn't be saying this," I said. "After being on the business end of a false accusation, I don't particularly want to paint a target on anyone else's back."

"Who?" Hadley asked.

"My boss. Cosima Tate."

Hadley slapped his forehead with greasy fingers. "Yes, of course! The woman who takes over the agency after Lowell's death and makes millions! Why on earth didn't I think of that before?"

I got the feeling he was being sarcastic.

"Okay, so you've already looked at her," I concluded.

"Up and down, Ms. Drake. No offense, but she was a far likelier suspect than you. Unfortunately, she has what we call an alibi."

"Maybe she hired a hooker to take care of Lowell."

"Hookers as a general rule aren't a murderous lot. They're usually the ones who wind up dead."

"Well, I'm afraid I can't think of anyone else who benefits from Lowell's death," I said.

"Nor can I, but we're reviewing his recent deals now. If you think of anyone else, I hope you'll call me."

"Of course."

Hadley finished his chips and crumpled the bag. He shoved his hands in his Burberry pockets and headed for the Tube.

I was a little discouraged, because I had a fantasy of Cosima being led away in shackles and strip-searched. That would have been an easy solution to my problems. Still, I was pleased that one of the storm clouds hovering over my head had cleared. On the other hand, it made me wonder which of my other enemies had it in for me. And Lowell, too.

32

I WOKE UP on Sunday with one thought in my head. Darcy.

Tonight was the night I would parade through the lobby of the Hilton on Park Lane in my fur coat. Jaws would drop. Men would swoon. Flowers would be strewn in my path. I wondered if I had the guts to wear nothing under the coat. That would be the sexy thing to do, but with my luck, the taxi would get in an accident on the way to the hotel, and I would be forced to use my fur coat to cover the bloodstained victims. I would stand there naked on the street in front of all the American tourists. Someone from South Dakota would ask me directions to Speakers' Corner.

Go naked? I think not.

I was nervous. Even a little scared. This was not my typical, no-strings-attached rendezvous. Nothing screws up a simple affair faster than an old-fashioned case of love. I wasn't sure what I would say or what he would say or who would say it first. In an odd way, I felt as if we were strangers now who needed to get to know each other all over again.

Hanging around my flat was doing nothing to calm my nerves, so I gathered up some of the materials from Dorothy's box and headed out for the Boathouse, which is a pub near the high street that is one of my favorite haunts. They have an upstairs, outdoor patio overlooking the Thames that I adore. On weekday evenings, you can't get near the place for the crowds. Jugglers and street performers do their thing by the water. They've known me for years, and they always manage to get me a corner table under a canopy, where I can sip bitter, stare at the river through my sunglasses, and do whatever work I feel like doing.

I ordered tempura prawns to go with my beer. It was much colder today, but with an unexpected appearance by the London sunshine. I checked my voice mail, but there was no retort from David Milton to my in-your-face message of the night before. Maybe he hadn't heard it yet, or maybe he was going back and forth with Saleema about his reply. I called my father, got his machine, and thanked him for saving my arse with the coppers. I checked e-mail, too, and was puzzled. No one sending little notes of encouragement. No one buzzing about industry rumors. No one bothering me about their contracts.

Strange.

I made sure I had signal on my mobile, and I did. I began to have the tiniest feeling of unease.

When I finished my prawns and my first beer was half empty, I began to sift through the ten-year-old panda papers from Dorothy's agent. By the time my third beer was half empty, I was no closer to finding something to back up my fighting words to David Milton. In truth, I wasn't sure what I expected to find. I saw Dorothy's original query letter, talking about the book she had written. I flipped through the pages of the signed first edition. *To Berta, who made this all happen.* Berta was Dorothy's first agent, a sweet but supersized woman who had worked at a literary press before launching her modest agency in Buffalo.

Unpublished writers will throw themselves at any agent who gives them the slightest encouragement. The trouble is that many agents can get you a deal, but then you drown in the midlist, wondering why your career isn't going anywhere. What you really want from an agent is great contacts, and the only way to build a high-powered Rolodex is to live in London or New York. Not Buffalo. That was the problem with Dorothy and Berta. Dorothy got published, but she wasn't going anywhere, not until Berta's weight got the better of her heart and Dorothy called me.

The first edition in my hands could probably fetch a couple thousand dollars on eBay. They're hard to find because so few of them were sold. With all due modesty, it wasn't until I entered the picture that Dorothy started selling, thanks to the movie deal I landed that put Butterball and the other panda boys on the big screen.

My BlackBerry buzzed and did a little dance on the table. I grabbed for it, anxious to get an e-mail to break out of my dry spell, but my face fell when I saw that the sender was David Milton. I opened the message.

AM ATTACHING CHAPTER TWO. JUDGE FOR YOURSELF.

Cocky bastard. I opened the PDF attachment and saw more of the same—old paper, old ink, old typeface, old words that were just like Dorothy's first edition but not quite. Just the way it would have been if Dorothy had modeled her panda epic on a novella by a dear friend. At first glance, Milton's fake chapter two was as convincing as fake chapter one. I read a page and then gave up, not wanting to put myself in a worse frame of mind.

I finished my beer. Shivered a little when the wind blew. Stared at the water. Watched the jugglers. Ordered a bacon, brie, and cranberry wrap to follow my prawns. While I waited, a shadow fell across my face from a woman standing between me and the sun.

"Sunday afternoon at the Boathouse," a familiar voice said. "You never change, Tess."

She was small. Hands on her hips. Jeans and heels. Designer shades. Dark skin. Long black hair.

She was about the last person on earth I expected to see. Saleema.

I have never been involved in a physical altercation with another woman. Well, once, actually, in college. A history teacher accused me of sleeping with her husband. You will probably not be surprised to learn that the accusation did have some merit, although in my defense, he assured me that he and his wife had an open marriage and that she regularly slept with her students. Turns out that was not entirely true. I apologized profusely, but we still wound up pulling hair, knocking over chairs, and sending two glass-framed watercolor paintings crashing to the floor of her office.

The dean, after consultation with my father, recommended I spend the following term abroad at NYU.

As Saleema towered above me at the Boathouse—at least as much as a five-foot-tall woman can tower—I wondered if I was in for another fight. When she took off her sunglasses, her eyes were two cold black dots. She pulled out the chair opposite me, sat down, and swept her lustrous hair back. I was already gauging the distance from the balcony to the tables below and wondering if I would survive the fall.

"I saw you at the play last night," Saleema said.

"You were there? I didn't see you."

"That's because I saw you first."

We were off to a good start. I signaled the waiter for another beer, and Saleema ordered a glass of cabernet. When our drinks came, we sat in silence for several minutes. I wasn't sure what she wanted, and I didn't know why she was here.

"One question," Saleema said finally.

Her pretty lips were scrunched, and she tapped the side of her wineglass with purple fingernails.

"Okay."

"Did you sleep with Evan in New York this week?"

Shit!

I thought about lying, but I didn't figure she could be any madder than she already was.

"Yes."

Saleema nodded. "I wondered if you would try to bullshit me about that."

"You already knew?"

"Evan made a point of bragging about it."

That son of a bitch.

"So are you going to slap me again?" I asked.

"No, I got that out of my system. You can be a slut with whomever you want."

I wasn't sure how to respond to that without making things worse, so I said, "Exactly why are you here, Saleema?"

My ex-friend stared out at the river and didn't reply immediately. After she took another sip of wine, she said, "I talked to Guy."

"Okay."

"He told me all about Dorothy and this David Milton. The one with the fraudulent manuscript."

"Do you think I'm stupid, Saleema?" I asked.

"About some things, yes, I do, Tess. When it comes to men and sex, you may be the most stupid woman I have ever met. But I've never said you were anything but a great agent. That's why I couldn't believe it."

"Believe what?"

"What you said to me in New York. That was the name you threw at me. David Milton."

"So?"

"So do you really think I would try to defraud you and your client? Do you honestly believe that?"

Ten minutes ago, I would have said yes. Now I'm not so sure.

"I think you would do just about anything to beat me," I told her.

"Well, you're right about that. We're agents. We compete. I'm not ashamed of it. And, yes, I made a special effort to go after some of your clients after the whole thing with Evan. But a fake manuscript? If you think I'd go that far, then you have gotten way too paranoid."

"Are you telling me you've never met David Milton?"

"I've never heard of him," Saleema said. "I told you that in New York."

"He did pro bono estate work for victims of 9/11," I said.

"So what?"

"So your secretary needed legal counsel after the attacks."

"Her attorney was a man named Joshua Mintz," Saleema said. "Do you know how many lawyers provided pro bono work back then? Hundreds. Probably thousands."

"What about Guy?" I asked.

"What about him?"

"I saw the two of you together."

"You think he and I are *both* in on it?"

"You hate me. And Guy knows Dorothy's writing style forward and backward. What was I supposed to think?"

"God, you really are paranoid. Get a clue, Tess. Not everything that happens in this world revolves around you."

I shrugged. "When have you known me to believe it didn't?"

Saleema actually laughed. Not loud. Not long. But she laughed.

"I appreciate your coming here to tell me this," I added. "You didn't need to do that. You could have let me make a fool of myself."

"You've never needed my help with that."

This time I laughed. But I knew it meant something for her to come here. It was a crack in the ice.

"I'm sorry," I went on, "for a lot of things."

Saleema took a long breath and stared at the table. "I know."

"Remember when I said I missed you?" I asked. "I do."

"We're not friends anymore, Tess."

"I'd at least like not to be enemies."

She stood up. "Maybe someday. Not now."

"You want to stay for lunch?"

"No, I can't." She hesitated, halfway being staying and going. "How's your father?"

"Fine. I'm still disappointing him."

"That's why we have fathers," Saleema said.

I knew she didn't want to leave. Not really. Just like I knew I didn't want her to go. Despite everything, it would have been easy to slip into our old routine, the way we did when we were best friends. We could have sat there all afternoon. She could tell me Hollywood stories. I could tell her about Darcy. We could get drunk, loud, and obnoxious with our laughter.

But she was right. It was too soon.

Her phone rang, breaking the awkward intimacy between us. She looked grateful for the interruption. She answered the phone and said, "Yes, Guy, I told her. Just so you know, she thought we were in it together. I told her that Tess Drake orbits the sun, not the reverse."

She listened, and her eyebrows knitted in confusion, and she hung up.

"Guy said to tell you something," she said.

"What?"

"He said that Filippa wasn't totally out of line to question his ethics. What does that mean?"

"Guy tried to get me to kick back part of my commission on Dorothy's next deal."

"Seriously?"

"That, and I should spend a naughty weekend with him in Brighton."

"That son of a bitch," Saleema said, looking genuinely angry.

"He's a greedy goat, but what else is new? You don't have editors and authors proposition you all the time?"

She shrugged. "True."

But I knew what it was. It was the old Saleema. The one who rushed to defend me, the way I always did her. The one who loved me. After all these years, that was the moment when I fully understood why Saleema had been so ferociously angry about Evan. It wasn't Evan's betrayal that had knocked out her foundation. It was mine. And I felt guilty all over again.

If she knew what I was thinking, she didn't go there.

"Take care of yourself, Tess," Saleema told me.

"You, too. Give me a call next time you're in London."

She didn't answer or make any promises. Instead, she cocked her head and said, "Filippa? What's that about?"

"Oh, that's one of Guy's little jokes," I said with a sigh. "After we did the film deal for *The Bamboo Garden*, we had to change the name of one of Dorothy's characters to keep the producer happy."

Saleema nodded. She left without another word, and I watched her go. I began to understand all the ways I had sabotaged my life, and I wondered if I was being given a chance to repair the damage.

I took a last swallow of Young's bitter.

And then it hit me.

Filippa.

33

I KNEW THAT GUY was innocent, because Guy of all people would never have made that mistake. Whoever David Milton had hired to craft his fraudulent manuscript was good. Very good. But I knew something that he didn't. The edition of *The Bamboo Garden* that fills the shelves of bookstores around the world includes a delightfully over-the-top, Disney-worthy villain who goes by the name of Filippa.

The woman who tries to destroy the pandas.

The woman children love to hate.

Except Dorothy didn't come up with the name Filippa. Neither did Tom Milton. I did.

The first edition, the one that sold about a hundred copies, the one that collectors snap up for big bucks on eBay whenever one comes available, used a different name for the villain. Liudmila.

So when I got back to my flat and opened up the attachment of chapter two that David Milton had sent me, I held my breath. Because in Dorothy's book, that's the chapter in which her villain first visits the London Zoo. Her wonderfully wicked genius. Liud-mila to a handful of early readers, Filippa to the world at large.

I scrolled down the screen, reading through seven pages of brilliant forgery, until the very last paragraph, the one where we meet her, the one where she appears outside the panda cage for the first time. And there she was.

Filippa.

I reacted like a Chelsea forward landing a tie-breaking goal. Hands in the air. Did a little dance. Wiggled my butt at the screaming crowd. If I had been Brandi Chastain, I would have stripped off my shirt and waved it in the air. It's not often in the art of dealmaking that you can count a win rather than a draw, but this was a win, pure and simple. Victory. David Milton was exactly what I thought he was: a cheat and a fraud. And I could prove it.

I called Dorothy to tell her the good news. No answer, as usual.

I thought about calling David Milton to gloat, but I wasn't going to give him any chance to repair his mistake. He'd learn about it soon enough. Tomorrow I'd chat with my IP lawyer and let him carry the ball the rest of the way.

Victory.

I got up and paced restlessly back and forth across my carpet, out to the terrace, through the kitchen, back to my desk. I was keyed up, stressed out, scared, and I didn't know why. I should be relieved, and, yes, I was, but there was something more. Then I realized what was happening. What this all meant. The last obstacle had been cleared from my path. I didn't have any reason to wait now, any more excuses to delay and procrastinate. I was ready. At my meeting with Cosima in the morning, I would drop the bomb and tell her she could bury me if she liked, but I was gone. Sayonara. Adios. Auf Wiedersehen. Tomorrow I would launch the agency.

The Drake Media Agency.

My agency.

I looked at my hands. They were shaking. It's one thing to dream about it and fantasize about it, and it's another to do it. But

I was going to do it. I was terrified. That's how you know you're
doing the right thing.

I called Emma. "Pack your bags, girl."

"What? Why?"

"Tomorrow's the day."

"Really?"

"Really."

I explained what I had found about David Milton, and she
whooped with excitement.

"What about Dorothy's next deal?" Emma asked. "Will Cosima try to go after it?"

"What deal?" I replied, laughing. Thank you, Guy.

"Oh, Tess, this is fabulous. Do you think everyone will come
with us? I still can't figure out why no one is writing back."

"Don't worry about it. I told everyone we were on hold when I
thought this Milton thing would derail my plans. Once I make it
official with Cosima, we can start getting representation letters
out to all the clients."

"Have you written something?"

"I'll do it right now."

"God, this is exciting," Emma said, with the naïveté of someone
who's at the beginning of her career and can go anywhere and do
anything. For me, my joy was tempered by the gravity of what I
was doing. Sally's warnings flitted through my brain. Cosima's
threats, too. I wondered if I knew what the hell I was getting myself into.

"Yes, it is, darling," I told her.

"Have fun tonight," Emma said. "I told Jane to look for you."

"Tonight?"

Emma giggled. "Remember? Darcy?"

Tonight. The Hilton. I had almost forgotten.

The queen is not a fan of the Hilton on Park Lane. In a city of low
buildings, the Hilton is notoriously tall; and on those rare days
when the fog clears, guests on the higher floors have a southern

view of the private gardens behind Buckingham Palace. I suppose this means that Liz can't take a morning stroll in her curlers and bathrobe anymore, sipping coffee from her I LOST MY HEAD AT THE TOWER OF LONDON ceramic mug.

Just kidding.

However, I am not the queen, and I love the Hilton. When clients stay there, I make a point of meeting them for breakfast in the executive lounge, where we can sit by the window and watch the traffic on Park Lane and the joggers in Hyde Park. The Hilton is the most American of the London hotels, but, to be honest, it means the service is better than at almost any other hotel in the city.

A town car picked me up in front of my flat at nine thirty. There was no way I was getting into an ordinary cab in my Julien Macdonald. I wanted a leather backseat caressing my bottom, with no chewing gum, no cigarette ash, and no crumby remnants of chips and crisps. Besides, if you are wearing a full-length mink, you want to make an entrance like a star.

I couldn't bring myself to go naked, but I didn't wear much. My sexy, knee-length red dress. Killer heels. Pearl earrings. Armani sunglasses, even at night, because that's what you do. Under the dress, I went for a white lace thong, so you know I was feeling horny, because I don't really like the idea of a shoelace wedged up my arse.

Over all that, the fur. Wrapped around me like an Eskimo blanket. The London temperature had turned cold again, but it could have been the hottest day in July, and I still would have worn the fur. It's so elegant I didn't know if I even had the courage to show it off in public. If you wear something like that, you have to walk the walk. Pretend to be someone you're not. When I got out of the elevator at my building, Samur didn't even recognize me at first, and when he picked up on the streaky colored hair, his mouth fell open.

"Ms. Drake," he told me, "you are looking gorgeous."

And I was.

On the drive through the city, I was jittery. Embarrassed.

Aroused. You can't help feel like Cinderella going to the ball, wondering if everyone's going to realize you're just a char girl. I am not exactly short on confidence, but confidence is as much an act as anything else, and sometimes you wonder if people will see through your costume.

The Hilton parking lot was crowded. I mean jammed. Taxis, limousines, top-hatted bellmen, photographers, ridiculously handsome men, unbelievably young and gorgeous women. Furs aplenty, but nothing like mine, I have to say. The hotel was hosting a party to celebrate the seventy-fifth anniversary of the British Film Institute. Hundreds of rising stars, falling stars, and comets flaming out. All of it live on BBC One.

The truth is that real stars hate televised galas, because they're more work than fun, and the unwashed media is there to excoriate every flaw in your makeup and outfit. You smile and parade for the judges like a sheepdog at the Westminster show.

Woof, woof.

I had to wait fifteen minutes for my town car to make it to the entrance. In the meantime, I peered through the smoked windows. I saw a kilt-clad Sean Connery. Gwyneth Paltrow, looking more and more like Blythe Danner every day. I mean that as a compliment. Daniel Craig in a tux. It was practically a James Bond convention. Jane Seymour, she of the long, long hair. Cate Blanchett. I wondered if Tom Cruise was here. He'd think I was stalking him.

And then it was my turn. As the town car slid smoothly in front of the entrance, an efficient bellman swung open the rear door.

"Good evening, ma'am," he told me with a big smile. He was young and fit. Moroccan maybe. I could forgive him for the "ma'am" comment. His hand was soft as he helped me out of the rear seat. His eyes took in the fur and my legs, even though I'm sure they train him not to look. I was happy that he couldn't resist a quick glance.

I slipped off my sunglasses. Took a breath. This is the moment when you expect to trip and spill forward, which I surely would have done if I had skipped the dress under the fur. Wind up on my face and show the world my arse. But no. I sashayed into the hotel lobby as if I owned the place. Behind me, I heard people murmuring about me, about the fur, about who I was. I thought about going back to tell them. I'm Tess Drake of the Drake Media Agency.

The lobby was chockablock with jewels, breasts, fur wraps, Gucci purses, and bubbling flutes of Dom Pérignon. Movie soundtrack music played above the burble of the crowd. Something from a Hitchcock film, I think. I had my eyes on the bank of elevators, but getting there was no small feat. I excused myself through clouds of Dior perfume. Smiled at stars, who smiled back, assuming they knew me from somewhere. I told Connery he looked fabulous. He did.

I was about to slip into the privacy of the nearest elevator and head for the twelfth floor when I felt a hand on my shoulder.

"You're Tess, aren't you?"

I stopped and turned to find a Sienna Miller look-alike flashing a big fake smile at me.

"That's right," I said.

"I'm Jane. Jane Parmenter."

"Oh, yes, of course. Emma raves about you, darling."

"Emma's sweet," Jane said, in the way that you say a West Highland terrier is sweet as it licks your face.

I didn't like her. Not that I would ever tell Emma that. But some women exude insincerity like body odor. I am all too familiar with young, ambitious actresses like Jane, who are C-listers scraping their nails against a sheer rock face to climb to the B-list. God help anyone who gets in their way. They will smile at you and pander to you and lie to you, and as soon as they don't need you, they will step over you like a used tissue on a sidewalk. It's not like I can entirely blame them. Beautiful girls like Jane get used all the time for their bodies in this business, so why not use everyone else? You learn the behavior that works in this industry.

Yes, she was stunning. Even more so in person than in the one photo I saw in Emma's copy of *Hello!* Makeup expertly applied, hydrangea lipstick so glossy I could see myself, capped teeth as white as Himalayan snow. Hollywood blue eyes with a razor sharpness to them. She was about my height, jagged short blond hair in the kind of cut that cost three hundred pounds to make it look like you did it yourself. Some skilled surgeon somewhere had done wonders with her breasts, packing them with gel like a stuff-it-yourself bear at a gift shop.

She wore a flaunt-it turquoise and white dress, with wild silk covering one leg and the other leg bare to her upper thigh. Two straps the width of dental floss struggled to keep her breasts inside the swollen cups of the bodice. A diamond-and-aquamarine necklace dangled into her cleavage like a spelunker exploring a dark cave. Every few seconds, one of the feckless straps slid down her arm, and she had to tug it back into position on her shoulder.

"What a party," Jane said.

"Yes."

"That's an amazing coat," she added.

"Thank you."

It was small talk, and that was all. We both knew the score. We weren't going to be friends.

"Emma tells me you called Godfrey Kahn," Jane said. She looked annoyed rather than grateful.

"I did, but don't count on me. I only know a couple of his execs."

"I'm sure a referral from you can only help," she said in a way that told me she was sure I could do her no good whatsoever. Which was probably true. I didn't tell her that the only way for her to get the part was to get on her knees in front of Kahn and do what good little actresses do.

"Good luck," I said.

"Any advice for me?" she asked, which was a polite question and nothing more.

"Just keep doing what you're doing."

Jane's eyes wandered. She was looking around carefully to see if anyone was watching us. It's a political calculation for hangers-on. Did I have enough clout to make it worth being seen with me?

"Lots of popzees tonight," Jane said. "I keep throwing myself at them. Maybe one of the pictures will hit the tabloids. That can't hurt, right?"

"Absolutely."

Except she wasn't going to see herself in the tabloids unless she stood behind Jessica Alba again. The popzees are smart. They know who sells. They're happy to take your picture, but don't expect a C-list face in the Star Tracks of *People*. It doesn't matter if you're DDG. In this room, everyone was gorgeous.

"I'd kill for that coat," Jane said.

I'd kill you first, girlie.

"Yes, it's stunning, isn't it?"

"It's a Julien Macdonald, right?"

"That's right."

Jane nodded. "I think I saw Paris in that coat in LA last fall."

What a smarmy bitch. I didn't know what I was going to say to Emma. It's hard to tell someone that you think her girlfriend is a shallow poseur, but I knew Emma was going to ask. The fact is, I had a hard time imagining Jane with Emma. Emma's body beautiful, but she doesn't have the glamour face, and I didn't think Jane would be satisfied with anyone less perfect than herself. Which made me wonder what game she was playing with Emma and why she was wasting her time.

"Are you staying for dinner?" Jane asked.

"I'm not here for the party."

"No?"

"No, I'm meeting a friend."

"Ah," she said, lips folding into a smile. She studied my mink again and recognized it for what it was. Sex candy.

I really wanted to get away from this girl.

"Well, I'm afraid I have to go," I told her.

"I understand," she said, giving me a wink.

Jane extended a limp hand for me to shake, but her Fendi clutch was in the way, and as she shifted it, the purse spilled to the floor. She bent over in the nimble way that girls do, stretching to retrieve it, and when she popped back up, more popped than she was expecting. It was the classic wardrobe malfunction. The starlet nipple slip. Jane's strap took a journey halfway down her arm, and the loose cup of her dress followed it, sagging into ripples of silk that exposed her left breast completely. It was inflated and round, powdered and pink, all perfectly manufactured by Dr. Doubledee with a puckered brown bull's-eye in the middle.

Jane appeared unaware of her girl's grab for the limelight, but all hell was breaking loose around us. Popzees can spot a bare breast like a sniffer dog finds drugs. Dozens of cameras clicked into action, capturing six images a second and blinding me with explosions of light. Any actress who spies a camera knows what to do, and Jane turned on the smile, put her arm around my waist, and swung to offer the cameramen an unobstructed view of the left slope of the twin peaks.

"Jane!" I said.

Smile. Flash. Click, click, click, click, click. Jane even waved.

I tried to reach over to correct the malfunction, but Jane didn't know what I was doing and seemed to believe I was groping her in front of the world's cameras. Which I was. I reached, she flinched, and my hand, which were aiming for her dress, wound up squarely over her breast, as if I were giving it a tender caress.

The cameras, already busy, went crazy.

The feel of my fingers on her nipple must have finally alerted Jane that something was wrong, because she looked down, screamed, and yanked up her dress, only to scoop up my hand with it and leave me with my fingers still clutched around her breast, which was now back inside the marginal protection of the silk cup.

I tried to withdraw my hand, got it tangled up in her spaghetti strap, and spilled Mt. Jane into view again.

"Oh, shit," we said in unison.

By now, the entire lobby was watching the show. At least two television cameras had the whole thing on video. Sean Connery was laughing so hard I thought he was going to lose his kilt. I shoved my hands into my pockets, felt my face glowing bright red, and watched helplessly as Jane repositioned her breast one more time. There was a collective moan of disappointment when she was decent again.

"What's your name, honey?" one of the popzees shouted.

Jane was no fool. "Jane Parmenter," she replied immediately. "P-a-r-m-e-n-t-e-r."

"Are you an actress?"

"Yes!"

"How about you, ma'am?" the same photographer called to me.

Ma'am again?

"Sod off. S-o-d-o-f-f."

Behind me, the bell for the elevator dinged, and the doors swung open. I dashed inside, eager to escape.

The last thing I saw as the doors closed was Jane grinning at me. She was happy, and she had reason to be, because she was about to get her wish. In a matter of minutes, she was going to be a tabloid star.

34

I WAS NOT EXACTLY IN THE RIGHT FRAME of mind to meet Darcy, but I hoped that my distractions would fade as the elevator hummed upward and the noise and glitter of the lobby vanished. I tried to forget about Jane Parmenter and think about the man who was waiting for me. I sighed, closed my eyes, and chanted the sort of mantra that Buddhists use to relax. *Ommmm.* Or in my case, I suppose it should have been *Wiiiiine.* Alcohol please, lots of it, and fast.

I got off in the quiet hallway and took a moment to compose myself. My mouth was dry, my nerves rattled. Even in the luscious coat, I felt a chill. I was glad no one was here to see me.

It shouldn't be this way, because I've met Darcy dozens of time, here or in the Mayfair flat. One big difference, though. We had now admitted we were in love. Normally I never confuse emotion with sex, but here I was. Room 1216. On the other side of the door was the man who made my heart race. I didn't know if I should knock or turn tail and run like a furry white rabbit until I was back in Putney.

I knocked.

He answered immediately, all tall and handsome, silver strands in his mane of dark hair, his white dress shirt untucked and half unbuttoned, his hands holding two glasses of red wine. Like he could read my mind.

We stared at each other. Neither spoke. I wasn't sure what I expected to see in his eyes, but it wasn't there. No hopeless passion. No schoolboy crush. We were adults, and I realized that he was as frightened as I was of what was happening.

Standing in the doorway, I didn't know what to do.

That was when I began laughing. Uproariously. Snorting, coughing, falling-against-the-wall laughing.

Darcy had no idea why. "Tess? What is it?"

I tried to speak. It wasn't easy. "If you must know, I've just been feeling up another girl's tit in front of half the fucking British film industry."

I laughed until half the bottle of red wine was gone. It was a good thing, because it broke the ice and let me relax. When I nestled into his shoulder, everything felt natural again.

"Do you like the coat?" he asked.

"That's like asking if I like chocolate. Or orgasms. Or you. I *love* the coat."

He bit his lip and looked uncomfortable. "Good."

That was as close as I came to saying it again. He didn't say it at all. The clock ticktocked past that awkward moment, and I understood the game we were playing. We were going to pretend it had never happened. I had never said the words. He had never written them down. We were simply going to go back to the way things were. Past imperfect.

I wondered if we could pull it off. It sounds like the smoothest, easiest option when you're in the moment. But tomorrow has a way of making you miss what you thought you had.

Was I disappointed? Right then and there, no. It sounds selfish, but I had other things on my mind. Having Darcy in my life, the way we had been a few days ago, was just fine. I didn't have it in me to love any more than that right now, and obviously, neither did he.

I guess you can turn the clock back for the cost of a fur coat.

"Are you naked under it?" he asked, teasing me. The old Darcy.

"Give me five seconds," I said.

"Go ahead."

Like a magician, I turned my back and extracted myself from my dress, leaving behind the heels and pearls. I twirled. Played the coquette and gave him a peek. He liked what he saw. His hands snaked inside.

Soon the coat was extraneous, a soft, expensive pile at our feet.

As we entwined on the sofa, I realized I was lying to myself. I loved him. It hurt my soul how much I loved him. But I didn't say it this time. Not when we were sated. Not when we finished the bottle of wine. Not when we made love again in the hotel bed. Not when we spooned in the aftermath and began drifting to sleep. I wanted to say it, because I wanted to see if he would say it back. But I didn't ruin the moment. You don't have to talk to me about making the same mistake twice. I kept my mouth shut.

That was okay. We had time. Time to work our way back to where we had already been. Time for me to dive past the craziness of the past few weeks and of the weeks to come. Time to see where our hearts would lead us, although for me, I already knew.

Something felt different inside me for the first time in a very, very long time. I was serene. Confident. Happy. I stared through bleary eyes at the clock by the bedside and saw that it was a minute past midnight. My life had changed. No more worries about Lowell. No more worries about David Milton. Nothing but the future.

There are days when your world comes together like the pieces in a puzzle, your sins vanish, your opportunities flourish, your enemies drop away, and you put the bad things in your life behind yourself as if you were turning the page in a book.

There are days like that.

Unfortunately, as I was about to discover, this was not one of those days.

IV

35

MY TÊTE-À-TIT WITH JANE PARMENTER landed the two of us on the home page of TMZ.com by morning. They chose a particularly unflattering photo of yours truly, with my furry white arm groping Jane's breast and my mouth wide open as if I meant to bend over and suckle on her discreetly pixilated nipple. The headline read, "Brit Film Gala Reveals 'Breast of Show'."

Nice.

It was bad enough that Jane's errant dress strap had made me the butt of bad jokes in Hollywood, but the rest of the media world was laughing, too. When I surfed over to the *Bookseller* Web site, there I was again. Openmouthed, fondling. Ditto for *Hello!* and the *Telegraph*. Rebekah Wade of the *Sun* left me a voice mail in such snorting hysterics that she probably needed oxygen.

Needless to say, word of my encounter raced throughout the industry with all the speed and prickly discomfort of an STD. When I arrived at the office, Emma smothered a giggle as she said, "Good morning." Several people applauded my arrival. My colleagues, displaying their usual tact and sensitivity, had enlarged the TMZ photo and taped a five-by-three-foot poster to my door. My mouth was the size of a grapefruit. Jane's breasts looked like basketballs. I smiled through gritted teeth, left the poster where it was, and went inside and closed my door.

Emma followed me. Her face was deadpan. "Do I have to worry about you moving in on my girlfriend?"

"Do I look like I find this funny?" I asked.

"I'm sorry. Really. I was concerned when Jane didn't come back to my place after the party, but then I saw why this morning. What on earth happened?"

"Watch for yourself. The whole thing is on YouTube."

"Oh, I know. I saw it. They were running video on the BBC this morning."

"Please tell me you're kidding," I said.

Emma winced. "Um, no."

I felt an urge to shoot someone.

Emma sat down and leaned across my desk. She whispered even though the door was closed. "Is today the day? Are you doing it?"

"Yes."

"That's brilliant!"

"Well, the timing could be a whole lot better, thanks to last night's little traffic accident with Jane's D cup."

I could see the news reports on my press release now. Tess Drake, last seen feeling up a starlet's naked boob at the BFI party, announced today that she was accepting clients for her new entertainment agency.

"Oh, no, it's perfect!" Emma assured me. "Everyone will know who you are."

"The Breast-Dressed Girl in London?" I suggested sourly. That was the photo caption on the *OK!* magazine Web site.

Emma lectured me with a wag of her index finger. "Tess, you know as well as I do that bad publicity is just as helpful as good publicity. Maybe more. Who cares how many boob jokes they make as long as people remember you?"

I groaned, but I knew that she was right. I had given the same counsel over the years to clients sued for trashing hotel rooms, clients arrested with transvestite hookers, and clients caught in amateur videos of their Caribbean sex romps. Being infamous is the same as being famous in today's gossip-hungry world. Even so, it's a lot easier to give the advice than it is to get it.

"How do you feel?" Emma asked. "About launching the agency, I mean."

"Like I could throw up," I said honestly.

I didn't really care about the tabloid trash, which was just a bit of fluff that would be pushed aside by the next celebrity scoop. By the end of the day, Amy Winehouse would be back in rehab, or Angelina Jolie would have adopted nine more children. If anything, worrying about my debut as a lesbian porn star kept my mind off what I was about to do. In fifteen minutes, I would march into Cosima's office and say sayonara to the Bardwright Agency. Au revoir to ten years of my life. I had been test-driving snappy ways to drop the bomb on the bus ride across the city. Hasta la vista, baby. Good-bye and good luck. Feel free to kiss my arse as I go.

Beneath the bravado, though, I was a jittery wreck. You can dream about the joys of being free, but it's not so easy when you're ten thousand feet up and the ground below looks really small. I wanted it to be over. Say the word, pack my bags, and start my new life. Let Cosima tell me what a terrible mistake I was making and then go ahead and make it anyway.

"How was last night with Darcy?" Emma asked. "Did you see him?"

"Yes."

"God, you must have felt so sexy in that coat!"

"I didn't wear it long," I admitted.

Emma giggled. "Was it fabulous?"

"Fabulous but strange," I said.

"Strange? How so?"

"Strange like it's not just a game anymore. It's real between us."

"That's good, isn't it?"

"I suppose it is."

Darcy was gone again when I woke up. No note. It didn't bother me, because I knew the score. I could love him and sleep with him, as long as I didn't expect anything more. That had been our arrangement from the start. So why did some part of me scream that I was a whore in a fur coat? I loved the man and wanted to say so again and again. I wanted to hear him say it back. I wanted to marry him.

God almighty, did I really just think that? What's wrong with me today?

I heard fingernails tapping on my door. Marty Goodacre, Cosima's faithful basset hound, poked his head inside. His brown teeth grinned at me. Coffee sloshed over the top of a mug clutched in his nervous hand.

"Lovely photo, Tess," he chirped.

"Fuck off, Marty. What do you want?"

"It's time for your one-on-one with Cosima," he reminded me cheerily. "She's expecting you."

"I'll be there."

"Well, don't be late—it's a busy day. I've been ringing up reporters all morning for a press conference at noon."

"Press conference? About what?"

"I'm sworn to secrecy!" Marty sang in a high-pitched voice.

I remembered Guy telling me about rumors of an earthquake at Bardwright, and I didn't like that the ground was already shaking and I still had no idea what was going on. It also worried me that Marty seemed insufferably pleased with himself. The tittering that normally followed each of his sentences was louder than usual.

"Did Cosima sign a new film rights deal with Sony?" I asked. "Is that what you're announcing? I saw her talking up the suits on Saturday night."

"Film deal? Oh, no, it's bigger than that, much bigger." Titter, titter.

"Just keep the reporters away from me, okay? I'm in a pissy mood."

"How is that different from your mood on any other day?" he asked.

"Good-bye, Marty."

"Remember, Cosima needs to see you right away."

"Instantaneously," I said.

"Honk, honk!" he cried, squeezing the photo of Jane's breast like it was the rubber bulb on a bicycle horn. He shut the door.

"What an arsehole," Emma murmured with a shiver.

I didn't care about Marty, but I did want to know what this press conference was about.

"What's the big secret?" I asked Emma. "Have you heard any buzz around the office?"

"Not a word. Cosima must be keeping this on a short lead."

I frowned. It made me think Cosima knew what was coming—me quitting, taking Dorothy with me, going for a big splash in the press. She had obviously ginned up some announcement of her own to steal the news from me. I wondered what it was, but it didn't really matter. She could have the headlines today. Tomorrow would be my story.

"My insides are water," I said, standing up. "How bad is it to leak shit on the floor when you're resigning?"

"You are too funny."

"I'm not kidding."

I wasn't, either. I wondered if I had time to hit the loo before I made the march to the corner office.

"This is your moment, Tess. Really it is. I'm so excited for you."

Emma leaned over and kissed me on the cheek as I steadied myself with both palms on the top of my desk. I breathed in and out until I was calm but dizzy. Emma held the door open for me, and I squared my shoulders and headed for the hallway, wobbling on my heels. I skipped the loo and squeezed my arse cheeks closed. This wasn't going to take long. How many words does it really take to say I quit?

I walked gingerly, not wanting to fall on my face. Remnants of my morning eggs and toast burped into my mouth, and I swallowed them back down. I could feel my deodorant dissolving into sticky white balls. My nose began to run. I was a portrait of self-confidence.

I wondered how Cosima would react to my big farewell. Maybe she would offer to double my salary. Maybe she would break down and cry and beg me to stay.

Or maybe not.

Her door was closed. From where I stood, I could see Marty, who watched me with a smirk from inside his office. I ignored him. He was number two on the list of things I wouldn't miss around here. Number one was behind the door.

I knocked and heard Cosima's voice, cool and aristocratic. "Come in, Tess."

I went inside and closed the door behind me. Cosima's desk was stretched diagonally across the corner of the office with two windows behind her overlooking the National Gallery. She sat with her head down, red pen in hand as she pretended to edit a contract. I shuffled my feet and studied the photographs all over the walls. Cosima with Ian Rankin. Cosima with Gordon Brown. Cosima with Jamie Oliver. Cosima with Keira Knightley. Cosima's expression was identical in every photo, as if she were molded out of Madame Tussaud's wax. Maybe that was what they used in plastic surgery these days.

"Have a seat," Cosima said, not looking up. Her reading glasses were balanced on the pointed tip of her nose. Her hair looked particularly black today, as if she had spent the weekend having the dye freshened at her salon. She twirled the pen in her hands, and I saw the painted nails of a new manicure, too.

The desk surface was so smooth I could see myself coming closer. She had objets d'art on the desk and on the window ledge. Romanian crystal. Asian jade. Native American wood carvings. I clung to the back of one of the guest chairs and decided to stand.

"I want you to know this isn't personal," I told her. "This is about me, not you."

Cosima ignored me as if I hadn't said anything. I chose my next words carefully, because I wanted to get them exactly right. I'd been dreaming about this moment for a long time.

I've decided to start my own agency.

I'm resigning.

I'm giving you my notice.

I'm going out on my own.

I quit, you bitch.

As it turned out, none of those was quite appropriate for what happened next.

Cosima put down her pen and took off her glasses. She closed the manila folder in front of her and pushed it neatly aside. When she leaned forward, her fingers formed a little church steeple.

"How ironic," she said. "I was just about to say the same thing to you."

"What?"

"It's not personal."

I blinked and had no idea what was going on.

That was when Cosima smiled, the way a shark probably smiles as it gets ready to feast on your leg.

"You're sacked, Tess," she said.

36

I REALLY WISHED that I had visited the loo first.

"Excuse me?" I blurted out.

"You heard me."

Yes, I had, but I couldn't believe it. Was this her little game? Her way to sabotage me in the press? You can't quit, Tess, I'll sack you first. I expected to see Donald Trump bolt from the closet and bark, "You're fired!" as if this were some kind of reality television show.

"Are you out of your fucking mind?" I demanded.

Cosima reacted with Zenlike calm. "I'll miss that obscene little mouth around here. Really, I will. You're always so entertaining. Like that titillating photo of you in the tabloids today. So emblematic of your taste and style."

"Fuck you," I said.

"There you go again. I love your coarseness. What a shame it doesn't fit with the new direction of our agency."

"I quit," I said, about fifteen seconds too late.

Cosima laughed. "You don't get it, Tess, do you? That's too bad.

I'm very busy, so I'd appreciate it if you could pack your things as rapidly as possible and vacate the premises. You can give me your key to the building right now. No offense, but I've asked a security guard to assist you as you gather your personal effects. Can't have you nicking the staplers, can we?"

I was dazed. Cosima knew it. She had landed a body blow, and I could see icy glee glowing behind her starchy skin. I wilted into the uncomfortable guest chair and squirmed.

"You knew I was going to resign," I said.

"Your plans aren't of much interest to me, Tess. However, my advice would be that you pursue a new career, because I believe you'll find that most of the doors in the industry are closed to you now. Perhaps you can parlay your recent fame into some exciting job opportunities. Maybe Britney Spears is looking for a new publicist for her upskirt photos."

She smiled wickedly.

I realized I was playing her game. Letting her rattle me. This was Cosima indulging in psychological warfare, because it was the only option open to her. Bragging to the world that she had sacked me didn't change a thing. The result was the same. When I walked out of her office, I would be free.

"Tell the papers whatever the hell you want," I snapped. "We can both spin it our way and see who wins."

"The game is already over. You lose."

"Don't be so sure."

Cosima clucked her tongue in sad dismay. "I've always found hollow boasting to be particularly pathetic. It really doesn't suit you, Tess. The fact is, I warned you not to get in my way. I gave you a fair chance to make the right choice. You could have been a partner here."

"And live in your pocket like Marty and Jack? No thanks."

Cosima's razorlike smile evaporated. "Exactly what do you know about Jack and me?"

That was a mistake.

I had been careful never to mention Jack's name around Cosima, and this was the wrong time to bring it up. As much as I wanted to throw it in her face, I couldn't do that to Jack. Even so, I wondered if it was too late, if she already knew. I tried to read her face to see if her desire to destroy me was really payback for my affair.

"I have two eyes, Cosima. I can see that the men around you walk funny. Like you've got their balls locked up for safekeeping."

Cosima restored the veneer of politeness to her face. She picked up her red pen again and reached for her half-frame glasses, ignoring me. "That will be all, Tess."

I fired back. "All? I don't think so. I haven't even begun. Clients aren't your chattel. They can go wherever they please. I've talked to every one of my clients in the past week, and they're all prepared to bolt from Bardwright and sign on with me."

"Clients," Cosima replied, nodding. "Yes, I suppose we should have that discussion now. You'll be contacted by our counsel, of course, but it's better if we're clear about this from the outset. I wouldn't want you to put yourself in any legal jeopardy in the next few days."

"What are you talking about?"

"I'm warning you explicitly not to contact any of the agency clients. Anything you say, or any incentives you offer, would almost certainly constitute a trade secret violation based on inside knowledge you've obtained as an employee of Bardwright. I don't like to pile it on, Tess, and I know you'll be struggling financially anyway, so you don't need a legal judgment against you to add to your woes."

"They're my clients," I insisted. "I recruited them. You can't tell me not to call them. You're crazy."

"If they were, in fact, your clients, that might be true," Cosima said. "But they're not. They're Bardwright clients."

"Not if they choose to leave."

"True, but they already chose to stay. They're represented by Bardwright now, not you."

"Excuse me?"

Cosima reached with obvious delight for another file folder on her desk. When she opened it, I saw at least two dozen pieces of paper neatly stacked inside. Without reading them, I could see that they were letters. Signed letters.

My heart sank.

"These are agency representation letters, Tess. As you'll see, they are all endorsed as of this weekend. I'll go through them with you one by one, so there's no misunderstanding, all right?"

She took the first letter off the stack. "Thomas Alcock."

My client. Former coach of the British World Cup team.

"Migdalia Vasquez."

My client. Investigative journalist.

"Dingo Dave Dressner."

My client. Radio disc jockey.

"Jean Paul Consaire."

My client. Chef and restaurant owner.

"Michael O'Neill."

My client. Actor.

"Anne Thompson."

My client. Novelist and member of Parliament.

And on and on it went. Name by name, she eviscerated my roster of clients. I tried very hard not to cry, and I cried anyway. I couldn't help myself. These were people I had called and e-mailed within the last five days, people who had sworn to me that they were with me, behind me, ready to stand at my side. People I had discovered. People I had made rich. People I called friends. And every one of them had signed the same boilerplate letter, formally assigning their representation to the Bardwright Agency and walking away from me.

Cosima continued until she had laid nearly thirty letters in front of me. They constituted the bulk of client relationships I had spent the past ten years building. The heart and soul of my business.

I understood now why no one was calling or writing me back. No one had the guts to say it to my face. Welcome to the Drake Media Agency, everyone. The agency with no clients.

I couldn't pretend I wasn't shattered.

"How?" I asked.

"Oh, please, Tess. Clients are neurotic little things—you know that. Scared of their own shadows."

"What did you do? Threaten them?"

Cosima tut-tutted me as if I were a child. "I don't need to threaten anyone. There's no need to be so dramatic. The simple truth is that no one wants to join a losing team, Tess. They stick with winners. They want to be represented by an agency that has influence."

"Impossible. These people were ready to join me. They told me so."

"Well, they may have said that to spare your feelings. I understand. But clients are creatures of self-interest. You know that as well as I do. Who wants to worry about whether their next publishing contract will be renewed? Who wants to worry about being blackballed? Not that I would suggest anything of the kind, but if people get it in their heads, they may get a little scared of the consequences. And fifteen percent is a lot to pay an agent, too. Ten percent is so much more attractive. You'd be amazed, Tess, at how many clients will sell you out for five percent."

Unfortunately, I knew she was right.

I should have expected it. These people weren't my friends. They owed me nothing. I had gone out on a limb, and they had sawed it off behind me. Not that I could really blame them. They could go with me and take a chance or pick the safe route with Cosima and save five percent. Easy choice.

It's not personal. It's just business.

I was so stunned to see the parade of letters laid out before me that I didn't notice at first that one name was missing.

Dorothy Starkwell.

I reviewed them all again, one by one, to be sure I hadn't missed it. I thought maybe Cosima was holding the letter back, waiting until I asked, so that she could hammer the final nail in my coffin. But her folder was empty. My heart took off again; I let out the loud breath I had been holding. I knew Dorothy. She would never sell me out. In the end, I had kept the one client who really mattered. As long as I had her as my flagship for the agency, then I could start from nothing and build my roster all over again. Cosima probably didn't realize that David Milton wasn't hanging over our heads anymore. Dorothy and I were free to do a deal with Guy that would give me what every agent needed more than anything.

Time and money.

I smiled in triumph. "I don't see Dorothy's name here."

Cosima leaned back in her chair, and I experienced the briefest moment of panic, expecting her to withdraw a letter from inside the top drawer of her desk. Instead, I relaxed as I realized she had no more aces to play. She shrugged, as if it were a matter of no importance, but that was all pretense. She had lost the client she wanted most, and she knew it.

"I'm not concerned about Dorothy," Cosima said.

This time I was the one laughing. "Oh, please. Dorothy is the crown jewel. It must drive you crazy that she's a woman of principle and you can't buy her like all the others. She's not for sale. Dorothy would never walk out on me."

"Maybe so, but you've always been your own worst enemy, Tess."

"What do you mean by that?"

"I mean that you're reckless. Foolish. Headstrong. That's why you're so easy to defeat."

I ignored her, because I knew she was right. "Did you try to get Dorothy and fail? Did she tell you she was sticking with me? I'm sure that was a terrible blow to your ego."

"I haven't been in contact with Dorothy at all. However, if she does choose to retain you as her agent, don't think for a moment that I'm a fool. I know perfectly well that you've already negotiated an eight-figure contract with Guy, and you've done so as an employee of this agency. So her next three books will stay here at Bardwright. You're not going to make a dime off that deal."

"There's no deal," I insisted. "Talk to Guy. Say it slowly with me, Cosima. *There's no deal.*"

"So you say."

"That's right."

I stood up. I wanted nothing more than to be away from her, away from Marty and Bardwright and all the clients who had betrayed me. I was ready to start over. Me and Dorothy.

"Don't forget your key, Tess."

I dug in my pocket for my office key and tossed it on her desk with a clang. Cosima got a little smirk as she palmed it. "I wouldn't be discouraged if I were you," she told me. "You see, I gave you a little gift. As I was taking away all your clients, you'll be pleased to know that I didn't bother contacting Oliver Howard. You're free to keep him."

I didn't say a word. I walked away and slammed the door. I could hear her laughing at me as I left.

37

EMMA MET ME in the hallway. Her eyes were big saucers of confusion and concern. "There's someone in your office. A security guard."

"I know."

"What's going on?"

I lowered my voice, although I'm not sure why I bothered. "Cosima sacked me."

Emma's big eyes got even bigger. "She did *what*? Are you kidding?"

I shook my head.

"Oh my God, Tess. This is crazy."

I threw open my office door. Everyone watched me in shocked silence, and I figured that Marty had made sure they all knew the score. Tess Drake was on her way out. Humiliated. Beaten. I ripped down the poster of Jane Parmenter and me and crumpled the paper in my hands. Inside the office, a security guard stared at me nervously. He was a kid, no more than twenty-four.

"Get the hell out of here," I said.

"I'm sorry, ma'am, but it's my job to stay."

"I said, get out."

"Ma'am, please don't make this difficult."

I might have cut him some slack if it weren't for the "ma'am" thing. I'm getting tired of that.

"You can give me five fucking minutes to myself, all right? You can watch me through the window if you want to make sure I don't put any Post-it Notes or paper clips in my purse."

He frowned and slid past me. I gestured Emma into my office and closed the door.

"It gets worse," I told her. "All our clients are basically gone. All except Dorothy."

"No way—that can't be true."

"They sold me out, the bastards. Oh, hell, it's not their fault. Cosima made sure they knew I was about to be hung out to dry in this business. She doesn't play anything but hardball."

"Do you think she knows about Jack? Is that what this is about?"

"I don't know. I hope not, for Jack's sake."

"So what does this mean?"

I shrugged. "Thank God for Dorothy, that's what it means. I have to call her right away."

"I am so sorry, Tess. I don't know what to say."

I could see a flicker of doubt in Emma's eyes. She was thinking of her own self-interest. Everybody does. It's the way of the world. If I had no clients, could I run a business? If I had no money, how could I pay her? She wanted to go with me, but there was a voice in her head telling her not to be stupid.

I decided to make it easy on her.

"Listen, Emma, Cosima's beef is with me, not you. She's not going to hold a grudge. If I were in your shoes, I'd stay right here. Hook up with another agent. If things go the way I want, then you'll be my first call to bring you over to my shop."

Emma shook her head fiercely. "I'm with you, Tess. You know I am."

I put my hands on her shoulders. "That's sweet, and I love you for your loyalty, darling. But you need to think about you. Okay?"

Emma nodded. She teared up and wiped her eyes. "Okay."

"Give me a minute, all right? I want to be alone with all this."

"I understand."

Emma slipped out the door quietly. I studied the office in which I had spent the last ten years and from which I was about to be banished. In truth, I had little to pack. There wasn't much of me in this place. Just files. Books. Things that were easily left behind and forgotten. Most of them were from clients who were no longer mine.

When you've been knifed in the back, it's hard to smile and say it feels good while the blood squirts out of you. Even so, I told myself I wasn't going to cry about it again. Better to fight back. Better to get pissed as hell. Except I didn't even have it in me to get mad. I barely felt anything at all. I stood there, shell-shocked, trying to count my blessings.

I realized it was a short list.

Dorothy. Darcy. Sally. And Oliver, of course, but Oliver and I weren't going to get rich off each other. My father. I needed to call him but not yet. Not until I was done and gone and home and drunk.

Ten years, and that's the sum of my labors. I wasn't doing cartwheels of self-congratulation. I had spent the last few days imagining that I was in one place, only to discover that I was somewhere else altogether. Lowell, God rest his soul, was probably up there, or down there, laughing at my dilemma.

That was also the moment life decided to pile it on. When you are sliding downhill, you build up momentum. I felt like the Bode Miller of bad news.

Emma knocked softly and poked her head inside. "I just thought you should know, I found out what's going on around here."

"Going on?"

"The press conference."

I had forgotten all about it, but I didn't figure that the press conference had anything to do with me. There wasn't much news value in my getting the sack. Well, that's not true—the tabloids would eat it up. But Cosima would be content to put that gossip out the back door, not call in reporters to announce my demise. She wasn't going to make me a martyr.

"Cosima is announcing an expansion," Emma said.

"Of what?"

"The agency. Bardwright is opening a branch office in New York."

"Ah, so that's the big secret. Well, she's wanted to do that for a while. Now that Lowell is gone, Cosima can go ahead and conquer the world."

I said it without much interest or care. Now that I was out the door, it didn't affect me for better or worse. Cosima could open Bardwright offices in LA, Paris, and Sydney, and it wasn't going to change my situation.

Then I got an uneasy feeling, because we were talking about New York. Dorothy was in New York.

I thought about Bardwright crossing the pond to the United States and how Cosima would love to follow up that announcement with a big client and a big, splashy deal.

I thought about her looking so unfazed that the one client of mine who really made a difference at Bardwright was the one who had slipped through her fingers.

I thought myself into a panic.

"Get in here and close the door," I told Emma. "Help me get Dorothy on the phone."

"It's still early in New York."

"I don't care, just get her. Right now."

We retreated behind my desk, and Emma punched the buttons on my phone. I told myself I was acting crazy for nothing. This was Dorothy. Other clients may not know the meaning of loyalty, but Dorothy wouldn't throw me over for five percent. She'd be offended at the very thought of it. Dorothy had said it herself. I'd have to kill someone before she went with another agent.

Even so, I wanted to hear her voice. I wanted to tell her about David Milton. I needed some good news and reassurance.

The phone rang in New York. Emma had the call on speaker-phone.

Dorothy picked it up on the first ring. I couldn't remember another time when she had done that. It was almost like she was sitting by the phone, waiting for me to call. That was my first clue that I was schussing past the next flag on the way to the bottom of the mountain, an avalanche racing behind me.

"Dorothy, it's Tess," I said.

I waited for the onslaught. The torrent of Dorothy babble, filling the first ten minutes of our conversation with pleasant inanities. The latest stories about the kinkajou. The digestive problems of her poodles. Everything that meant nothing about anything, which was how Dorothy's scattered but wonderful mind worked.

Instead, there was silence. Complete silence. She didn't say a word. I thought I had lost the call.

"Dorothy, hello? Are you there?"

"Yes, I'm here, Tess."

She sounded strange. Bereft. Upset. Unlike Dorothy. My stomach began to make revolutions like the London Eye.

"Are you all right? You don't sound like yourself."

"I didn't sleep a wink. I've been sitting here all night. I'm so upset."

I remembered that she had every reason to be upset. David Milton and his manuscript were still weighing on her mind.

"Well, I can make you feel better, darling, because I have fabulous news. The best. David Milton is a total fraud, and I can prove it. You don't have to worry about it for another minute." I explained my brainstorm about Filippa and Liudmila and waited for her relief and gratitude to burst through the phone.

I was seriously disappointed.

"That's nice," she said.

Nice?

"Dorothy, do you understand what this means? You're completely in the clear. The allegations, the threat of a lawsuit, they're gone."

Dorothy sighed long and hard. "Yes, I'm pleased, of course, but I knew all along there was nothing behind this. You sound so surprised. It makes me wonder if you doubted me."

Doubted her? Maybe a little.

"No, no, that's not it at all," I insisted. "But now we can move forward without any legal obstacles. I can sit down with Guy and work out the final terms on your next deal."

There was another stretch of silence.

"Yes, well, about that."

I waited. Dorothy didn't say anything more. Emma, standing above me, turned ghostly white.

"Are you there?" I asked. "Dorothy, what's wrong?"

Her voice, when it came, was pained, as if the kinkajou were gnawing on some delicate part of her body. "Tess, you know how hard this is for me."

"What?"

"You know I love you."

"Of course, I do. What is it?" I was having trouble breathing.

"I would never have imagined myself saying this, Tess, never in a million years, but I've decided we have to part ways."

Emma gasped and slapped both hands over her mouth.

I didn't reply. I opened the bottom drawer of my desk, where I kept an emergency pack of cigarettes. It was the pack I had left there, unopened, for the five years I had been smoke free. I removed it, along with the lighter next to it, and unwrapped the plastic around the box. With a slap, I popped a fag from the pack and took it between my shaking fingers.

Fuck being a nonsmoker. Fuck my lungs. Fuck the indoor smoking ban. I lit up and took the sweetest drag of my entire life and blew out a cloud of smoke.

I stared down at the speakerphone.

"Did you talk to Cosima?" I asked with a pretend calm. "Is that what this is about?"

"No, I didn't, but I have to tell you, I have already made other arrangements."

"Other arrangements? Are you serious? You've talked to another agent?"

"Yes, I have."

I inhaled smoke and closed my eyes. "And that's it? Without talking to me? Without discussing whatever is wrong? I can't believe this, Dorothy. I can't believe you would do this to me."

I heard sniffling through the phone. Dorothy was crying. "I know, Tess, but after what you did."

"What I did? What on earth did I do? Who have you been talking to? I can't believe you would listen to lies about me and walk away from our relationship without even giving me a chance to set the record straight."

"There's nothing to set straight, Tess," Dorothy told me, in a quavering voice so defiant that she sounded like a stranger. "I saw it. I saw that disgusting, horrible photograph. That was all I needed to see."

"Photograph? What are you talking about?" Then I saw the crumpled poster in the middle of my office floor. "Oh, for God's sake, do you mean the picture with me and that actress? Dorothy, her dress slipped. I was trying to help her fix it. It's not like I'm some kind of pervert who goes around molesting women. I can't believe this is what has you upset."

"It's not that."

I squeezed the cigarette so hard that some of the tobacco squirted onto the desk. "Then what the hell is it?"

"I saw that grotesque, revolting thing. Don't try to deny it, Tess. Don't try to make excuses. You know perfectly well it's the one thing in this world that I could never, ever forgive. I don't care who it is, or how much I love them, I could never accept it."

"Dorothy, what are you talking about?"

"You were wearing a *fur coat*, Tess! Fur! You!"

The breath left my chest in a rush.

"Oh, no. Oh, my God. Dorothy, look. Please listen."

"Don't say a word. Do you have any idea what it did to me to see you with those dead animal skins draped all over your body? Did you give a thought to the creatures that died? I could never be associated with anyone who would allow innocent animals to suffer in that way. Never. And you, Tess! Knowing how I feel, how could you! How could you hurt me like that!"

"Dorothy, I am so sorry. I didn't think. It was a hideous mistake."

"I'm sorry, Tess, I can't talk about this anymore. I'm just devastated."

"Give me a chance to tell you what happened."

"No, I won't. I can't. Tess, this is a part of my life where there are no second chances. You of all people should know that."

And I did. She was right. I knew it. I had said as much to Cosima. Dorothy was a woman of principle, and I had trampled her principles the moment I slid my arms inside that coat. I had lost her, and I had no one to blame but myself.

38

"OH, TESS," EMMA MURMURED when I hung up the phone.

I shook my head and kept smoking, like the prisoner facing the firing squad who knows what's about to happen. I didn't want sympathy. I just wanted it to be over.

"Maybe she'll change her mind," Emma said.

"No, she won't."

I knew Dorothy. She wasn't going to change her mind. Not about this. I had crossed the one line with Dorothy that you never could cross. I may as well have taken a pistol and shot the damn minks myself. I wanted to call Julien Macdonald and ask if he'd never heard of polyester.

I crushed out the cigarette when there was an inch left. I already wanted another one. Just like that, I was a smoker again. Dad wasn't going to be happy.

"What can I do?" Emma asked.

"You can make nice with Cosima and Marty, darling. Save yourself. I'm history."

"Don't say that."

"Emma, sweetheart, I have no job, no clients, no deals, and soon enough no money. This wasn't exactly my plan."

"You could go to your father. He'll help you."

And, yes, he would, but Dad is the last person I would turn to for a handout. It's one thing to admit to yourself that you're a failure, a screwup, a suicide bomber sans dynamite. It's another to admit it to your father.

"I haven't quite exhausted all my pride," I told her.

"So what are you going to do?"

That was the big question. What the hell was I going to do? This afternoon, this evening, tomorrow, this week, this month, this year.

"I have no idea," I said.

Maybe I'll go to Italy and visit my mother. Her life revolves around sex and Chianti, which isn't such a bad way to pass your days. Unfortunately, my mother ekes out her modest living as a bar singer when she's not sleeping with swarthy artists, and my singing voice would clear out the patrons at a karaoke bar. So even that option isn't open to me.

I heard impatient tapping on my office window. The young security guard pointed at his watch. I held up five fingers, asking for an extension from the warden. He didn't look happy.

"I should call Jane," Emma said.

I nodded. "Go, go."

Emma opened the door but stopped without leaving. "Who do you think Dorothy is going to use as her new agent?"

"I'm sure she's going to be the first client of the New York office of the Bardwright Agency," I said.

"But she told you she hadn't talked to Cosima," Emma pointed out.

"That's true."

I was confused, but only for a moment. Then the answer was obvious.

Saleema was in London.

Saleema, who has wanted to ditch her New York agency for years and run her own shop.

Saleema, who was probably in the building right now, ready to be trotted out in front of the press as the lead agent for the US wing of the Bardwright Agency. The lead agent with a big new client.

She had told me flat out that she was waiting in the wings for that moment when I made my mistake with Dorothy. I hadn't made her wait long. Give me a rope, and, sure enough, I'll find a way to hang myself.

The strange thing is, I didn't even blame her. The blame game stopped at my door.

"See if Saleema is in the office," I told Emma. "I bet someone around here knows where she is. Tell her I want to congratulate her."

I heard a new voice.

"You don't have to do that," a woman said from my doorway, squeezing in front of Emma.

When I looked up, I realized I was wrong. So very wrong.

It wasn't Saleema standing there. It was Sally Harlingford.

"The congratulations go to me, Tess," Sally said. "I'm the one heading up the Bardwright office in New York."

I haven't been speechless many times in my life, but that was one of them. It occurred to me that every time I thought I had fallen to the bottom, the ground gave way underneath me again. I remembered thinking not so long ago that Sally would sell her soul for a one-way ticket to New York. Apparently she had. I just never believed she would sell *my* soul to get there, too.

Sally slipped inside and closed my office door, then leaned back against it. She sniffed the air. "You're smoking again. You shouldn't do that."

I still had nothing to say.

"I see the look on your face, Tess," Sally went on. "I am sorry, believe me, but business is business. I told you that. You had your chance to stay here. You didn't heed my warnings."

I felt as if I were seeing her for the first time. A woman in her late forties, alone, who loved the finer things in life and couldn't afford many of them. A woman who, like Guy, must have grown bitter watching others taste the things that she couldn't. For her, this opportunity must have felt like grabbing the brass ring on the carousel. I knew the lifestyle she wanted, but I didn't realize how far she would go to get it.

"We were friends," I said when I could speak.

Sally's aristocratic chin nudged upward in defiance. "Oh, don't trot out that tired guilt trip on me, Tess. We're big girls. Saleema was your friend, too, wasn't she? That didn't stop you from sleeping with her fiancé. So don't pretend that you've ever let friendship get in the way of what *you* want. This is my chance. This is what I've wanted all my life, and now I have it. I won't apologize for that."

"You better watch your back, Sally. You're in bed with the devil."

"Cosima's not the devil."

"No? Did you know what she was doing? Stealing all my clients? Were you part of that, too?"

"Cosima was looking after the best interests of the agency," Sally replied. "That's her job. If you expect anyone to treat you with kid gloves in this business, then you're more naive than I thought. Cosima didn't steal your clients. They made a choice. If they didn't trust you enough to stay with you, then whose fault is that?"

"She threatened them," I said.

"She wooed them. Persuaded them. Enticed them. That's how we do it. You're no different."

"What about Dorothy?" I asked.

"What about her? If you want to blame someone for losing Dorothy, look in the mirror. I didn't wear the coat, Tess. You did. So don't get on your high horse about loyalty when you're the one who handed her to me."

I saw a flush in her face that looked like pride. I had never appreciated how jealous she must have felt of me over the years. How much she wanted the things I had. Now she had beaten me, and she was relishing her victory.

"I'll sue the agency," I told her, because I didn't know what else to say. "I was the one who negotiated Dorothy's next deal. We both know it. I deserve a share of the commission."

Sally shook her head. "Deal? What deal? You've been clear with everyone that there was *no deal*. And now you want to say that there was? Please. You can't have it both ways, Tess. Walk away with a shred of dignity, all right? Sometimes you win, and sometimes you lose. This time you lost big."

I walked up to Sally until we were nose to nose.

"What about Lowell?" I said softly.

Her face twitched. Just a little. "What about him?"

"My God, Sally, did you kill him? Was it you? Tell me you wouldn't do something so vile."

I saw cruelty in her eyes, and it was probably the most horrible thing I had ever seen in another person's face. It was there and gone in a flicker, but I knew I was right.

"Vile? If someone really killed Lowell, then they did the world a favor. He was a pig."

"Did you hate him that much?" I asked.

"I did, in fact, but that doesn't mean I killed him."

"No?"

"No."

I wanted to believe her. But I didn't.

"I can talk to the police, you know. They have DNA. If you were with him, they can prove it."

Sally shrugged. "Tell them to test away, darling. I would sooner die before I got on my knees in front of that man again. I've been there, and believe me, I had no desire to repeat the experience. Besides, like I told you before, Lowell preferred girls who are a lot younger than you or I."

"I'm not bluffing."

"Neither am I. Don't make a fool of yourself, Tess. I was at a party the night Lowell played his last sex game. Cosima was with me. Fifty people saw us there."

"That's convenient."

"Yes, it is. You're following a dead end, so let it go." Sally glanced at her watch. "I have a press conference to attend."

"I hope you can live with yourself."

"It's easy to live with yourself in Manhattan. Believe me, I'll sleep like a baby."

I thought about slapping her. I didn't. There was nothing to do but let her leave.

Emma reappeared, chewing on her fingernail and sending eye darts after Sally. I wanted to tell her to stay away, that I was radioactive.

"Are you okay?" she asked. Then she said, "I'm sorry—that's a pretty stupid thing to say. You know what I mean."

"I'm all right, Emma."

"How could Sally do that to you?"

"If I were in her shoes, I probably would have done the same thing," I said.

"No, you wouldn't."

No, I wouldn't. God knows I've made my share of mistakes. I've been stupid and selfish. But I like to think that I know what I will and will not do.

"You'll bounce back," Emma told me. "You will. No one can hold you down for long."

"That's sweet of you, darling."

I wasn't in the mood to be cheered up. Oliver told me that if the worst thing I ever experience in life is to lose everything and start over, then I'm pretty lucky. But you know what? I don't feel so lucky.

Emma looked sheepish. "I know it's a bad time and all, but can I ask you something?"

"What is it?"

"Well, did Jane say anything about me when you saw her last night?"

I wasn't about to tell Emma what I really thought of Jane, or that Jane had dismissed Emma the way a spoiled child casts off an old toy. She didn't need to hear that right now. "I'm sorry, no, we didn't talk long."

She dropped her dress, I grabbed her breast. End of story.

"Oh," Emma said.

"Is something wrong?"

"It's just that I can't reach her. I've been trying and trying. I just called again, and her number is out of service."

"Blame it on T-Mobile," I said. "I'm sure it's a glitch."

"I guess, but it's weird. I mean, I called Godfrey Kahn's office to see if they had another contact number for Jane, and they said they had never heard of her."

I wish I could say I was surprised.

"I'm sorry, darling, but look, Jane's not the first wannabe actress who lied to impress a girlfriend. So she's not really up for a big part. Does that make a difference to you?"

"Of course not. I just can't understand why she would lie. I mean, she's way hotter than me. She didn't need to impress me. I couldn't believe she'd even give me a second look, you know?"

"Don't sell yourself short," I said, but I was being kind. Emma has the body, but in the BP world, it's true that she doesn't really fit in. You have to have the perfect bitch-in-a-bag attitude that says you're better than everyone else. Emma is too sweet. Too innocent. Not a player like Jane. Girls like Jane don't generally come after girls like Emma unless they think there's something in it for them.

I stopped.

Little cold feet tiptoed up my spine.

"Emma," I murmured, "who was it that told you about that nightclub where you met Jane?"

"What? Oh, it was Sally." Emma froze. "Oh, no. Oh, Tess, no, you must be wrong."

I stared at her, and she stared back, and we both knew. I wasn't wrong.

I thought about Jane Parmenter and that flimsy, floppy dress, and her bending over and spilling her breast out next to me. And the cameras clicking like crazy. What a horrible, hideous coincidence that it would happen then, with me in that damn fur coat, and photographers everywhere to broadcast my picture all over the world. I mean, okay, it was my stupid mistake to wear the coat at all, but without Jane and her nipple slip, Dorothy would never have known about it.

Sure, I might be paranoid, and it was all just a coincidence. Bad luck. Bad timing.

Or maybe it was all a setup. Maybe I had strutted into the lobby of the Hilton with a target hung on my back and Jane Parmenter poised to intercept me like a laser-guided, silicone-stuffed missile.

I thought about something else, too. Something worse. If Jane was part of the conspiracy, maybe Emma and I weren't the only ones fooled by her performance.

Lowell preferred girls who are a lot younger than you or I.

That was true. Lowell liked flowers that were freshly picked, not three-day-old roses. He thought girls came with a label that read, "Best if used by age 25." If Sally and Cosima had wanted to dangle an irresistible morsel in front of Lowell, they couldn't have done better than Jane. Lowell would have done absolutely anything if he had a girl like Jane naked in his apartment. Like climbing onto a chair as part of a naughty sex game, only to have the chair kicked out from under him.

"Tell me this isn't my fault," Emma said.

I watched her crumble like the naive kid she was, finding out for the first time that there are heartless people in the world. She trembled and began to cry for herself and for me. I put my arms around her.

"It's not your fault. Don't think that."

"Tess, I'm so sorry," she whimpered.

I murmured that everything was okay.

But nothing was okay. My heart seized. I felt sick.

Not about Jane. Not about Cosima. Not even about Sally or Dorothy.

It wasn't the knowledge that my plans lay in ruins or that my clients and friends had betrayed me. It wasn't the uncertainty of having nowhere to go and nothing on which to build a future. In the end, none of that mattered. I realized that in the days since

Lowell had died, only one thing had been real to me. Only one thing had wormed its way inside my heart. Only one thing had really changed my life.

I had fallen in love. I had said it to myself and said it aloud. I had let someone into my soul. That was the one thing I had never believed anyone could take away from me.

And it was all a lie. I knew that now.

Because when I thought about that damn coat draped around my shoulders, I realized that the trap they had laid for me didn't begin or end with Jane Parmenter. Or Sally. Or Cosima. There was one other person who had to know about it, who had to be in on the setup, who had lured me to the spiderweb with a gift and a note that told me exactly what I wanted to hear.

Darcy.

Darcy had been part of it, too.

39

I COULDN'T STAND to be there anymore. Not for another minute. Not for another second. I flew past the security guard in the hallway, who shouted after me. I ignored the stares of the agents and assistants at their desks and bolted for the rear stairwell that led out of the building. This was the end. I had no intention of setting foot inside the Bardwright Agency again.

On the ground floor, I crashed through the alley door and wandered into the London streets, blind with rage and humiliation. Black cabs blared their horns at me. The day was dark and threatening, and a smoggy, stinky haze filled the air. In a fog of depression, I followed Charing Cross into Trafalgar Square, where I collapsed on the steps of the National Gallery and buried my face in my hands. There were hardly any tourists wandering in the square that afternoon. Just me and the hundreds of pigeons and the awful clouds.

Darcy.

I knew I hadn't made a mistake. There was no other way to piece together the puzzle of what had happened. Darcy had sent

me the coat as bait. He had lured me to the Hilton, and Jane Parmenter had waited for me there in front of ten thousand cameras.
I had played right into all their hands.

Worst of all, the son of a bitch had let me make love to him one
last time. It would have been better to leave me with an empty
hotel room and a note that read, "The joke's on you."

Part of me never wanted to talk to him again, but I had to hear
him admit it to me. I had to hear the words from his own mouth.
If he stabbed my love in the heart, maybe it would finally die. I
took out my cell phone and punched in his number. I wondered if
he would duck the call, knowing it was me, knowing that I knew
the truth. But he answered.

"Hello, Tess," Jack said.

God, that voice. I hated myself that it still twisted my insides.

He didn't pretend. He wanted me to hear his regret, how sorry
he was. As if that changed anything. As if it mattered to me that he
felt bad.

"You bastard," I spat into the phone. "You goddamned bastard. How could you let them do that to me? How could you be
part of it?"

"Tess," he began, but I wasn't finished with him. Not by a long
shot.

"Did you think I was kidding? Do you think I say that to every
man I fall into bed with? I loved you, Jack. I never let myself be
vulnerable with anyone, and I did it with you. I laid it all on the
line. And what did you do? You played me. You lied to me. You let
me think you gave a damn about me."

"I did. I do. I wasn't lying, Tess."

"Oh, go fuck yourself, Jack. Don't tell me you didn't know.
Don't pretend you weren't a pawn. Cosima told you exactly what
to do, and you did it."

"Please let me explain."

"Explain what? How you let me make a fool of myself? Did you
and Cosima have a good laugh about that?"

"God, Tessie, it wasn't like that at all. You make it sound like I
had a choice. Cosima knew. I don't know how she found out, but

she knew all about us. She confronted me last week and gave me an ultimatum. If I didn't help her, I would have lost everything."

"You had a choice, Jack. You always did. You could have left her."

I heard him breathing. He struggled for something to say, some way to protect himself. I realized for the first time that he was a coward. I had been in love with a fantasy, something out of *Pride and Prejudice*. There was no Darcy. There was just Jack, a slave with golden handcuffs, whose tailored suits and expensive cologne were more important to him than me.

Admit it, Jack, I wanted to say. Admit I was nothing to you.

"I wish I was as strong as you are, Tess," he said in a quiet voice. "But I'm not. I don't have it in me to start over. I made a devil's choice with my life a long time ago. You knew that. I told you from the beginning."

I didn't feel strong at all. I felt hollowed out. I felt like vultures were picking away at what was left of me. Even so, he was right. I should never have expected him to be more than he was. I had built him in my mind out of soft clay.

"Please believe me, I had no idea what she was planning," he went on when I was silent. "She didn't tell me. I never thought she would be so . . . so vicious."

"Do you think that makes you innocent?"

"No."

"If she had told you what she was going to do, would you have done anything different? If you knew she was going to destroy me, would you have cared? Would you have suddenly found some glimmer of decency in that selfish fucking heart of yours?"

"I don't know," he said. "I'd like to think so."

"Don't flatter yourself, Jack. The answer is no."

"Tess, it won't mean anything to hear how sorry I am, but I want to say—"

I cut him off. "Don't bother. Don't try to make yourself feel better. I only want to know one thing. Did Cosima tell you exactly what to put in your note, Jack? Was it her idea for you to tell me you loved me? That was the biggest lie of all, wasn't it?"

He didn't answer. That was answer enough for me.

"Make sure I never see you again, Jack," I said.

I slapped my phone shut. I pressed my hand against my chest because the air was coming in raggedly, as if my body were rejecting each breath. It takes a lot to wound me. I keep the walls around me pretty tall and thick. I use my little jokes to make believe I don't care, but I do. My walls were rubble now, broken down, nothing but ruins. I cried again, and I hated myself for it. I hated giving them the satisfaction of beating me so completely.

I don't know how long I sat on the steps. An hour, maybe. The day went on, getting darker. Eventually, I got up and walked with no destination in mind, wandering through the square and along the path to St. James's Park. Buckingham Palace was ahead of me, all formal and forbidding. I thought about stopping at the gate to tell Liz that this was her fault, hers and the prime minister of Tuvalu. If they hadn't blocked traffic that fall day, I would never have gone into Hyde Park, would never have met Jack, would never have turned him into Darcy. The walls would still be barricaded around my heart.

Oh, but who am I kidding? I always have someone else to blame. I'm where I am because of three people. Me, myself, and I.

My phone rang. I took it out and checked the caller ID and saw it was a reporter from *The Guardian*. Good news travels fast, and bad news travels even faster. I thought about skipping the call, but it was time to face the music.

"Hello, Gerald," I said, putting on my cheery voice. The voice that says all is right with the world.

He wasn't fooled at all. "Tess Drake. Rumor is you just got the ax at Bardwright. Say it ain't so."

I drew in my breath and prepared to fight. I wasn't really ready for this, but life doesn't wait until you're ready. "Cosima can call it whatever she wants. I don't care. The fact is, I've been planning to leave Bardwright for weeks. I'm opening my own agency."

"I can print that?"

"Yes, you can print that. Print it in big bold letters. Today is the first official day of business for the Drake Media Agency."

He had the good manners not to laugh in my face. "Except I hear your client roster is a little thin, Tess. You lost everyone to Queen Cosima, didn't you? Including the big fish, right? I understand that Dorothy Starkwell dumped you over that stupid photo. Bad call, wearing the fur coat."

I could have told him I was set up. I could have told him about my conspiracy theories. Hell, I could have dropped hints about Lowell and foul play and a disappearing actress named Jane who must have been paid cold hard cash. There was a juicy story in all of that. But I wasn't playing the game. I was done with dancing to other people's music.

"Damn right," I confessed. "That was stupid of me. You know me, Gerald—I've done stupid things and done them proudly. But that was my number one mistake, and I managed to do it in front of the whole world. All I can do is learn from it and move on."

"So what are you going to do?"

"I already told you, Gerald. I'm opening the agency. It starts today. Clients welcome."

"What about money? Don't you need money for that kind of thing?"

God, yes. But I didn't say that.

"If you worry about everything you don't have before you do something, you'll never do anything," I told him.

"Well, good luck, Tess," Gerald said.

"Thanks. I'll need it."

I hung up. Fifteen seconds later, the phone rang again. It was *The Sun* this time. Five minutes later, *The Independent*. Then *The Bookseller*. *The Daily Mail*. *The Mirror*. I talked to all of them, and I told them the same thing. I was on my own and open for business. I'm sure no one swallowed my line. They would announce my downfall in the headlines tomorrow, but I didn't care. I wanted to scream it to the world. Today, right now, Tess Drake is responsible for Tess Drake, and no one can do a thing to me if I don't let them.

Big words. Big talk. It covered up the reality that I was scared to death. Scared and alone.

When I was sick of talking to reporters, I silenced my phone and sat down on a bench. I had been walking and talking for so long that I didn't even know where I was, and when I looked around me, I realized I had marched all the way to Hyde Park. I was on a bench near the Serpentine. My ego must have drawn me here as a cruel joke, as a reminder of the day I had met Jack. It seemed like a lifetime ago, and it was. I had lived and died an entire lifetime since then. The question was whether, like a cat, I had a few more lives left in me.

From the bench, I stared up into the sky. At that moment, just to add insult to injury, the clouds decided to open up and pee down rain. Everyone else had the good sense to get out of the downpour or put up an umbrella, but I sat there and let it soak me to the skin. My multicolored hair lay plastered on my face. My drippy makeup turned me into a clown.

The people who walked by, huddled underneath their nylon bubbles, looked at me as if I were crazy. They were probably right. I guess you have to be crazy to be in this business at all. I guess you have to be crazy to have an affair and fall in love. All you can do is laugh when it bites you in the arse.

So I laughed.

Laughed and laughed and laughed until, when I finally stopped, I began crying again.

It turns out Saleema was right after all. She told me I would wind up sitting in the rain, wondering how I fucked up my life so badly. And here I was. I could pretend for the newspapers, but, honestly, I didn't know what I was going to do. We all think we're invincible, and it sucks when life reminds us that we're not. I thought about how I got from there to here and how things had gone so badly off course. I reflected on my life since that first morning, sitting on the bus and hearing that Lowell was dead, and I asked myself if I would be better off if I could punch rewind and go back to that moment and start over.

If you could correct all your stupid mistakes, would you do it? Or are we the sum of everything we do wrong?

My BlackBerry buzzed. Even when I silence my phone, Emma

can reach me in an emergency by sending me a text message. To-day, however, my definition of an emergency was pretty fluid. I ignored her message and sat there feeling sorry for myself.

I thought about calling Saleema. Partly to tell her she was right, because I knew she'd appreciate the irony. Partly to ask her for a job or to suggest that the two of us do what we had dreamed of doing all along—set up shop across the pond, Drake and Azah, a transcontinental agency. Partly just to feel like, if I asked for help, someone would toss me a life ring and reel me in. I didn't do it, of course. It was too soon. I had misjudged Saleema along with ev-eryone else, and, once again, I had no one to blame but the wet girl on the bench.

My BlackBerry buzzed again.

Leave me alone, Emma.

I took stock of my situation, which was a mistake, because I real-ized the state of my world was even more dire than it looked on the surface. I live hand-to-mouth like everyone else. A few bucks on the dole wasn't going to pay my rent. What did Sally say? You can cherish your ideals for a while, but in the end, it's all about money. Gerald said the same thing. What about money? I thought about Oliver, teetering on the brink of starvation from day to day, and wondered how he found the courage to wake up every morning. Of course, some days, he thought life wasn't worth the trade-off for his misery. I never wanted to sink so low.

I stared at the rain sheeting down across the Serpentine.

I thought about calling Dorothy. Partly to grovel and ask for forgiveness. She might even say yes. Partly to yell at her that she could blame me for a few dead minks, but she was wrong to let my one mistake outweigh everything else I've done for her. Most of the good she's been able to do in this world is because of me. Her audience. Her wealth. Thanks to me.

And, by the way, I'll wear any damn coat I want.

But I didn't call. It was over.

I thought about calling Oliver. Or Guy. Or the clients who had sold me out. I didn't call any of them. Not yet. I didn't want pity or pep talks or excuses. All I wanted was to get back to basics. To do my job. It sounds crazy, but I've always believed that I was put on this earth as a go-between for the people who have something to say. I'm the woman who gives talented people their day in the sun. I can't sing. I can't dance. I can't crunch numbers. I can't even remember who I'm meeting for lunch on Friday. But I can make deals.

Which I can do from the back table at Caffè Nero if I have to. Who needs money?

Buzz, buzz, buzz.

Oh, for God's sake, Emma.

I extracted my BlackBerry, and, sure enough, there was a text message waiting for me from Emma. Well, fourteen of them, actually. I didn't need to open the messages, because I could see the lineup on the screen, and they all said the same thing.

TURN ON YOUR DAMN PHONE.

So I did.

It occurred to me that if news of my demise had made the rounds of the media, it had made its way to my father at *The Times*. He wanted to talk to me. I really wasn't in the mood for paternal sympathy, but if he wanted to call, so be it.

I didn't have to wait long. Two minutes later, my phone rang. Hello, Dad, it's your failure of a daughter here. When I checked the caller ID, however, I didn't recognize the number. I made a mental note of the newspapers that hadn't checked in yet to dance on the grave of Tess Drake and wondered which one was calling now.

"Drake Media Agency," I answered the phone, like I was sitting in my corner office. "This is Tess Drake."

"Wow, the lady herself. You're a tough person to reach."

I didn't have a clue who this man was.

"Sorry," I said. "Busy day."

"Sure, okay. So how are you?"

"I'm having the most miserable day of my godforsaken life, and I'm sitting here in the pouring rain like an idiot," I said.

Okay, no, I didn't say that.

"I'm just great," I said, because that's what you say when people ask.

"Fantastic. Terrific. Listen, you were right."

"Of course, I was," I said.

He laughed. It was a breezy, attractive, familiar laugh. "Cool. I like you, Tess. I like your attitude. So what's it going to take?"

"What do you mean?"

"I mean, the film rights. What are you looking for? Normally, I'd have Felicia get the conversation started, but it sounds like the two of you aren't exactly the best of friends. That's okay. I love her, but the woman can be a chore sometimes. So I thought I'd call you myself."

"Felicia?"

"Felicia Castro. My agent."

I had a little stroke.

"I'm sorry, who is this?"

He laughed again. "It's Tom."

"Tom?"

"Right. Remember, we met in New York?"

"Tom."

"You got it."

"Tom, could you hang on for just one second?"

"Sure."

I squeezed the phone against my palm so there was no chance of anyone on the other end hearing anything at all, and then I shouted loud enough that I'm pretty sure they could hear me in Piccadilly Circus. *Holy shit!*

I came back on the line, cool and calm. "So, Tom, you read *Singularity*."

"I did. It blew my mind."

"I knew it would. I was worried that Felicia snatched the book away from you."

"She did, but that just made me more curious. So do you have a number in mind for the film rights?"

"I do," I said.

I was thinking about five hundred thousand dollars, but you always let the other guy go first.

"Well, I was thinking an even million," Tom said. "How does that sound?"

"Pounds or dollars?"

"Let's say pounds."

"Let's say one point five million," I told him.

He laughed again. "That guy in New York was right about you. You've got balls."

"One point five million pounds is a bargain, Tom. You'll never regret it."

"Yeah, all right. I'll make it work. I want to meet this Oliver Howard, you know."

"I think that can be arranged," I said.

"Can you be civil enough with Felicia to work out the rest of the details with her?"

"I'm the soul of restraint."

"Yeah, I bet you are. Don't worry, I'll tell Felicia to retract the claws. I'm in London next month, so tell Oliver dinner's on me. You come along, too, okay?"

"It's a date."

"See you later, Tess."

"Thanks, Tom."

And that was that.

Some deals are done over coffee. Or wine. Or at a funeral. Some are done in the rain in Hyde Park. Anyway, I may have lost Dorothy and her pandas, but I still have one client. And one big deal. The Drake Media Agency wasn't just a figment of my imagination.

I wondered how Oliver was going to react to the idea that I was about to make him a millionaire. And that the publishers who had turned down *Duopoly* were about to open up their wallets and start begging me for the rights.

Like I said, this is what I do.

Okay, I know it's just a start. I've climbed one rung back from the bottom, and I have a long way to go. Knowing me, there are probably a thousand new ways I can screw up my life tomorrow. Put me in a fur coat, and point me at the next disaster. But not today. Today, I have a new job and a new boss.

Me.

I called Emma. She could barely get the words out of her mouth. "Did he reach you? Did he reach you? Did he reach you?"

"He did."

Emma screamed. A full-throated, high-pitched scream. "AAAAGGGGHHHH!"

"Listen," I said, cutting her off. "What I said before still goes. You're better off staying where you are. Okay? I'm telling you to stay put and not do anything stupid like me."

"Right."

"We're clear about that, okay? Stay put."

"Right."

"Good. Because I can probably scrape together enough to pay you for three months, but it would be crazy to give up what you've got for an agent with practically no clients and a reputation for fondling breasts in public."

"I'm in."

"I said no."

"I'm in."

"You're not listening to me, Emma."

"I'm in."

"Then get the hell out of that fucking place and come meet me at my office," I told her.

"Where is that?"

"I'm on a bench in Hyde Park."

"It's raining," Emma protested.

"Didn't I tell you not to take this job? Now come on, get over here."

"I'm on my way."

I hung up.

Now I had a client, a deal, and an assistant.

Good thing, too, because there's a lot to do. My day's just starting. I have to call Oliver. I have to get back on the phone with his original publisher and launch a reprint of *Singularity*. I've got to get them on the hook for a multibook follow-up deal, too. Six figures per book, minimum. I've got to write a press release and run it by Cruise and start feeding it to the entertainment media. I've got to nail down the details with Felicia and get the deal signed.

Oh, and there's a little debt I owe to Lowell. I have to call my Burberry-wearing, greasy chip–eating detective, Nicholas Hadley. Tell him to track down Jane Parmenter and stick one of his cotton swabs in *her* mouth. He just might find some interesting DNA if he can get past all that Botox.

So sorry, I can't sit around here talking to you. The agency is up and running. I've got to start knocking on doors and drumming up new clients. It's not like there's a slow day in this business.

Now you know.

This is my life.